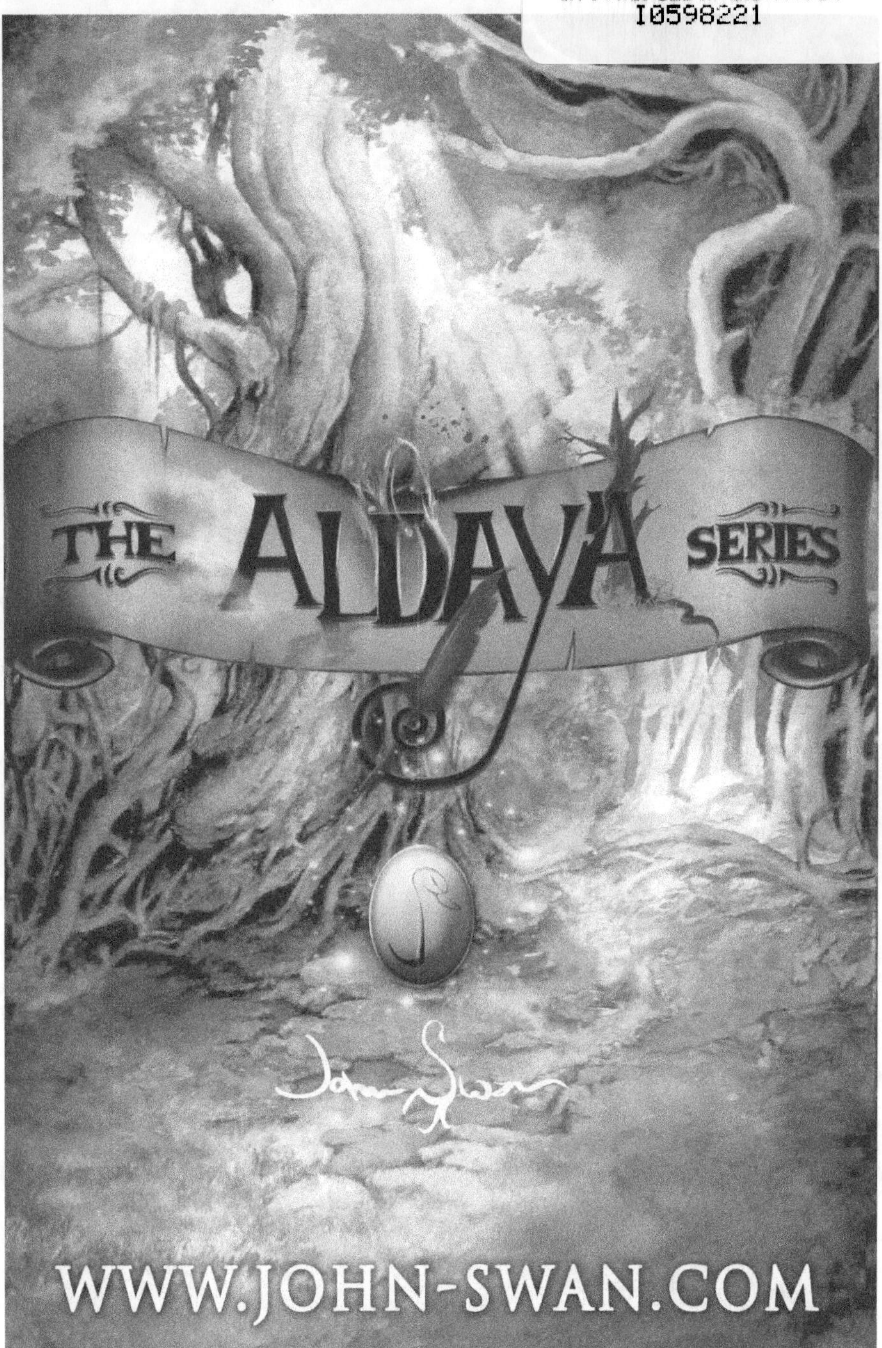
THE ALDAYA SERIES
John Swan
WWW.JOHN-SWAN.COM

Copyright © 2013 by: John Swan
First Print Editon, 2014

ISBN-13: 978-0-9906555-1-0

Published independently within the United States

Manufactured and printed in the United States of America

Cover Art and Design by Natalie Spasic

Chapter Illustrations, Custom Fonts, Banner, & World Map by Thomas Beck

Digital Renderings, Character Art, and Table of Contents by Mike Dumas

Edited with patience by John Harten

The dedication of this work is...

Firstly, to my family. Without their love and support, I would never have had the opportunity or means to finish.

Secondly, to Stevie Nicks, who has been my muse since childhood. Through her music, she has given me the strength to believe in my art and the courage to never give up on my dreams...

And lastly, but certainly not the least, to my beloved niece, daughter, sister, and best friend, Elizabeth. She left the Earth much sooner than expected, but her sprit will live on forever in my writing. She sat by my side on the white sand beaches of Oahu the day this story was born, and she still sits by me each night as I delve into the beautifully fractured world you are about to enter.

Lizzy, you will always be the Everyoung.

The Great Isle

# of Aldaya

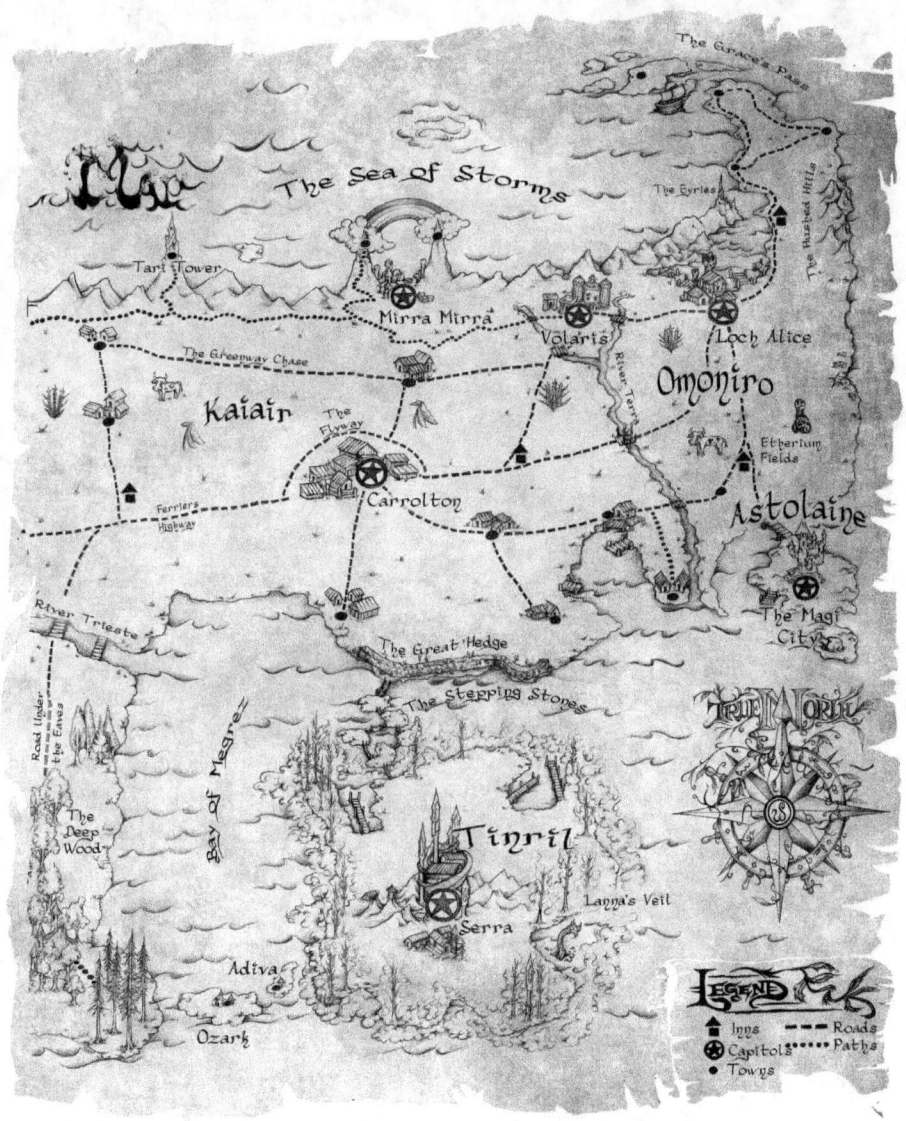

PROLOGUE

A Lullaby of Ages

IN A TIME BEFORE OURS, when the universe was much younger, a great civilization lived upon the surface of an infant world not much different than our own. It was tucked away in our same distant arm of the galaxy, with its twin moons shining unblemished in the night sky, and its surface full of spirits both great and small. Of these, some were strange and timid, and others bold and strong.

The most powerful were called the Esmë, and they came from the depths of the expanse and were armed with knowledge and a purpose, which was to create and bring forth their thoughts and designs into reality. And after much searching, on this remote and dust-ridden world, they finally found potential.

While the Esmë weren't numerous (no more than sixty in all) six there were that came before the rest, and they were responsible for the guidance and protection of the sphere in its earliest forms. With their power and intellect, along with the help of their kin, they molded and provided the base for all other things to come.

For ages they created and dreamed, and two great isles came to rest above the blue waters. Aldaya was first, and here the Esmë lived and labored in preparation for their most treasured work. And it was for them that the second Isle of Atlan was brought above the waves. The Esmë sat it gracefully upon great undersea mountains and filled it with everything that their children would need to build and grow. It was then that the five races of the free peoples awoke, and so began a period that their histories refer to as the Northern Dawn.

At its height, a utopia was achieved. There was no pain, sickness, or wealth beyond what was achieved by the growth of the spirit and mind, and the sphere shone like a beacon out into the land of stars. But its radiance and splendor soon attracted the attention of another powerful spirit that was kin to the Esmë, known as Izman.

He was older and more powerful than all the others, save the Esmë queen Maia, and he had once worked side by side with her and the others on endeavors throughout space and time. But unlike his kin, Izman did not put the same value on his creations. This fundamental difference led them to part ways, and he had gone on alone, leaving the rest to their own devices. But even with all of his power and intent, Izman could still not achieve alone what his counterparts had together. And gradually he became envious of them and their fair children.

So from his dark realms out beyond the stars, Izman boldly appeared and approached the Esmë and the free peoples of the sphere with grand words of peace and cooperation. Many rejoiced at his coming, and for a short while the twin isles prospered greatly with his aide. However, Izman became so enamored of the potential for his own power that he began to introduce his own wicked designs; abominations and perversions that mocked the grace and beauty of the others' creations. To the dismay of the Esmë, their great works began to unravel, and for the first time fear and doubt crept into the world.

A shadow then fell over Atlan, and the age of wonder ended. Confrontation soon developed, with Izman refusing to leave the sphere and continuing to tighten his grasp in the north. A great and terrible war ensued, and although the Esmë eventually overpowered him, Izman achieved one last foul deed before his capture.

He, and the most powerful of his wicked designs, dove deep into the ocean and assailed the undersea mountains beneath Atlan, causing it to fall. That day is remembered as the Sowing of Sorrow, for no other event would ever exceed what was lost during those final hours as the northern isle slowly disappeared into the Encircling Ocean.

Soon after, the Esmë caught Izman, imprisoning him and those they would not destroy deep near the core of the sphere. Here, in enchanted chambers so dark that no light would ever again reach them, they were to be left until the ending of days. But not all of Izman's foul craft had been caught or exterminated, and with three of his most powerful accomplices still at large, the Esmë worried for the safety of their children and their home upon Aldaya.

But then something happened that has yet to be explained by record or by memory. Just shy of forty years into the settling of the northern refugees upon Aldaya, the Esmë vanished. The grace of their magic faded, and the places that were once filled with its power fell silent. The free peoples had been left to their own devices, and for 1086 years not a trace of the gods could be found beyond that of relics and myth.

During this time the dark spirits that had escaped the wrath of the Esmë and hid in the lightless places of the world had silently kept watch. They now heard the call of their master from the deep, and crept back out into a fractured world that seemed ripe for the picking.

From the Scrolls of Bronwyn
Shamaness of the Wanderers
Year 1,068 of the Twilight Age

I

Uŋexpected News

I T WAS A BEAUTIFUL LATE summer evening, and far in the southern regions of Aldaya the sun was beginning to set over the territory of Alamarayn. Its vast pink and white beaches brushed up against the calm warm waters of the Southern Ocean, where dolphins played in the blue surf along with its tan-skinned people. It was considered by many to be the greatest realm on the Isle, not only for its beauty and temperate climate, but also due to its excellent stewardship.

The capital of Alamarayn was the fair city of Alastria, being crowned by a great white marble palace that sat upon a low hill. Its terraced walls and golden domes were set in such a way that it looked as if a giant wave had been frozen in time and entombed within white marble, and it inspired awe in the minds of any who laid eyes upon it.

It was properly called the Seat of the Seas, and high upon the balcony of its tallest tower stood the High Lord Éolan, looking out towards the water and watching the sun slowly sink towards the horizon. He was tall, tan of skin, and his brown hair framed a face that he knew the people below both respected and loved. Although he looked young, Éolan was much older than his people thought by just glancing upon him. His deep blue eyes were what gave that away, seeming to hold ages of wisdom and experience behind them.

The silver buttons of his white shirt were undone down the middle, letting the breeze hit his thin, muscular chest. As a breeze drifted up from the sea, he closed his eyes and stood silently. Dusk had always been his favorite time of day in the capital, especially when the dark orange and purple rays of the sun reflected off the polished white marble walls. It made the whole palace, and most of the white city that stretched out below, seem to glow.

As Éolan opened his eyes and looked down, he could see the hustle and bustle of the day was winding down. The vendors were beginning to pack up their stands and head out through the gates towards the coastal villages, while the shop owners that lived in the city were preparing for the evening crowds by lighting their lamps and opening their sunshades.

Éolan had always admired Alamarayn, with its boulevards lined with tiny cafes, bakeries, and shops packed full of goods from all around the Great Isle. Many of the streets and covered bridges were fully canopied by flowering trees and vines, and in the few open spaces great groves of palms dotted the cityscape, swaying in the warm trade winds blowing in from the sea.

Being built on the upper delta of the Culann River, the waterways wound like snakes throughout the city. These gave birth to the wide canals on the lower tiers, which ran through the heart of the capital and fell through great turbines that generated much of the city's power. And as Éolan watched the large ferries, paddle barges, and small gondolas ferrying lovers and visitors to and fro, daytime business began to give way to the night markets and the pursuit of pleasures.

Looking back out towards the horizon, he once again closed his eyes as the breeze drifted up from the south. With it came the constant drone of the summer cicadas from their unseen hiding spots and the calls from the gulls overhead. He had always loved the nighttime sounds much more than those of the day, and after a few peaceful moments the sun finally sank below the horizon and he turned and headed back into his apartments.

They were one of the few things he liked more about the palace than his estate in the northern city of Nausica, where he governed as Steward. His rooms here were large and airy, with a constant breeze from being so high off the ground. On the walls hung some of his most prized pieces of art. Amongst them were a few lovely paintings, but most were in the form of finely woven tapestries.

Éolan admired his collection, and had always enjoyed finding new images and meanings woven deep into their backgrounds. Many were from here in Alamarayn, and filled with images of water gods, mermen, and other folklore of the seas. However, some of the rarest came from all over Aldaya.

Some were from the quarrelsome countries in the east, and filled with valiant battles between kings and queens. Two came from north of the Vellorian Mountains that few from the southern lands now dared to cross. The first was reminiscent of the deep jungles, and woven mostly from greens, browns, and darker shades of night. The other was quite opposite, and was woven with fiery reds and bright yellows that represented the sand lands. Yet the rarest of all hung in a glass case on the far wall and hidden from the light of the sun. Its charred remains were one of the only pieces of history that remained from a land now entombed beneath the waves, and looking at this one always made Éolan sad.

Coming in from the balcony, he took a deep, patient breath as he watched the three palace servants scurrying around his apartments. They were hurriedly packing the large open trunks upon the bed with clothes and papers, along with anything else that would be needed for his journey. But as he was about to return to the balcony, there was a knock at the door, and excitement flooded him for a moment. "Come in!" he said.

He had been hoping it was his husband, Callan, but as the large doors swung open a tan, curvy woman swayed in pushing a small food cart. She dismissed the three servants with a smile and quick wave of her hand before parking it alongside the large willow desk. Éolan caught her eye and she shook her head slightly. "He has not returned yet, meh lord."

Éolan nodded and forced a smile as he sat down, but he knew she wasn't fooled. He missed his husband, and as much as he had hoped to see him before leaving the palace, it looked as though it wouldn't happen.

The woman, named Chessa, was one of two senior assistants to Callan, and Éolan's favorite person in the palace (besides his husband of course). Being the Premiere Elect, his spouse had achieved the highest position one could come by in the Alamarayan leadership. Naturally, he had many servants, errand runners, and advisors, but Chessa seemed to be all of them wrapped into one.

When Éolan stayed at the palace, she also doubled as his aide, being the only one whom he implicitly trusted and enjoyed being around. It was no secret that he preferred to try and do things on his own. He had never been as comfortable as the other nobility when it came to the service workers making a fuss over him, but Chessa had always been different.

She was dark of skin, very short, and quite round. She had more teeth of gold than of white when she smiled, which she did often. She was in her middle years, spoke with the thick accent of her island home, and always smelled like the ocean. Like every day that had passed since Éolan had met her, she was dressed in her usual garb. It consisted of a large floral-patterned sheet that tied at the shoulder, and was always accented by various sorts of large tropical flowers tucked somewhere in her hair.

Today's choice was a large pink one called *summer's tide*. It was pinned neatly behind her right ear and looked quite vivid against the sea-foam cover-up. It smelled sweet as she placed a steaming cup of light brown kuva down in front of Éolan. He took a sip of the bitter and aromatic brown liquid before adding some creamed syrup, and eyed the large plate of mango and pineapple that his stomach didn't seem to have room for.

"I got a message for you, meh Lord," she said as she glided over to the cart and retrieved a small scroll. For her size, it had always surprised Éolan how light she was on her feet.

"Eh, I think you're not gonna be too happy. It's seemin' that the premiere will not be back until tomorrow, late night."

Éolan smiled. Chessa insisted on delivering messages in person, but usually told him the contents before he had a chance to open them. It had always interested him how she knew what was inside, yet the seals never seemed to be broken. "Thank you, Chessa. I'm sure he's just been held up again," he said.

Éolan was disappointed. He hadn't seen his husband in two weeks, and tomorrow morning he himself was leaving to spend at least a week at the Charis Vale. Months ago his presence had been requested for the annual gala that started the autumn term of the institution, and he had accepted. It had been quite a number of years since his last visit, and he had been excited about seeing some of his old companions and friends. But that was before all the rumblings in the East had started again, drawing the scrambling leaders to the summit in Volaris in hopes of avoiding a war that none of them could afford.

While the political news was troubling, the selfish part in him was frustrated that Callan had been forced to attend at all. Threats of war from the four Eastern territories were old and when one of the quarrelsome leaders didn't get exactly what they wanted, they threatened the invasion of their neighbor. It was like dealing with a group of young children in a sandsquare, children that had never learned to share. Although, after the recent skirmish between Endmoor and Sansori had resulted in the death of one of the King's sons, perhaps the summit was needed.

Oh well, Éolan thought, as he pushed the yellow fruit back and forth on his plate. *Too late to cancel now.* Chessa picked up on his downcast mood and took the opportunity to chime in.

"Don't be getting too down, meh Lord," she said as she came over and patted him on the cheek. "You will see your *Hy'eya* soon. Take a walk out to da palace gardens and breathe in da air. I'll finish da packing."

Hy'eya was a word from the islands. The closest translation was "lover eternal," although Chessa always said the translation didn't do the meaning justice.

As he took a sip of his kuva, he contemplated a stroll, but he knew the gardens like the back of his hand. They were beautiful, but had become boring. A walk alone out in the city, inconspicuously strolling by the shops and listening to the street musicians, was what he desired most. But there was nothing liberating or relaxing when moving about the city surrounded by six guards in armor, and he immediately abandoned the idea. He had snuck out alone before, but the capital city was not safe like Nausica, and he didn't seem to have the energy tonight.

In truth, the only thing he wanted now was to rest. He was never able to sleep well when he was on the cloud clippers. They were always too noisy, and he liked to be in control of his faculties while flying that high above the ground. But he knew that Chessa would not be leaving the room until his things were packed and he had gotten some fresh air.

"Maybe a walk to the gardens and back would do me good," he said as he smiled at the kind woman.

"Hey-o! Dat's da spirit. Now move that tiny bottom of yours. And stop by da kitchens for a bite to eat. You barely touched your dinner."

Chessa liked to point out that she didn't think Éolan had enough meat on his bones. But with that being said, if Chessa had her way, everyone alive would be at least fifty pounds overweight. Or as she called it, "healthy."

As Éolan neared the doors and his hand was about to close around the handle, it turned by itself and opened, nearly knocking him over. It was the other of Callan's senior assistants, a man named Baylin Tennon. He was quite the opposite of Chessa, and Éolan had never particularly cared for him. He was tall, bald, and always dressed in black robes. His demeanor was distrustful, and his sincerity was sickeningly sweet and too eager for Éolan's liking.

"Another message for you, Lord Éolan," he said courteously.

"Hey you! I'd think you would have heard of knocking before?" piped up Chessa.

It was no secret that the two detested each other, and when Chessa finished Baylin simply looked at her for a moment and turned his large nose up. "Is there anything else?" he asked Éolan through his smile.

Éolan had already ripped open the parchment, read it, and was moving towards his desk to hurriedly jot down a response.

"Yes," he said, finishing in a hurry. "I am going to need you to send this off tonight. Use the carrier it arrived on. It will be the only one able to find her."

Baylin's demeanor perked up at this. "May I ask who *she* is, my Lord?"

Éolan frowned. Everyone in the capital knew that man had a flair for gossip and loved being privy to information that was clearly none of his concern. But just as he was about to politely move on, someone else in the room decided not to miss out on her opportunity.

"Oh-ho!" piped up Chessa.

Éolan slowly closed his eyes and inhaled deeply, giving a slight shake of his head and trying hard not to smile.

"Now we are asking da High Lord his business, are we? Well, I can tell you that if we were in my land, I'd put you out on da street," said Chessa.

"Well, then the sea gods must be shining down on me today. Because we aren't on one of your quaint little islands and you certainly aren't in charge of staff here in the palace," Baylin said. His smile was a work of art, and not a tinge of anger came through in his voice. But his eyes said volumes.

Chessa slowly shook her head up and down in agreement.

"Lucky for you, Mr. Baylin. Lucky indeed." They both went silent, but Chessa never let him out of her sight as she continued the packing.

She had always been convinced that he was a dangerous man, which was something she had warned both Éolan and Callan of many times. Éolan could sense it in him as well, but Callan had always kept him in his service and Éolan could understand why. He did his job flawlessly.

"Please make sure it is sent off immediately," Éolan said as he wax-sealed the letter with his signature blue wave and handed over the envelope.

"Yes, my Lord. Is there anything else?" Baylin said through his smile, which Éolan had always noticed never touched his eyes.

"That will be all, thank you," Éolan said.

Baylin cleared his throat and said, "If you need anything at all before your departure tomorrow, please call upon me any time. As the premiere's *first* assistant, it is always my pleasure to make sure all of the proper arrangements are seen to." His large nostrils flared as he pursed his lips and bowed low before gliding out of the room.

Éolan sighed.

"Ha!" blurted Chessa just before the door slammed. Now that Baylin was gone, she had made her way into the bathing room and began gathering the things Éolan could do without in the morning.

"He looks like a great bat swooping around here all da time," Chessa chuckled. "And by da way, just what is da Queen of da Wanderers wanting at this time of night?" she asked.

Éolan sat back down at his desk and gave her a coy sideways glance before continuing. She had seen the seal of the Black Rose upon the envelope, and as Éolan set it and its contents aflame in the burning dish, he decided there would be no harm in answering her question.

"It seems the peace talks in the East have not gone as well as we had hoped. The Grand Marchioness, Bronwyn, was requesting sanctuary for her and her people on the high northern plateau of our lands. It seems she no longer feels safe on the plains."

Chessa opened the doors to the large willow wardrobe and disappeared inside. "And you said yes, I'm thinking?"

"I did indeed," said Éolan, leaning back in his chair. "We have plenty of space and her people are mostly self-sufficient. But they are slow to move and have many women and children with them. If war actually begins this time, I don't want them caught in the crossfire."

"You're always so kind and understanding, meh Lord." Chessa shut the wardrobe and made her way across the room before gingerly falling to her knees. She then plopped onto her belly and slowly started to scoot under the large bed. "That's why da Premiere loves you so much, I think." She was trying to get out Éolan's lined traveling cloaks that he used when venturing north during the winter months.

"Chessa," said Éolan shaking his head slightly and smiling. "It's late summer. What would I need those for?"

"You're heading to da mountains, meh Lord. My cousin Taia tells me your teeth can break from chatterin' up there! Unless you've got some like mine." She poked her head above the side of the bed and smiled, revealing the array of golden caps that covered many of her teeth.

II

Early Bird Gets a Wagon

THE NEXT MORNING ÉOLAN AWOKE with a start. His whole body was shaking and his breathing was labored, and after the disorientation wore off he sat up and drew back the blue curtains from around the four-poster bed. It couldn't have been much past five and the sun was not yet over the graying horizon, but he could already hear distant commotion in the city below. He took a deep breath as he smashed his head back down onto the feather pillow.

There had been a time when he had answered to no one, with the only deadlines and expectations being those which he had set for himself. But that life was distant now, and although he wanted badly to stay tucked in, he knew if he lay there much longer he would fall back asleep and be late for everything that needed to be done before he left the palace. If he only got his feet on the ground and stood up, he would be fine.

Twenty minutes later, he slowly stretched and made himself get up and head towards the washroom. As he passed the full-length mirror he stopped and stared at his naked reflection. His muscular body was covered in a cold sweat and he seemed pale. He didn't like when Callan was away from him, and his dreams always seemed to become much more intense in his absence. But it wasn't until he was done rinsing off in the grand pearl tub and lying there with his eyes closed did his dream begin to come back to him.

It had taken place somewhere deep in the Endless Marshes to the east, and in an old canoe had lain the body of a girl. She was young, perhaps fifteen, and all the colors in the dream were muted shades of grays and blacks save her golden blond hair. She was ghostly pale, almost to the point of being translucent, and cold to the touch. Éolan had been having similar dreams of the girl off and on for many years, but lately they had become much more frequent.

Sometimes she had been deep in a cave or on the mossy floor of a long-forgotten forest. Other times she was atop a snowcapped mountain, or drifted alone in the endless ocean. But no matter what the location, it was always the same pale girl.

At the end of the dreams she usually disappeared into thin air or drifted just out of reach. But for the first time ever it had ended differently. Éolan had approached the girl's canoe and she had stayed within reach. As he had leaned over the boat, something drove him to grab her hand and open it. Inside was an old, ornate, key, and when he tried to take it, her hand had suddenly clamped shut around his.

A strange cat that he hadn't noticed at first now lay next to her, and its emerald eyes had locked onto him and a low growl had come to his ears. As he looked back at the girl's face, her eyes popped open and blazed with purple light. She screamed and jolted up, sending an echo through the marshes and flinging Éolan backwards and into the black waters.

Tentacles and claws from the swamp creatures had then started trying to drag him to their lairs in the black water. As his head went under, all noise ceased except something just on the edge of his hearing. It was a strangely familiar voice that kept saying the same thing over and over, but he could barely make it out. But as he was dragged deeper and deeper down into the muck, the louder it grew. By the end, a woman's voice was screaming, "HELP HER!" so loudly that it rattled his brain.

The creatures let him go, but he was clawing desperately at his own ears, fearing if the screams grew any louder that his head might explode. Suddenly, the voice stopped, and he felt the urge to open his eyes under the water. The black mud blocked everything from vision, yet he could still see one thing. The girl's purple eyes glowed just in front of him and were slowly fading away, and that's when he had woken up.

As he lay in the warm water watching the bubbles in the tub disappearing, he tried not to focus on the uncomfortable feelings associated with the dream. Instead, he was trying to figure out why last night had been different. He had never seen the girl in his waking life, nor did he understand why he recognized the shrieking voice that had appeared. His gaze drifted outside the open window as a big puffy white cloud rolled by without a care. Éolan wished he were that cloud, just able to drift above the world for a short while.

A deep gong sounded, letting the city know it was now six o'clock and telling Éolan it was time to leave his bath. He immediately went under water, pretending not to hear it, and when he finally emerged into his room, he looked around. His bed was made and his outfit had been laid out for him, and Chessa was walking around opening the curtains and singing to herself in her native tongue. Baylin was standing at the ready by the desk with the morning correspondence and trying his best to seem diligent.

"What can I do for you this fine morning?" he asked.

"Just the post please," said Éolan as he began to dress.

Baylin cleared his throat, and after a quick but smug glance towards Chessa, began reading off the senders from the stacks of scrolls and envelopes. Nothing that had to do with Éolan came up until the last letter. "Oh, this one looks to be from the premiere, my Lord. I must not have noticed or I would have given it to you straight away."

As Éolan rushed over and took the letter, Baylin smiled sourly. "Thank you, Baylin. That will be all," Éolan said, breaking the seal of the white swan and beginning to read.

The man bowed and swooped towards the door and left while Chessa kept up her humming and tidying.

The letter read:

My Hy'eya,

I am sorry about the brevity and timing of my letter, but it looks as though I won't be home in time to send you off. I cannot reveal too much of what occurred at the summit in Volaris in case this message is intercepted, but I fear our efforts will not have many lasting effects. Something strange is afoot in the east and troubles me, but I'll talk to you more about it in person. That stubborn ocean storm is still swirling over Endmoor, and the admiral has suspended all clipper travel until further notice, making it impossible for me to return before your departure. I have corresponded with the other stewards to inform them of my delay in the hopes of making your exit smoother, but that is not a guarantee. Now that you will be traveling by coach for a large portion of your journey, I have arranged to have Chessa travel with you, along with a guard that Captain Selar will have ready.

I miss you, my love. Try and make it back from The Vale as soon as possible. Be safe in your travels.

All My love.

This doubled the bad news for Éolan. It was official: he wouldn't see Callan, and he now had to travel by coach across the river lands. He would have to make it to Iccobar, the foggy capital city of Endmoor, and hope that the storm had passed by then so he could catch a clipper to the north.

He slipped himself into the rest of the outfit Chessa had laid out for him and fastened his signature blue cloak about his shoulders. *Traveling used to be so much easier with the mirrors,* he thought as he kissed the now folded up letter and put it into his inner pocket. That storm had now earned him three extra days of travel, most of it going to be looking out the window at nothing but endless mist and complemented only by the putrid smells of the swamps. If it hadn't been so long since he had been to Charis, he wouldn't have been going at all. As he gathered his journals and other important papers and was organizing his traveling bag, he thought about the journey ahead. At least he would have the company of Chessa.

"Well, it seems that the minister wishes you to accompany me to the Vale. I'm assuming you have proper attire for the journey?" Éolan asked as he turned towards Chessa. She was helping herself to the bowl of chocolate covered nuts by the door, but nodded as she dusted off her hands onto the particularly loud salmon-colored wrap she was wearing.

Éolan smiled. "Have our things sent down and I'll meet you at the main entry as soon as I can."

Chessa bowed and followed Éolan out of the room as he began to make his way towards the central part of the tower, but quickly veered off to the servants' stair and out of sight.

When he reached the center part of the tower, he took a seat on the *dobo*. It was a cushioned bench seat that moved up and down the stairs when carrying heavy loads. There were many that ran at the lower levels, carting those who couldn't make the climb of the tower multiple times a day, but this one was reserved for the premiere's apartments. And although he usually preferred to walk, Éolan knew it would allow him to move quickly enough and avoid being stopped too many times.

As the chain rattled and he began to make his way down the wide curving staircase, he stopped it for a moment and looked over the thick marble railing. He could see down to the floor of the main hall ten stories below, and it was milling with activity that he knew he must navigate through to get to his coach. But before that he had to make his way past the floors of the stewards, and that was not an easy task.

Although he held the same rank as the others, even less than some, many still looked to him for news and advice because they trusted him. Éolan had no desire to be involved in politics, but the Steward of Nausica held a seat on the council, and with it came duties he would rather have avoided.

He reached the ground floor in short time and approached where Chessa, Baylin, and Captain Selar stood near the entrance. Chessa was instructing two footmen where to take his trunks. It was far busier than normal today, whether it was from the rumors from the east or just being the first of the week, and the great hall was packed with people. The other members of council wore their midnight-blue robes with their white belts, and foreign dignitaries and palace servants rushed to and fro.

Éolan strode towards the door and, with a nod towards the group, they began to follow. Captain Selar was half a foot taller than Éolan and perhaps twice as wide, and all muscle. He quickly fell in stride as they exited through the large ornate iron and pearl doors. "Captain, it is a pleasure to hear you will be accompanying me on my journey," Éolan said.

They marched down the stairs and he saw four mounted guards in front and four more in back. He paused and shook his head slightly. "Although I think I must disagree with you on the number for my escort."

"Just following orders, my Lord," the man said, but Éolan swore he saw a smile creep into the sides of his mouth.

It was no secret that Callan was a bit overprotective, and Éolan usually obliged, but this was excessive. "Captain, I will permit two in front and two behind to appease the premiere, not including yourself, of course. But not one more."

With a nod the captain strode off and dismissed the other part of the guard and started issuing instructions. As Éolan neared the coach door a gangly and awkward young man came barreling around the front of the horses, making them rear upwards out of surprise, and nearly tripped over himself as he clumsily yanked open the door.

"Allow me, my Lord!" the young man exclaimed. For a moment Éolan paused and looked back at Chessa and Baylin as if they had an explanation. But the crystal clear voice of the captain rang out again.

"Alrik, I told you to stay at your post!" he said.

The lad turned red.

"I apologize, my Lord. This is Alrik, and he is under my training to become an escort for the premiere. He will be accompanying us to Iccobar, if that suits you."

Éolan could tell the young man was embarrassed, but under that helmet he also saw bravery and loyalty behind his naïve brown eyes and would gladly give the young man a chance. He smiled and nodded cordially to Alrik. "I take it this will be your first time as an escort outside of the city?"

The young man grasped his sword hilt and placed the back of his left hand up to his forehead. "Yes sir!" he said.

Trying his best not to smile, Éolan said, "Well, I accept nothing less than professionally trained men and women in my guard. I hope to not be disappointed."

As the blood drained from his face a bit, Alrik opened the door even wider and let out another "Yes sir!" so loudly that Chessa had bite her lip to keep from laughing.

As she and Éolan climbed into the roomy coach, they settled back into the dark blue satin seats and prepared for the long journey. He looked out of the window and upwards in admiration. Although his time here was less now than it had once been, he did love the Seat of the Seas. Its high ancient walls held many memories for him, and as he looked up towards the rooms he shared with Callan, he smiled.

He settled back into his seat and pulled the golden handle

that dangled down from the ceiling. As the sound of a little bell rang up towards the driver's stoop, the captain's voice rang out once more. The coach jerked forward, heading north and east towards the river lands of Endmoor.

III

Dreams within a Willow

AS SHE DRIFTED ALONG UNDERNEATH the brilliant night sky, Mim felt content. She had always admired the stars, and as they disappeared from her view, she felt sad. But the room she entered was beautiful, more the size of a great hall, with shelves that climbed from floor to ceiling and filled with amazing pieces of art and books. A woman stood above her, her kind purple eyes shining with love, and she had radiant golden hair just as Mim had. She disappeared, and as Mim sat up the woman was now seated with her head turned away and staring into an ornate crystal hand mirror. Upon it were etched images of gods and goddesses dancing under the night sky and beneath ancient trees.

As she began to sing, the mirror began to glow, as did the woman's eyes. The song was a tale of eight sisters that guarded the heavens, and the melody was so beautiful that Mim floated upwards and over to the woman's lap. Her reflection showed a toddler, but Mim knew it was her and giggled. The woman began to laugh as well. She let go of the mirror, but instead of it dropping and shattering on the marble floor, it stayed suspended in the air.

The woman spoke a phrase in a beautiful language that was foreign to Mim's ears, and the mirror began to glow brightly once again. As she finished, her reflection then took on a life of its own, and as the woman began to sing, so did her reflection. The harmony between the two was beautiful, and when the song was done the reflection stared back and smiled. The woman told it goodnight and the reflection nodded lightly before disappearing.

She put the mirror into a small silver chest with an ornate lock and a key sticking out of it. After closing the lid she slipped the key on a silver chain and fastened it around her neck. She then took Mim back to her bassinette and laid her down, but just as her head hit the soft pillow, the room shook violently and the stained glass window across the room shattered inward.

As she jerked awake, Mim nearly lost her center and plummeted down from her perch in the giant willow and into the black waters below. As she tried to regain her balance, she scraped her hand along the branch and sent her companion off to the side with a loud screech. "Mother of the king!" she shouted loudly.

Draped in her grey cloak and hidden within the reedy leaves, she was all but invisible save the fishing line hanging down from the branches. It was one of many that she had rigged to the huge trunk of the old tree, helping her to increase the chances of a good catch. Each line had its own bell or scraps of tin that would rattle when a fish began to tug at the other end, alerting her of a bite. And it was one of the bells jingling from above that had stirred her from the drowsiness of her recurring dream.

As the ringing grew louder, she wasted no time to pull out the tiny wooden invader that had found a home in the palm of her hand. She quickly scaled the branches of the tree and came to the correct bell and began to pull. The most important thing at the moment was to get whatever was attached to the other end of the rope. She drew the line up out of the water, but as the hook came into view it was empty of both fish and bait. "Ugh" she groaned as she sunk against the large trunk. "Well, there went breakfast, Jess!"

As she peered over to her right, her cat sat quite far below. With her dark brown and black fur, even her bat-like ears were barely visible from this high up. But her emerald eyes shot daggers through the misty air, and with a sultry look she turned away and settled grumpily down onto the branch to which she had been thrown down.

"Fine, be that way then. Dirty rotten..." Mim continued on in a frustrated mumble as she scaled the different branches to pull up all of her lines. She was unsure of the time, since the clouds were thicker than normal today, but by the lighter shade of grey around her she assumed dawn must be well on its way. Once done she nimbly climbed down and dropped silently into her leaky boat, where Jessel waited patiently for her ride back to dry land. Mim paddled swiftly and quietly, making sure not to disturb the swamp any more than needed. She knew what lived in the black waters, and none of the creatures were friendly to intruders.

As she left the cover of her willow, large raindrops began hitting the hood of her cloak and Jessel quickly curled up beneath it to try and stay dry. Mim pulled it more tightly around them and paddled onwards towards the house. Usually the ride lasted only a few strokes, but the storm had raised the water level almost to her shed. Within the last day she had begun to wonder what would happen if the water started seeping inside, but that was one of her lesser worries, and she had resolved to deal with it when, and if, it happened.

She thought about her dream for a moment but shook it off. She had been having it for as long as she could remember, and dwelling on it for too long started to make her sad. She never got past the shattering of the window, and although it used to bother her, the older she got, the more she felt that she might not want to know what happened next.

After a few more paddles the house loomed into view. Much of its former white stone was now a rough patchwork of shabby masonry, and its four walls leaned inward slightly due to the foundation slowly sinking into the wet earth. This skewed its features, giving the heavily draped and sagging windows of its three stories the look that all Endmoor now shared, one of neglect and sadness. It was called the Inn, although Mim had never understood why. It had been a very long time since it had been the host to weary travelers, mostly because no one traveled to her tiny town of Slaidburn anymore.

But Mim wasn't heading for the main house, and instead docked her leaky craft against the wall of a small cypress shed that had been built off of the back. She tossed Jessel in through the half-open window, which had long ago been swollen and stuck in its track, and clambered in after her. Mim preferred to use the window when possible, and when the water was this high it was even easier than normal. It allowed her to go in and out without having bother with those that lived in the main house.

As her feet hit the ground, a distant bell tolled six times, telling Mim she was late. She began rushing around her small room, and after undressing ran to the small metal washbasin on the floor in the far corner. As she began to clean off the mud and gunk from the swamp, the water quickly turned from clear to black, but she didn't have time to change it now. Just then there came a knock at the door and a gruff voice rattled in through the keyhole.

"Wake up, ya little prit!" It was Warly, the middle-aged buffoon that was the caretaker of the Inn. One of his tasks was to make sure all of the girls in the house were up on time for work, although she rarely ever needed it.

"I'm already up, Warly!" she shouted as she dipped further down into the cold water. She wouldn't put it past him to try and sneak a peek of her through the crack in the door.

"Wha' was that? Ya need me to come in and wake ya up proper?" he wheezed.

"I said I'm already up, you old goon! Now get away from my door before I go and tell Jennah what you're up to!" Mim said. She launched one of her worn shoes at the grey door as hard as she could, and it fell with a thud to the rough floor with more of the flaking paint.

Warly laughed deeply, which triggered a coughing fit as he hobbled off. Mim hated the way he always talked to her. He was nearing fifty, and probably the most unattractive man she had ever laid eyes upon. Half of his teeth were gone; he had one good eye, a bum leg, and reeked of *vexor* from dusk to dawn. Mim had always threatened to report him to Jennah, but deep down she knew he was harmless.

Jennah was the lady of the house, and had inherited it from her aunt after she had passed on. It now served as a castaway home for girls like Mim, who each paid a small amount for a room to keep them dry and warm at night. Of the ten women living in the main house, Mim was by far the youngest. Many inside had children of their own now, and with each new child the house grew more crowded and made the solitude of her shed all the better.

Jennah was very charitable and well respected, although many claimed she dabbled in swamp magic that kept her ageless. The use of the *craft* was frowned upon by much of the world now, and although not illegal like in other lands, some of the more conservative townspeople distrusted her. However, most of that came from the wives of the worker men who had wandering eyes. But as Mim thought about it, in the three years she had lived in her shed, Jennah really hadn't changed much. But Mim liked to keep to herself, and didn't see her too often.

Once Mim was sure of Warly's departure, she jumped out of the water and quickly dried off before throwing on her work garments. They were a little too baggy and worn, but clean, and she hurriedly tied the strings on her shirt, waist, and shoes before running over to the mirror. All that remained was a jagged shard than hung down dangerously from the frame, but it was all she had and looking decent was one of the only requirements of her job.

The reflection shot back an image of a young girl, no more than fifteen, and who looked a lot like the woman in the dream. Mim had always wondered if those vivid images were the last moments she had with her birth mother. Although she never fully understood it, she had always felt that the dream was more of a memory than random images. As a child, thinking about the woman had made her terribly sad, and forgetting it seemed to be the best thing for her to do.

As she ran her three-toothed comb through her hair, she smiled. She always liked it this length and it would still have quite a while to grow before she had to cut it again. The wig maker in town paid a good amount for it because he knew it was the best he could get, and it was in high demand. It was pale gold, and when the sunlight hit it a certain way, it seemed to shimmer. It made Mim laugh when she saw some of the older women in town with wigs made of her hair upon their heads. Even though they tried to fool everyone, they usually avoided Mim's gaze as they passed by. But her hair was not her most striking feature; that was her eyes.

Slightly oversized and almond shaped, they beamed back purple with a bright blue ring around the outer edges. It seemed the ring grew a bit smaller with each passing year, with the purple taking up more of the center. Mim had never seen anyone else with purple in his or her eyes before, save the woman from her dream.

Talula, one of the women that Mim worked with, had always said she thought Mim was part swamp fairy. She highly doubted that for one of two reasons. The first was that fairies weren't alive anymore, and had disappeared long ago. And the second being that in the old stories they could do wonderful things with their magic, like make flowers bloom and trees grow tall. Mim wasn't too hard on herself, but she knew she didn't do much that was considered wonderful, and she certainly wasn't flying around making flowers pop out of the ground. So the fairy explanation was definitely not the right one.

Pulling herself away from the mirror, she made her way to her bed and sank to her knees and reached under. She jiggled a board loose and pried it up. Inside was a small space just large enough to hold a coin purse. This was where Mim hid all of her extra earnings, and she checked on it every day before she left and the moment she came home. So far she had saved up thirty endins, which to her was a small fortune.

Its purpose was to someday get her out of Slaidburn, and although she didn't know much about life outside of her small corner of the world, she was sure that there were better places than this. Unlike many of the poor people in her town, she had dreams that someday she would travel and learn. It was a long shot, she knew that, but she had vowed to herself that she would never give up on it. But the coin also gave her the security that if she ever needed medicine from the apothecary in town, or emergency food for her and Jessel, she would be able to get it. She counted it quickly, and after reaching thirty she stuffed it back into its hiding space and headed towards the door.

She stopped to pet Jessel, whose long brown body was stretched out on the end of the bedding pile. But her cat wouldn't have it, and she put her large bat-like ears back against her head and sauntered over to the opposite end of the bedroll and sat facing the wall.

"Well, fine then. If you can't spare a scratch I might just forget your scraps at work tonight, you big sourpuss."

Jessel immediately turned around and walked merrily up to Mim's hands.

"That's a girl," Mim whispered into her ear as she bent down and flung the cat up and over her shoulder.

Jessel purred for a moment and butted Mims head with hers before jumping down and snuggling into the bed fluff for a nap. Mim stood up and made her way towards the door and grabbed her grey cloak, which had already dried. Lady Jennah had knitted it for her as a solstice present last year, and it was warm and nearly waterproof. Mim loved it, and as she threw it over her shoulders, she took one last look at her room before making her way out into the hall and creeping towards the front door.

As she made her way through the house, she noticed it was still quiet. Besides Warly, she was always the first up and first out in the morning, which she liked. It's not that Mim didn't care for the other women in the house, but she got particularly tired of hearing about all of their problems that none of them ever did anything to fix.

Inside smelled extra damp today, and the heavy maroon drapes and carpets were now traps for mold and mildew more than anything else. An open window would have solved much of the problem, but they had all been swollen shut years ago. The only thing Mim did like about the Inn were the ornate carvings etched into the frames of the doors and windows. The odd symbols were connected with vines, and looked as though they spelled something. But anytime Mim mentioned them to Lady Jennah, the woman either feigned ignorance or ignored her completely. After a while, Mim had taken the hint and decided to quit asking.

As she neared the front door, she heard Warly start to descend the crooked stairs from waking the girls above. She hurried and snuck out before he saw her and stepped into the pouring rain. As she backed up under the eaves, a large clap of thunder rumbled above her and the rain got harder. "The Water Bearers be damned," she murmured with a sigh.

She took off her worn black shoes, rolled up her pants, and pulled up the hood of her cloak over her blond hair. Stepping into the rain, she quickly made her way through the puddles and flooded holes as she headed towards another long day at the Last Stand.

IV

Eppalong Wynd

ONLY ONE LANE IN SLAIDBURN still remained on its southern edge and held its ground against the encroaching black water, and it went by the name of Eppalong Wynd. The right side sat on a bit of a rise and this was the only reason the marshes had not engulfed it completely. No one lived on the left, and a great gray wall now blocked the empty shells of the former houses. It stretched east and west along much of the territory of Endmoor, splitting it like the trade road did a few miles to the north. The locals called it the Veil, and although it looked solid, it was not made from stone and mortar like other walls, but of dense grey fog. Beyond it was nothing but the bogs of the Endless Marsh.

No one knew exactly what was within, because the few that entered had never come out again. But the locals said that a curse lay over it, trapping those that died within its boundaries to stay there and wander the mists until the end of days when the Esmë would return to free them. And ever since she was a child, Mim had listened to tales of people hearing strange melodies drifting through from the unseen. Some of the elders in the village claimed it came from the sirens, which were ancient swamp demons from the times when magic still dwelt in the world.

But Mim had never believed much of it, and those tales had become more folklore now than reality; stories that parents would use to scare their young children into obedience. But Mim had never heard anything herself, and she lived closer to the Veil than anyone. However, that didn't help remove her fear of what lay beyond, and when she made her way up the Wynd, she always kept to the right.

The only light on the street came from the few scattered oil lamps that hung from rusty iron poles. The little bit of electricity that still existed here was used in the town square only, and the outlying areas had gone back to lamplight long ago. However, they were set so low that they looked like floating orbs and really did nothing for navigating. This made it particularly treacherous at night if you were unfamiliar with the gaping holes in the road. The caretakers had long since forgotten about the huge cobblestones that made up the lanes in Slaidburn, and they were cracked and jaggedly misplaced all the way up to the doors of the mildewed wooden cottages.

If possible, the other structures along the Wynd looked even worse than the Inn. With wealth being a thing of the past, and most of the hardwood being used up over the years, the old shacks were pieced together with various types of softwood and thatch, which gave the area its nickname of the Quilt.

When Mim arrived at the back door of the Last Stand, it was half past six, and the kitchens were already full of huge steaming pots on the stovetops and fresh loaves of sweet bread cooling on the counters. The scents made Mim hungry and the heat from the ovens took the dampness out of the air. It always amazed her how much Miss Barley got done before she arrived, and many times she wondered if the woman ever slept.

She had gotten lucky today, and a small breakfast was on the little side table by the door, which consisted of a hunk of fresh baked bread and *skurash*. Mim knew it was just a mixture of yesterday's leftovers, but it always tasted so good she never complained. After all it was a free meal, and with no fish this morning it was well received. Miss Barley always took care of Mim when she could, and that hadn't changed since the day they had met. Mim easily owed her life to the woman.

Being without parents, Mim had gone into the care of the six elderly widows that lived near the center of town. They took care of the abandoned children in the Quilt, and after being found near the edge of the marsh and brought into town as a baby, they had cared for her as long as they could. But by the age of twelve she had been thrust out to live on her own and to make room for others. Twelve was the age of decision down here, and if you weren't wealthy enough for education you went into service or begging. But no one helped her find an actual job in service, or how to beg properly, which had been up to her as well. But luckily, after a month or so of sleeping in trees and surviving on scraps from rubbish piles, fortune smiled down through the clouds and gave Mim a chance.

One day, one of the old widows who had cared for Mim, named Nony, had been walking down the street in Slaidburn and dropped her basket of food. This sent the contents scattering across the street, and the starving children that lived in the alleyways quickly ambushed her and had begun taking her things. Mim watched as the woman tried to snatch up her precious goods, but the kids were too quick and too many. She knew the woman was kind, for she had often read to Mim on nights when her loneliness had become too much. And it had made her mad to watch Nony struggle against the children, many of whom she had raised and given a fighting chance at some sort of life. So she decided to show the best of her character and help out an old friend in need.

She had jumped down from her perch in the trees and chased off the kids with her sling before helping the lady pick up her things. Nony was so grateful that she gave Mim a large, bright red apple, which she devoured on the spot. But Mim's good deed got her more than an apple that day; it got her noticed.

A woman had watched the scene from across the square and admired Mim. Her name was Tella Barley, and she was the owner of the aptly named Last Stand Tavern located in the Quilt. She also happened to be in need of a young kitchen helper, and Mim's heroic deed had caught her attention. Although it didn't pay much, the position guaranteed a meal and a roof overhead. Mim had started the very next day and had been there for nearly three years now, being paid just enough for her tiny shed and a few articles of clothing.

Mim treasured that moment as she finished her breakfast and hopped down from her stool. She began stirring the daily concoctions on the stoves and checking the loaves still in the ovens before Miss Barley returned from the storerooms. She was a middle-aged woman with greying hair, which was always braided and put into a bun on the back of her head. She was heavier set, most likely from all the years she spent in the kitchens, but light on her feet. She had toughness about her, but it was the same kind that all people who lived this far south seemed to have. Her eyes were deep brown, and by all accounts, she had been a beauty in her youth.

"Morning, Miss Barley," Mim said.

"Mornin', Mim," she said.

This was generally all they spoke until the breakfast crowd came through around seven. Until then, Mim went around doing her usual duties in the kitchen before heading out into the dining room. Once out front she had to make sure the lamps were lit and all the tables set.

Right at seven, the workers would come in to eat before heading to the north for their various jobs in the rift fields and mines, with many of the jobless right on their heels. The Last Stand had become more of a relief kitchen than a dining establishment over the last few years, and Miss Barley was now given a stipend from the capital that was used for public food aid. She stretched it well, and most people left content and able to make it until their next meal.

The first of the people were just beginning to head through the front door, and as usual none of Mim's co-workers were on time. Although breakfast was usually cut and dried, Mim couldn't fill the dishes, serve all of the people, and clean the tables alone. She yelled back to the kitchens, "The crowd's arriving and I'm all alone out here, Miss B!"

Distantly, she heard the response she knew she would get. "Just make do, Mim!" And so the day began as usual, with Mim running herself ragged trying to do everything alone out front until someone decided to show up.

At half past seven, Mim heard Talula barrel through the back door. The young redheaded woman was one of the sweetest people she had ever known, but was constantly late.

"Sorry, Miss B!" she said breathlessly. "The youngest was up all night with a chill and I..." suddenly her voice trailed off into nothing, and Mim knew why. Miss Barley had just given her famous "I don't give two meals and a coin purse, just get to work" look. Mim had gotten it a few times herself, and although it wasn't meant to be mean, it sure got you on task quickly.

"Hurry up, Talula, ya lazy cow!" screamed Mim. She knew the woman had three young kids at home, but she was getting steadily behind and the cramped dining room was looking particularly cluttered.

"Hold your horses, ya little swamp rat!" Talula said, smiling through the service window. She then came bursting through the door with her large tray in hand and immediately began clearing the tables.

As Mim ran into the kitchens to get more pots of food, Candy arrived to start on the dishes. She didn't even bother to defend her tardiness and just walked straight to the sink, nearly knocking Mim over, and started getting down to business.

"Well good morning to you too!" Mim belted as she waddled out of the door, heaving a pot of potato mash that weighed nearly as much as she did.

Unlike the girl's name suggested, the dishwasher was sour in both attitude and smell. Her dark greasy hair always seemed a week behind in washings, and the acne on her face generally kept her hidden in the kitchen.

After breakfast was done, it was time to start on lunch. Talula cleared and cleaned as Candy trudged along with the dishes and Mim worked with Miss Barley as they slaved over the upcoming meals. As usual, the old cook made a full lunch seemingly appear out of nothing, that afternoon's being a hearty vegetable stew with pieces of roast mutton and accompanied by her signature sweet bread. It was also delivery day, and at eleven the cart arrived from the market in Slaidburn.

To Mim's surprise, the delivery driver was not the usual sweet-tempered old man, but a young sleazy boy named Snife Bestlay. As he leaned in the doorway to the kitchen and smiled, a hungry look crept into in his eyes as he stopped on Mim. She saw nothing more than an oversized rat with his jagged teeth, huge nose, and scraggly-whiskered chin. No one liked the boy because they knew of his extra-curricular activities. Snife was in a group of young teen boys called the Night Runners. They preyed on innocent girls and drunken women dumb enough to roam the Quilt alone after dark.

"Just put the bags down by the door like usual and get out. You're stinking up the kitchen," she said.

Candy laughed and Mim smiled in triumph at the jab, but Snife didn't appreciate it. He seemed in an extra nasty mood this morning and as he started to cross the kitchen, Mim reached into her pocket and grasped the handle of the bread knife she had tucked away. But, as if on cue, Miss Barley came out from the pantries before things got nasty. She, like the rest, knew Snife's reputation.

"You listen to me, you nasty little boy. Filth like you is not allowed in this establishment. If you're delivering now, you will leave everything at the back door and we'll bring it in ourselves. Understood?"

Snife sneered and turned to leave.

Miss Barley smacked him on the back of the head with her wooden spoon. "When I ask you a question, I expect an answer."

Mim's love for the woman grew.

"Yes you old cow, I get it!" snapped Snife.

Candy laughed and Mim glared at her. Lucky for Snife, he was quick on his feet because Miss Barley went after him again. As he ran out the door and clunked down the old wooden stairs that led to the alley, the cook turned her attention on the dishwasher.

"Candy, make yourself useful and go grab the other bags of grain and put them away. And if you think that boy is so funny, I'll keep you here until midnight and send you across the Quilt alone and see how you fare."

Candy's smile vanished, and she ducked her greasy head and went out to fetch the remaining supplies from the cart. The cook then turned towards Mim. "Be a dear and run out and make sure he leaves me a new order list."

Mim ran out the back door and into the steady rain that was still falling. She took off her shoes again, and trudged around the other side of the old supply wagon, putting out her hand. "Miss Barley needs a new checklist." Even though it was mid-morning, she didn't trust being alone with him one bit. He looked at her and smiled, revealing his nasty yellow teeth.

"What's in it for me?" His breath was rank and made Mim take a step back.

"I don't know. Maybe I'll buy you some mouth soap next week when I get paid."

The greasy boy's smugness faded. He reached out and grabbed Mim's throat. He pushed her back and she thudded against the brick wall. He leaned in towards her ear and spoke, his nasty breath making her want to vomit.

"You listen here, you tasty little thing. It would be in your best interests not to make enemies with me."

His other hand was now sliding slowly up her shirt, and for a moment Mim froze. Other girls might let him get away with stuff like this and not put up a fight, but not her.

She kneed him in the crotch, which sent him doubling back into the wagon. She then pulled back and planted her right fist squarely into his nose. This sent blood trickling down his face and him into a heap near the side of the wagon. He looked pathetic lying on the muddy road in a ball, and Mim looked at him pitifully, but shouldn't have paused. He kicked her hard in the knee, sending her bouncing against the hard bricks and falling into a mud puddle. He yelled and she covered her head with her arms as he lunged at her again.

As he jumped onto her, Mim once again tried for the bread knife in her apron but couldn't get her hands free. But behind Snife a red blur streaked across the alley and with a large thud he fell back onto the ground. Talula stood above him now, with a large iron pan held steadily in her hands. Then came another smack, and Mim looked up just in time to see Miss Barley sending the horse pulling the delivery cart galloping down the alley. Snife turned and yelled in frustration. With blood streaming down the side of his face, he got up and began staggering after his cart. Talula went after him, swinging feverishly as she chased him partway down the alley.

Miss Barley helped Mim up and started leading her towards the stairs that rose up to the door. She limped back into the kitchen and the old cook got her cleaned up and fetched a small glass of warm milk to help calm her nerves. She then walked over and grabbed her coat.

"Where are you heading, Miss B?" Mim asked, trying in vain to remove the mud stains from her shirt with an old rag.

"I'm heading to the market and then to the mayors and making sure something is done about that boy. And today!"

The look in her eyes was fierce, and as Talula began to protest, the woman just continued to march towards the back door. "Lunch is all but ready, just serve it!" And with a slam of the door she was gone.

When noon arrived, the much smaller crowd piled in. It was usually women and children, since most of the men were away at work in the rift gas fields up north. Lunch wasn't free either, costing two endins per adult and one per child. Although it wasn't much, this cut back on the amount of people that came in to eat. Today only about thirty were there, so lunch was a bit quicker than normal.

By two o'clock Miss Barley was back and working silently on dinner. Tonight looked like it was going to be particularly busy, and at five thirty people began lining up outside in the rain. When the doors opened at six the dining room filled instantly, but the filling of empty stomachs weren't all that the people had on their minds. The men were telling strange tales of war in the east, and of shadows settling in the Grey Mountains to the north. As she stopped by a table of burly men on her rounds, Mim picked up some of the conversation.

"...aye, and according to Gabdy, ten folk from Dane have gone missin' within the last week. Not a trace of them found neither. And there's word of the Gypsies massing up near the borders as well... "

She moved on, trying not to think about the poor missing people, or the strange Wanderers, but it was like this at every table. And while Mim only caught bits here and there, it was enough to make her feel uneasy.

As she stopped at her final table in the corner, an elderly woman named Ilanya sat there with her daughter, granddaughter, and great granddaughters. She had always claimed to be a viewer, being able to see things that had not yet come to pass. And although Mim didn't believe any of it, she was still put her off by the way the woman stared at her all of the time. As she quickly plopped the spoonful of the pork sausage casserole and hunk of cornbread on their plates and began to leave, Ilanya's bony hand grasped Mim's wrist and pulled her so close that only she could hear her whisper.

"A threat is coming for us all my dear, but you most of all. It has finally arrived, and now the veiled stars in the sky are in danger of going out for good."

Ilanya's daughter was now out of her seat and prying the old woman's hand off, while Mim did her best to smile and be polite. Most of the old woman's days and evenings were now spent sitting in the old wicker rocker on her front porch, mumbling tales filled with fairies and demons to any child who would sit with her. Sadly, even when no one was there to listen, she mumbled on anyway.

The only other hiccup was when Mr. Ol'Grady, the clockmaker, seemed to have reached his limit in vexor. This happened almost daily, so Mim wasn't surprised when she had to walk him out to the bench across the street. It was embarrassing, but most of the townsfolk were used to his behavior and felt sorry for him. Mim knew they all remembered clearly why he now acted the way he did, and wondered sometimes at their callousness.

Just shy of a year past, his wife and children had disappeared. Her name was Lena, and although she was never the most together-looking woman, she always had a smile and a kind word to say when she brought her three children in for mealtimes. She had apparently descended from one of the old wealthy families from the southern counties, whose money and property had long ago been swallowed by the swamp.

She constantly spoke of them and their old house, with their fortune being the center point. Mim remembered the woman talking about it almost to the point of obsession. She also never seemed satisfied with her husband's amount of coin, or him in general. It was sad watching him work so hard for a woman who didn't give him the light of day, but instead sat dreaming of a rich prince who would never come.

But one day on her way to work, Mim had seen Lena and her kids walking along the Wynd. They had looked strangely blank, and fearing for them, she had ran and gotten Jennah. But just as the two rounded the corner on the way back, they saw all four step through the Veil and disappear into the swamps. Mim had tried to go in after them, but Jennah hadn't let her, and they were never seen or heard from again.

Ol'Grady spent days standing at the edge, wailing into the mist for their return. His only answer was the silent swirl of grey that now stood between him and his family. Shortly after, he had turned to the bottle for comfort and hadn't put it down since. Mim had always given a kind ear to him when he wanted to talk, but he was now a ruined man, and she had never felt sorrier for another human being in her whole life.

When she re-entered the kitchen with the last of the empty dishes, Talula was in full-blown complaint mode.

"My achin' feet! I think everyone from Slaidburn to the capital ate here tonight. Not to mention it's colder than a well digger's backside on winter's eve back here! When did it get so chilly?"

Tossing her tray on the counter, she walked over and sat on the floor by the large, warm ovens and began rubbing her ankles. Mim yawned in agreement and began to wipe down the surfaces that Miss Barley was done with.

"Don't you worry Talula; you just sit on your big rump while I clean up. I really don't mind." Mim knew it was a little late in the day for such jokes, but she didn't care tonight.

Talula glared and her, and her response was to launch a large chunk of bread across the room, aimed directly at Mim's head. Mim caught it and threw it back towards Talula, who grabbed it out of the air and took a large bite with a smile as she continued rubbing her feet. Miss B came out and started harping on them about roughhousing. As she returned to the cupboards, Mim could hear her mumbling and trying to come up with new and inventive ways to make the food last the rest of the week. It seemed the market had shorted her order again, making it exceedingly difficult to manage.

After some prodding, Mim got Talula to start putting away dishes in order to help out Candy. The girls' hands were so wrinkled from the soapy water they looked as if they belonged to an old woman. And just as Mim turned her attention to a particularly stubborn stain on the prep stove, the bell rang in the kitchen.

Someone had just come in the front door.

Unwanted Guests

IM STARED OVER AT TALULA, and although it was probably nothing, anxiety crept into the room. Not many people in the Quilt were out this late, and after today's run in with Snife, she wasn't fond of someone just waltzing in at this hour.

"Didn't you lock the door?" she asked Talula.

"Of course I did! Maybe it didn't catch. It's probably Ol'Grady wanting another jarful. Just go out there and tell him to go home!" Talula said.

"I'm busy. You do it, you're the one in charge of the front."

She turned back to the stain she had been working on, but Talula was not giving up.

"No way! I'm done out there for today. And besides, I'm elbow deep in suds!"

"Well I don't care who it is." Candy said in a low voice. "We're closed and I'm not washing another dish."

She dried her pruned hands on her damp apron and marched through the service door, but as she began to tell whoever had entered to go home, she was quickly cut short.

The voice was low and strange, and although Mim thought it came from a woman, she couldn't be sure. It was empty and cold, and this made her and Talula rush to the door and press their ears against it to try and listen. Although they couldn't make out exact words, the strange woman's voice sent chills up their spines.

"Mim, I've got to get going before it gets too late. Candy can finish up herself," whispered Talula.

"No, wait! Don't you want to know who it is?" pleaded Mim.

"Tell me about it tomorrow," she said through a yawn.

And as the door shut, she could see Talula's red curls disappear into the mist. Mim huffed. A moment later, the voices in the dining room stopped and she heard Candy start to walk back towards the kitchen. She hurriedly began her duties again, acting like she had never stopped.

When Candy walked in, Mim turned to ask her about the guest, but the look on the dishwasher's face stopped her from speaking. Her eyes stared straight ahead, and she didn't seem to notice Mim or the fact that Talula had left. Her gaze was blank and she walked straight towards the cupboards in the far back where Miss Barley was still counting inventory. Mim took the opportunity to peek through the door and try to see the woman with the strange voice, but two tall figures in dark, mud-stained cloaks were with her and blocked her from view.

As Candy and Miss Barley came out of the stores, the old cook was furious. Candy had her by the arm and was leading her out into the dining room. No matter how the woman protested, Candy just kept walking with her hand clamped firmly on her arm and staring blankly ahead. When they entered the dining room, Mim again assumed her position at the door to try and hear what was going on. She cracked it this time and the voices were much clearer.

"My companions and I desire an evening meal. The fresher the kill the better," said the strange voice.

Who eats raw meat? thought Mim.

"I don't have anything freshly butchered to give you," replied Miss Barley.

Mim noticed she sounded strangely more distant by the second.

"Dinner ended at seven," Miss Barley said.

"I desire a meal," the voice said. "So march your old bag of bones back into the kitchen and find one."

It seemed like all air had left the building. No one had ever talked to Tella Barley like that. After the lifetime of hard work the woman had put in, feeding some of the most impoverished and hungry people in all the lands, she deserved to be treated better than this. By the door, Mim waited for the explosion she surely thought would come. She had seen Miss Barley throw grown men out of the front door for less, and surely this person was a goner. But as the seconds ticked away, nothing happened.

Fine, thought Mim. *I'll give this elite her meal and she can move on.*

She ran to the ovens and grabbed the large pot of leftover pork sausage from the day's dinner, and although it was mostly scraps, perhaps it would be enough to get them on their way. She then quietly tiptoed into the dining room and crept up behind Miss Barley. "Excuse me, ma'am, but this is all the meat..." As she rounded Miss Barley and Candy, she stopped dead.

Her words caught in her throat and she was unable to breathe. The woman at the table was the strangest looking person she had ever seen. Her body was thin and gangly, and her pale skin stuck out jaggedly in places as if it were trying to cover too many bones. Even sitting down Mim could tell she was tall, and her thin robes were midnight black and hemmed in places with dark maroon embroidery. Then Mim took in her face, and it was paler and more terrifying than the rest of her body.

Her cheekbones were set a little too pointy and high. The mouth was nothing more than a thin slit stretched too far across the length of her face. The nose looked as if it had been removed, shrunk, and poorly placed back on. And her eyes were ghastly and tilted upwards too far, and completely black with veins around the outer parts. Their color matched the hair that came down from her dark hood, which had jagged protrusions poking out at a few points near the back.

"Oh! I didn't smell a child," the creature said. As her black eyes met Mim's purple ringed with blue, she stopped.

"Well, what do we have here? How strange..." She got up from the table and circled her. At full height, the creature stood at least two feet taller than Mim.

"I can smell the sweet scent of youth a mile away, little piglet, yet somehow I had no idea *you* were here." A cold, pointy, finger ran across Mim's cheek and up to her temples. "And what strange eyes you have."

Mim was rooted to the ground and dared not move. Whatever stood before her seemed to be a demon that had jumped off the pages of one of Ilanya's stories, and as she glanced towards Miss Barley and Candy for direction, the two were expressionless. They stared ahead in some sort of trance. *What was wrong with them?*

A lightning bolt cracked overhead and the woman let out a high-pitched laugh. When her oversized mouth opened, Mim could see two rows of sharpened teeth that filled the inside: one in the front like normal, and another jagged row sitting just behind it. The two figures that accompanied her said nothing, remaining still and hidden under their cloaks.

As she looked down at the blond girl, for the first time in over a thousand years, curiosity crept into Morra's mind. The girl had no smell, and try as she might, Morra Losis couldn't sense a trace of her except with her vision. But even stranger were her eyes. Purple eyes like those she had only seen many ages ago, and the bearers of them had disappeared from the sphere before the Great War in the north had begun.

But yet here in front of her one remained, and she wondered to herself whether her queen would find interest in this young human. *Oh, most certainly,* she thought. This revelation was the only thing keeping her from devouring the succulent girl on the spot. But if she lost her now, she would have to hunt for her like mortals did, and that was certainly not going to happen. Then the most wonderful idea came to her mind.

With the centaurs it had always been the hunt, the Dwarves their precious jewels, and the Elves their knowledge. But with humans it had always come down to their desire for freedom and independence. And although she hadn't been awake for long, she knew in this age that true freedom could only be attained by one thing: wealth. She knew exactly what this poor little mongrel desired most just by looking at her torn outfit and dirty hands.

"Well, it seems that one servant around here knows how to appease a guest of status. And I have always prided myself on paying the help."

Morra Losis snapped her fingers and one of the tall hooded figures glided over, producing a large coin purse. She dipped her hand in and pulled out a large handful of endins and sprinkled them into the pot of meat with a smile. The taller creature then went back to standing by its twin before she drew herself closer to the girl once again.

"That is for the meat, dear."

She then reached into a pocket from the inside of her cloak and pulled out a very small black purse. It was made of a shimmery fabric and all over it were dark maroon shapes.

"And this is for you."

As her hand placed the small pouch in the girl's free hand, a tremor went through her. She could barely contain her appetite.

She grabbed Mim's jaw with one hand and effortlessly lifted her off of the ground, running her forked purple tongue up Mim's cheek. The pot dropped to the ground, sending pieces of raw pork and coins spilling onto the rough floors. Her grip was so tight that she felt the girl's jaws beginning to crack. She hadn't had a meal this intriguing in an age, and her resistance was crumbling to the need to satisfy her hunger. *What can one little bite hurt?* she thought.

But as she thought of her master, she quickly let go, dropping the girl back to the ground and turning back towards the table. As she bent down and picked up a raw piece of intestine and dangled it in front of her face, she said, "I just don't think this will do. I certainly do not eat off of the floor, and when I feed I have always desired something with a little more...spunk." She turned towards the dark greasy haired girl and let out a low gurgle, briefly revealing her jagged rows of teeth. Lifting her enchantment, the girl came out of her stupor, and after a moment began shrieking and backing away.

Mim turned and ran, barreling into the kitchen in a panic. She dropped the small black bag onto the counter, and thinking quickly, ran to the back door and kicked it open before running into the store room and hiding behind the bags of flour. As the creature came through the kitchen door it stopped and began sniffing the air, quickly finding the black bag upon the counter where Mim had dropped it. She smiled down at it and looked towards the open back door before returning to the dining room.

Even after the screams of Candy ceased and the ding of the front door bell told her that the demon woman had left, Mim stayed where she was for a long while. She wasn't sure how much time had passed, but when she slowly crept out from behind the bags of flour she still moved silently towards the dining room. Miss Barley was still there, standing in a stupor, but Candy was gone.

Mim ran to the door and pulled the wooden bar down to secure it before turning to the cook, and after a few moments of prodding she began to come too.

"What in the Esmë's name am I doing out here?" she said, looking around confused. "Mim, what's been going on? Where are Talula and Candy?"

Mim simply stared up at the woman, not having any idea where to begin or having the heart to explain.

"I think it's time for you to go upstairs and lie down, Miss Barley," Mim said. The old woman smiled blankly and headed into the kitchen. Mim watched her as she slowly grabbed her things and headed towards the stairs and out of sight.

As Mim stood there in the empty room, she had never felt so confused and alone. The walls seemed to be staring at her, wondering what she was going to do next. Her senses were heightened and anxious, and all she could think about was making it home safely. Coming out of her thoughts, she realized it was time to leave, but not just the Last Stand: the Quilt as well. The strange woman that had just left had taken an interest in her, and Mim had no intention of ever seeing her again.

She ran to the kitchen and grabbed an empty grain sack, stuffing it with two loaves of bread and a large container of the casserole that would last her for days. In the storeroom she also found an old canteen that was bound to come in handy. She swooped by the bin that held all of the extra scraps of cooked pork and picked out a few for Jessel.

On her way towards the door, she stopped at Miss Barley's inventory book and picked up the pencil. She couldn't write well, but she knew enough to jot down a quick goodbye. She hastily scribbled an apology note to the kind old cook, telling her that someday she would come back and repay her for all the kindness she had shown. She told her about the loaves of bread and casserole, and to just take it out of the week's wages that she would never be picking up.

She grabbed the sack of food and a spare box of matches off the counter, and just as she wrapped her cloak around her, a crash came from the alley. Mim blew out the last lamp in the kitchen and felt her way towards the dining room in the dark. Right at the door she placed her hand back onto the small purse upon the counter. The fabric was so soft it felt like liquid in her hand, and for a moment she thought of leaving it behind.

But as she picked it up, it jingled, and Mim's heart skipped a beat as she opened it. From the light that seeped in through the crack of the door, she saw a small purse full of golden coins. The light of the low flames danced off of them and reflected back into her eyes. They seemed to draw her in, and the symbols and designs on them were strange and unlike any she had ever seen.

She closed the purse and snuck out into the dining area, stopping to pick up the endins from the pile of meat on the floor. There had to be at least twenty, and Mim picked as many out as she could find.

Something creaked outside of the front entrance, and she looked around in case anyone else had seen her discovery. She knew no one else was in the room, but people in the Quilt would kill for the amount of money in the bag she now held. She tucked it in her grain sack and made her way towards the front door and undid the bracing bar.

As she tiptoed onto the street, her heart was pounding faster than it ever had, threatening to beat right out of her chest. Her mind was already racing with plans about what she could do with the money she had just found. She didn't know much about life outside the Quilt, well, anything really, but the amount in the bag would have to be enough to at least get her somewhere.

She had heard of many places that taught young people skills in service work, reading and writing, and many other trades. And even in this remote corner of the world, she had heard of the Charis Vale. It was where the wealthy lords sent their children to learn anything that they wanted, and then grow up to be successful like a shop owner, a full cook, or even a teacher! If she could only get in, maybe she could work off the rest of the cost.

And even if she did make it there, she didn't know what

she would teach. All she knew were some basic survival skills, how to fish, and a few recipes from Miss Barley. *Who knows, she thought, maybe there is a teacher for that there as well.* Talula had said they taught kids how to swim in pretty ways and play weird musical instruments. If they could teach useless stuff like that, then surely they had somebody giving a lesson or two in how to survive.

But one thing was for certain; she would put the coin to much better use than that horrid creature would, and throughout her journey she vowed to help everyone she could along the way. She was getting out of this terrible place, and with a renewed sense of purpose she gathered her things and crept out onto the Wynd, leaving the Last Stand for the last time.

Hungry Mists

ANY VIGOR MIM HAD BUILT up immediately took a back seat to the fear that set in as she took in her surroundings. It had to be close to midnight, and the fog that had enveloped the Quilt was thicker than she had ever seen. She couldn't see one foot in front of her, and the amount of noise she was bound to make as she tried to navigate across town to The Inn would attract everything terrible to her like a magnet.

Snife Bestlay and the woman with the black eyes stuck out particularly in her mind. But she had no choice except to cross the Quilt and get to her room and develop her plan. And there was Jessel. There was no way Mim could leave her only real friend here to starve in the marshes alone. And she wasn't about to leave the extra months' worth of pay still hiding under the loose floorboard beneath her bed either.

So, carefully and slowly she began, one foot at a time, creeping like a ghost through the fog. She had navigated the way many times at night and had it memorized. But what worried her most were the unseen potholes and trash that riddled the roads and alleys she needed to take. Her only defense this late was silence, and if she made too loud a noise it could mean the end of her.

Her only bit of guidance was the occasional glow from one of the old hanging lanterns that lined the wynd. The light from them didn't even reach her on the street level, and if anything added to the eeriness and did nothing to ease her anxiety.

As she walked on, the paranoia of the mists grew worse with each passing step. Every few moments she would stop and crouch down on her heels, swearing footsteps were coming up behind her. The thought would send her heart racing for a moment, but once the ambush didn't happen, she would rise and begin again. At the spots where the lamps would make the black turn to grey, she imagined seeing ghostly faces out of the corner of her eye, or feeling the breath of the dead on her neck.

She thought of all of the people that had died in the marshes trying to find their way out. It took all she had to keep her wits about her and not be consumed by her fear, but she was halfway home now and had to keep moving. Only three blocks before she hit the road that led over the bridge and down to the Inn, and that was one road she could skip down blindfolded.

As she was nearing the next eerie lamp, Mim heard something. It wasn't footsteps, but a distant wheezing that seemed to be coming from a bit farther up and to her right. She stopped, trying to discern what it could be, and crouched to the ground. She couldn't leave this side of the street; it would risk making too much noise. But going towards anything strange in this darkness seemed like asking for the Sister of the Moon herself to come and take her away to the halls of the dead.

This thought made her even more terrified than she already was, and her hands began to shake.

Suddenly, a flash of the blond woman from her dreams streaked across the inside of her eyelids. It was just for a moment, but it was definitely her. Then an image of Jessel wandering the mists without food or love shook Mim from her stupor. She had to get her, and if she were to make it home, she was going to have to go past that noise.

She slowly stood up and began to move forward. The noise grew steadily louder, and the fact that it wasn't moving actually made her feel a bit better. At least her target was stationary. Within ten steps she kicked something and it let out a tiny moan. There was a person on the ground and the noise was coming from their strange breathing. She was about to step over the body and continue on, but she had to make sure it wasn't Candy or Talula.

It was too dim to see whose body it was at her feet without risking some additional light. She reached into her bag to grab the matches she had nicked from the kitchen, but at the last moment stalled. What if she lit the match and it became a beacon for the terrors that lurked in the night? For an instant, she considered putting them back and moving on, but Mim owed her friends enough to check. She pulled in her cloak around her and fumbled with the match for a moment before lighting it. Luckily the first one took, and Mim cupped it in her hand and moved it towards the face of the person on the ground. As it got closer it revealed the drunken, face-down carcass of Ol'Grady.

The strange wheezing was from his mouth being partly blocked by the grass where he had found his bed for the night. *You've gotta be kidding me,* she thought. She put out the match and did her best to sit the man up against the light pole so he could breathe properly. As she looked at the sad clockmaker, a tear came to her eye. This is what life had become for people down here in the Quilt. There was nothing left but broken spirits, sadness, and drunken messes.

She dug into her bag and pulled out the purse she had found and slowly untied the knot on top and opened it, and for a moment she thought she heard the bag itself let out a sigh. But she dismissed it quickly and reached in to grab one of the strange coins. She pulled one out and tucked it into the pocket of the man and leaned in to kiss his forehead. "Use this well, Mr. Ol'Grady. Your life isn't spent yet."

She took back up the cautious tiptoe for another block or so before a terrifying noise came to her ears. Somewhere in the distance she heard the sobbing moans of a woman, accompanied by the grunts and laughter of the Night Runners.

Mim froze. The boys hadn't heard her, but they stood on the only bridge that crossed the Morrowyne River and led to the Inn. There was no way she could swim the river at night, with its deep and narrow channel being hazardous even at the best times. But Mim had to get home, and the only way to do it was to cross that bridge. Slowly and silently, she moved closer to the sobs and muffled screams of the woman.

The boys obviously had their prey gagged so she couldn't make too much noise, but it wasn't enough to silence her. Mim wished she could tell how many of them there were, and made out at least six distinct voices. When she got to the foot of the old stone bridge, a boy started talking and Mim instantly recognized the voice of Snife.

"This is what you get, you red-headed tramp. You should have known better than to mess with the Lord of the Night Runners. And we are going to stay here and keep this up all night until that little purple-eyed rat tries to make her way home. Then we are going to have some *real* fun."

Mim's stomach dropped to her feet and her hands clenched. The runners had Talula. Mim was so furious she wanted to run across the bridge and start beating in the faces of the despicable monsters, but it was at least six to one at the moment and the odds were definitely not in her favor. If she was going to help Talula, she was going to have to be smart, and after a moment of contemplation she had an idea.

She reached down to the ground and fumbled for some rubble that had fallen from the wall of the crumbling bridge. After she had collected a few nice-sized pieces, she walked to the center of the road and called to Snife. "Oh, stank breath, is that you?"

She launched one of the egg-sized stones into the mist, knowing she hit one of them after hearing a crack and a shout. Hopefully it had been Snife, but any one of the nasty kids would do.

"I wondered if that was you, but a few blocks back I smelled your nasty mouth and I knew you had to be close." she said.

Nothing but silence met her ears, and this angered her. She decided to quit playing around and quickly get down to the point. "If you want a real challenge, why don't you come and get it? Surely I didn't scare you too much when I kicked you around today by your wagon!"

As soon as the words came out of her mouth, she knew that had done it, and she turned and ran down the Wynd before ducking off to the side of one of the lampposts.

Snife screamed, "Get her!"

Mim was almost invisible in her grey cloak as they ran by. She counted four or five sets of feet, which meant that most of the boys were now chasing a ghost into the mists. As she expected, Snife had stayed behind to guard the bridge and his prize. Mim could hear him talking to Talula again, whispering about the terrible things he was going to do to the both of them once Mim was caught. *Over my dead body,* she thought.

She stepped out onto the Wynd and began to launch stone after stone towards where she thought Snife was. If Mim drew him away long enough, maybe Talula could escape and save Mim some time.

Snife said, "You aren't getting past me, you little pretty. You can throw all the stones in the world, but your friend here will pay for every single one." Following a loud thud, Talula screamed through her gag, and Mim stopped throwing.

Something inside her snapped. She kept one stone in each hand and marched across the bridge. A strange anger boiled up inside her, rage she had never felt before, and it scared her. It seemed to have total control and she felt as if she was possessed. Talula's sobs led her right to where she needed to go, which was right towards Snife Bestlay, who she now intended to kill.

She knew she had arrived only after tripping over the legs of her friend, and right on cue the rat lunged at her from the shadows, but Mim was ready for him. She closed her eyes and turned around, as if being led by some invisible force, and threw out her right hand. The punch landed somewhere on his face and sent him reeling back, howling in pain.

A second later he was on top of her, ripping at her clothes and doing everything he could to subdue her. In his fury he managed to rip her rucksack from her back, sending its contents dumping out across the road. The purse had fallen to the ground and opened, sending half of the gold coins onto the road also, which caused her to pause briefly. With a fist to the face she went down onto the hard stones.

She jumped up quickly and continued after him, landing another two blows somewhere on his head. He tried feebly to defend himself, but Mim was too quick and angry for him to contend with. She moved like a cat in the darkness and used it as her weapon. Snife landed a few more blows to her face, but her adrenaline masked any pain and Mim advanced on him.

The dueling pair soon reached the opposite edge of the bridge, and Mim realized she had Snife pinned against its low railing. From what she could see, he was ducking and trying to protect his head from the blows she was inflicting. As he backed up against the railing, she took a quick step back before planting her foot squarely into his chest. This sent him over the edge of the bridge, and with a splash he disappeared into the swirling black waters below.

With not a second to lose she ran back, scooping the coins

and food into the sack, while running towards Talula. When she reached her she knelt down and started untying the bonds that held the poor woman's ankles and hands. As she ran her hands over her, Mim sighed with relief that Talula still appeared to be clothed. She was bruised and beaten, but it seemed Snife was saving the most terrible part for when he had caught Mim too.

Talula appeared to be too traumatized to understand that Mim was trying to rescue her, and seemed to have given up and just lay there. Mim was still trying to move her when screams started echoing from the fog. They were coming from where the other boys had run off to, and their footsteps were rapidly approaching.

The screams continued to get worse, and Mim realized it wasn't their usual hollering of victory, but of fear. In between she heard that same guttural wheeze she had from the creature at the Last Stand, and with each wail the sound of running feet lessened. Mim started to panic, and the anger came back again, taking control. She didn't have to know what was lurking around in the dark and picking off the Night Runners to know she wasn't going to stick around and find out. She turned back towards Talula and gave her a healthy smack on the cheek. "Get up you old sow! I didn't risk my neck to save you so you could just lie here. Now move!"

As Talula began to stir, the footsteps began approaching again. One of the Night Runners must have escaped and was barreling towards them. As the limping footsteps got closer she was ready to fight again, but they revealed a young boy of maybe twelve who collapsed at Mim's side. It was Barth Miller, and everyone in the Quilt called him Barty. He was a kind boy, and Mim knew his family from the Last Stand. They were decent people, and it surprised her that he was out running so young. The flesh on his arm had been torn almost completely off, and he was missing an eye. It looked like some beast had mauled him, but had stopped mid bite.

Mim knew the boy was dying, and after a moment his heart stopped beating and Mim knew he had passed out of this horrible existence. A guttural screech came from somewhere ahead, and Mim felt Talula's hand clasp onto her shoulder. "Come on. We've got to run!"

A dark shadow appeared on the bridge just behind Talula, and just as a pale hand reached out towards her friend neck Mim shouted "No!" A flash of purple light blazed out of her eyes, and her voice reverberated in the air around them. The bridge beneath them shook and the fog rippled and swirled outward from where she was crouched, forcing their assailant back and out of sight. She returned to normal in an instant, but Talula stared wide-eyed. She was at a loss, as was Mim, but another screech echoed out from the fog as the bridge shook again.

"Come on!" pleaded Talula. "We've gotta go!" She grabbed Mim's arm and hauled her off the cobblestones and they started to run, knowing that if they didn't get inside somewhere fast they would surely die on the streets tonight. As they got over the short bridge, they continued straight before ducking into an alley on the right.

"I've got to get to my kids," Talula said, gasping for breath. "It's only two blocks that way, I can make it."

Mim began to protest, but the woman cut her off. "Mim, if they die without me there to protect them I could never forgive myself. But you've got to get to the Inn. That thing is following us, and if we split up maybe we'll have a chance." The red headed woman leaned forward and gave Mim a quick kiss on the forehead. "I'll never forget what you did for me tonight, my little swamp fairy." More screams and shredding sounds were growing closer still, and after a moment the two turned from one another and ran.

Mim darted across the alley and decided to take a shortcut she knew. As she ran, she thought about what Talula had just said. The monster in the mists did seem to be following them; but more precisely, following Mim. As she barreled out of the alley and back onto the Wynd, one of her feet found a wide crack in the road and wedged in. As she bent down and was trying to loosen the oversized shoe, a low cackle rolled up to her ears.

Looking to her right, Mim saw the outline of Ilanya's ancient figure rocking in her chair on her porch. Her arthritic hands held a tiny nub of candle, and it gave just enough light to show her face. What the soothsayer had proclaimed at dinner seemed to take on new meaning now. Whatever it was that was out in the fog, Ilanya seemed to have known was coming for quite some time.

"Ilanya! Get inside!" screamed Mim as she finally slipped her foot out of the crack.

The old woman's daughter rushed onto the porch and grabbed the woman and began dragging her inside. But Ilanya kept speaking until the door slammed. "You can't hide from it, child! It pierces your walls and knows the dark parts of your heart. That's where it feeds."

The temperature of the air suddenly dropped and Mim took off at full speed towards the Inn. As she approached the front door the few oil lamps that usually stayed lit at night were out. Mim barreled through the old wooden gate, knocking it off its rotten hinges, and grabbed for the front door. It was locked. She banged as hard as she could. Just as she had given up and was beginning to sink against the door, Mim heard the latch unlock. Warly's large hand reached out and grabbed her by the hood of her cloak.

Once inside, he clasped his hand over her mouth to keep her quiet, but Mim didn't have time to get tossed around by this brute. She sunk her teeth deep into his palm and he yelped as his grip loosened. "Something's following me!" she said.

"You lil' wretch! I gotta get ya to the hideaway with the other gals or you're as good as dead!"

"No, Warly, I have to get out of here!"

As she turned to start down the hall towards her shed, the front door exploded behind her, sending splinters flying into her back. The next thing she remembered was the smell of the mildewed carpet before suddenly being lifted into the air. She only had enough time to think, *This is it*, before everything went dark.

VII

The Third Floor

HE NEXT THING MIM REMEMBERED was light. It was distant at first, starting with a deep orange and slowly growing like a sunrise. As she tried to open her eyes, she winced and quickly closed them again. Her hearing was faint but also beginning to come back as well. There was a ringing in her ears, and she could tell it had been worse at some point while she was unconscious. She was lying on her stomach, and when she moaned lowly she heard the scrape of a chair and the shutting of a door.

As she fully opened her eyes, she realized she was in her shed and lying on her bed. She could feel something warm next to her, which she assumed had to be Jessel. Her cat's low purring was sending tiny vibrations into her side and it gave her some comfort. As she tried to move her arm to scratch her companion's head, her body reeled in pain. She had never hurt so badly in her life.

It seemed as though every muscle burned and every bone was broken. Her back was on fire, and her face felt swollen and puffy. At least she had survived. The last word echoed around in her head. As all of the memories of the previous night came flooding back like a tidal wave, her breath caught in her chest and tears came to her eyes.

The door opened and Lady Jennah came gliding through. She was more disheveled than Mim had ever seen. Her long dark hair was up in a tight bun, with haphazard pieces sticking out all over her head. The kohl around her eyes was nonexistent except for a few dark smudges, and her brown dress was dirty and wrinkled. A large bandage was on her right cheek, and dirt was caked under her chipped finger nails. It seemed as though Mim hadn't been the only one to have a rough night.

"Colette is bringing you something for the pain, honey, don't try and move. We couldn't give it to you while you were asleep because your breathing was so shallow we thought it might stop your heart," Jennah said.

Colette entered carrying a medicine bag. She was the town apothecary, and had great stores of things to mend all sorts of wounds and ailments. She was young and frightfully skinny, but her gauntness seemed to fit her focused demeanor. Without saying a word, she opened her satchel and began rifling through and picking out different glass vials of medicine and setting them up on the old wooden bureau.

"Stop, Colette, I won't be able to pay." Mim stopped as the image of the coin purse from the Last Stand flashed into her mind. *Where was it?* She looked at Jennah and the woman shook her head slightly and put her finger to her lips. She knew what Mim was thinking and warning her to keep quiet. Mim sighed and smashed her face down into her pillow and wanted to scream. All of her hopes and dreams had just sunk into the marshes.

"Quiet, Mim," Colette said. Lady Jennah has generously agreed to pay for your treatment. But before I give you something for the pain, I need to change the dressings on your back."

Mim could feel that she was riddled with holes from the splinters that had once been the front door. As she felt the old bandages peeling off, the cooler air hit the wounds and she sighed with relief. But it was only a few moments until Colette began rubbing oils and ointments across her skin that burned like fire, and any relief vanished.

Within a minute, Mim was chewing on her pillow to try and assuage the pain. She had one of her hands in Jennah's and was squeezing so hard she was afraid it might hurt the woman. All the while Colette was babbling in the background, assuring Mim that without the ointments she would most likely get all sorts of infections that wouldn't be so easily treated. Jennah filled Mim in on some important details that had happened while she had been out. Although she didn't feel like hearing any of it, at least Jennah was trying to get her mind away from the pain.

"Everyone in the house is fine, if you cared to know. Colette says Warly's hand is mending nicely. If he hadn't gotten you inside when he did, you'd most likely be dead."

Mim felt badly for hurting Warly, but that quickly passed as Jennah continued.

"You have been asleep for almost twenty-four hours, which Colette says was your body's only way of healing itself. Your concussion was so bad that we feared any comfort elixirs might have killed you. But every gray cloud has a silver lining. At least you were naturally knocked unconscious by the blast at the door while the girls and I removed the pieces of wood from your back."

Her tone barely hid the obvious sarcasm, but Mim was grateful. "Tell the girls thanks for me," she said, turning her head towards the wall. Jennah kept silent and it gave Mim a few moments to process the terrible events of the previous evening. They played out in her head, but as the images and emotions flashed by more and more questions began popping up. All of them were important, but none of them she could answer. *Why had the terror stopped at the front door and not laid waste to everyone in the house? Was it because of me? Did my eyes have something to do with it? Did I do something after I was knocked out?*

She turned and began to ask Jennah, but after another curt shake of the head, she began rambling on again.

"Talula made it home safely and has come by to check on you when it's been safe for her to leave her house. But on a sadder note, there is no sign of Candy."

If Mim's heart could have sunk any lower, it would have. "The death toll stands at six at the moment, with four more still missing. What was left of Snife Bestlay was found near the banks of the river at the edge of town."

A terrible feeling of grief and relief flooded over Mim. She wasn't happy that he had died so terribly, but at least he hadn't drowned in the river.

"Miss Barley is safe and sound and says she'd like a word with you when you're ready."

Mim was happy to hear about the old cook and could imagine she'd be more than curious about the note she had left.

"What is going on in the rest of town? I'm sure everyone is terrified," Mim said.

"Most people aren't leaving their houses unless they have to. Naturally, everyone has their own idea of what was behind it, ranging from swamp demons to the Lord of Nothing himself. The mayors are pretending to have things under control and saying it was some sort of animal attack, but are just as lost and bewildered as the rest of us. They set a mandatory dusk till dawn curfew and are 'investigating'. They also sent an emergency request to the capital for aide but who knows how long that will take. Until then, the mayoral guard is questioning everyone they can think of and making hourly rounds. Some of the men in town have formed groups to look around as well, but I honestly don't know what they hope to accomplish."

She turned slowly towards the window and looked out into the misty rain, lightly shaking her head back and forth. "You still can't see two feet in front of your face when you go outside."

Colette seemed to be going to extra lengths to cause Mim pain, and it was taking all of her self-control not to elbow her in the ribs.

Suddenly, a stabbing pain shot into Mim's hip and she looked down just in time to see the healer pulling out a large needle.

"For the queen's sake, Colette! Could you at least warn me before you do that?" Mim wailed.

The woman didn't even bother to look up and started gathering her things as Mim felt a wave of warmth radiate out from where she had been injected. Her body felt tingly and she began to get sleepy again. The pain was washing away and it felt wonderful.

"That'll knock her out for a few more hours," she heard Colette telling Jennah. "When she wakes again, give her half the dose I did, and continue to drop it down by half every six hours until the bottle is gone. I'll leave what's left of the wound ointments with you. Keep treating her back with them until the dressing starts coming off clean. She's healing much faster than I expected, so I don't know if she'll need all of it. If you have any left, let me know. I'll need them."

Mim couldn't keep her eyes open. "Wait..."she said, but the other two women didn't seem to be listening. Colette's voice was beginning to echo, as if Mim was dropping away from them into a deep well. "That'll be fifty endins in total..." All Mim could think about as she drifted out of consciousness was her money. As her eyes drooped shut, images of falling coins, demons, and thieves ruled her dreams until she woke up many hours later, deep in the night.

———◦◦◦———

Jennah sat asleep in a chair that was leaning on the opposite wall, and an oil lamp was burning lowly on the washstand. It was still raining outside and Jessel was gone, presumably out hunting. As Mim slowly tried to get up, pain shot through her again, but it was nowhere near as bad as before. The medicine had helped, and she felt good enough to stand. She was still groggy though, and had to steady herself on the wall before taking her first step. When she reached the chipped sink, she gazed into the shard of mirror hanging above it and took in her reflection. She looked terrible.

Her face was pale, except where the purple and yellow bruises from Snife's fists had landed. It seemed as though all the fat in her body had disappeared, which hadn't been much to begin with, and her skin was stretched tightly over her face. Her golden yellow hair was matted to the side of her head, but as she leaned closer to the mirror in the dim light she noticed the most drastic change of all; her eyes. All of the blue was now gone and had been taken over by purple. She dipped her hands into the wash sink and splashed her face before looking back up, as if that would change things.

The water was fresh, meaning Jennah must have filled it for her. She dunked her whole face into the basin, letting the cool water soothe her bruises. She stayed submerged as long as her lungs would allow, and each bubble of air that left her nose seemed to bring up another question.

Her body then let her know that she couldn't stand for too long yet and the lack of air wasn't helping her dizziness, so she grabbed an old pair of trousers on the shelf below and dried her hair. She snatched her comb and headed back towards her bed, and as she sat down and began brushing, she looked over at Jennah.

"Jennah, I'm awake." The woman continued to sleep on, breathing deeply. "Jennah?" Mim said louder. Once again, the woman didn't move an inch, and her chest rose and fell in the same rhythm. Mim sighed. She stretched over and kicked the leg of the chair. She hadn't meant it to happen, but the old support gave out and sent the woman sprawling onto the floor with a thud. Jennah rose, cursing and wide-eyed.

Mim hopped up and tried to help her, apologizing as best she could. "A tap on the shoulder would have done just fine, ya know," Jennah said. As she dusted herself off and bent down to retrieve the absent leg. She shoved it forcefully back into its position before sitting down once again.

"I didn't mean to knock it out of place, I was just trying to get you up. Now please, I don't have much time before I have to leave. Where is my bag?" She said it as calmly as possible, but the earnest in her voice we easily noticed.

"If you are referring to the purse I found in your bag with the supplies you lifted from Tella's kitchen, it is safe and sound under your loose floorboard."

Mim immediately jumped down and slid under her bed. Her back burned with a vengeance, as did her whole body, but she didn't care. She loosened the board and stuck her hand in, closing her fingers tightly around the purse full of coins.

As she heaved herself back onto the bed, she looked at Jennah. "Thank you," she said. For a moment Jennah just stared at her. "You don't need to be afraid to open up in front of me, Mim. From what Talula told me, I'm surprised you are holding up as well as you are."

The comfort was nice, but Mim had no desire to relive the night's events again and pressed on, wanting the answer to the biggest question of all. "The one thing puzzling me is why that monster decided to stop at *your* front door."

A low rumble of thunder echoed throughout the marshes. Jennah sat in her chair and stared back cautiously, as if sizing

Mim up. After a few moments of silence she spoke, but it was quiet enough to ensure that no one lurking around the house or outside the window could hear over the pouring rain.

"I can't tell you exactly why. But I'm positive it has something do with the old carvings above the doors and windows that you used to ask about. Whatever their meaning, I think it was the only reason that beast couldn't come inside."

Mim thought about it for a moment. In her head it didn't make much sense that the strange vines and symbols would be able to keep something from entering a house, but she listened quietly as Jennah continued.

"I inherited this house from my aunt and she was quite a remarkable woman. I remember sneaking around inside when I was young and seeing tons of things with the same designs on them. One of them was an amulet that she wore around her neck and never took off."

Jennah reached inside the neck of her dress and pulled out the oldest piece of jewelry Mim had ever seen. It was very ornate and rounded on the edges. Fine metal work was etched all over its surface with five symbols adorned the top, and a large purple stone set in the center.

"On her deathbed she gave it to me and said that I was never to take it off. She told me it would protect the wearer from forces of dark design, and that if I wore it I would be safe." As she looked down and turned it over in her hand she spoke distantly. "I have to admit, I never quite understood its power until now."

As the lamplight reflected off of the amulet, a strange feeling came over Mim. It was as if the old piece seemed familiar in some way. She knew she had never seen it, but something strange attracted her towards it. Jennah reached up and unclasped the catch that held it around her neck before coming over and putting it around Mim's.

"No, please I—" she began, but was cut off by a curt, "Sssh."

As soon as the cold metal hit her skin a surge of power flooded into her. As she looked over into the shard of mirror, her eyes were glowing, and a faint purple light radiated around the room.

Jennah gasped. "Mim! How long have you known about this?"

Mim didn't know how to respond because she honestly didn't have an answer. "When I was being chased here from the Last Stand was the first time anything had happened. But this…"

With an inquisitive look from Jennah, Mim described everything she could remember about the dream, the woman, recounted the meeting with the horrid creature at the Last Stand, the taking of the money, and finally when she had screamed and shook the bridge.

When finished, she sat back and closed her eyes, waiting for the barrage of questions. But when Jennah didn't say anything, Mim opened her eyes and leaned forward. Jennah was staring right through her, lost in thought. Mim had expected bewilderment and would have settled for surprised, but the woman showed no sign of looking the least bit thrown off by what Mim had just told her.

After a moment she spoke. "Even though you have been here for quite a few years now, we really don't seem to know each other very well. But I've had my eye on you since the day you stepped foot in this house. Put on something more decent and come with me. There is something I have to show you."

Mim got up and slipped off the flimsy gown that she had been put in for sleeping and threw on a very loose fitting shirt so she didn't aggravate her wounds. She slipped into her only pair of non-work pants, which were so baggy that she had to hold them up with her hand so they didn't fall to her ankles. She put the coin purse back into its spot under the bed and was ready to go.

When Jennah looked down at her, she frowned. "We need to find you some better clothes. And I would take off the amulet for now, unless you want the whole house seeing your eyes." Mim hurriedly took it off and shoved it in her pocket before

Jennah opened the door and they snuck out into the house. As the amulets affect wore off, Mim felt a brief withdrawal and she steadied herself against the door frame for a moment before walking after her.

It was late and everyone should have been asleep, but Mim could hear voices coming from different rooms as they passed. It seemed that many of the women had decided to bunk together for a few nights after what had happened, and she didn't blame them. With the amount of chatter coming out from under the doors, she was sure the recent events were all any of them were talking about.

As she and Jennah made their way along the hallway, the strange carvings above the doors and along the crown molding stuck out everywhere, with many in places that Mim hadn't noticed before. They were even embroidered on the curtains that draped the windows and carved on the warped baseboards that ran along the floors.

As they neared the front of the house, they turned to go up the spiral staircase. When they reached the second floor, they continued right and down the hall. At the end, a small inset on the left led them maybe five steps before coming to a halt at an old gnarled bookcase.

"Keep a lookout for me," Jennah said.

Mim was confused but walked back to the corner to keep an eye on the hallway. She gave the all clear before the woman grabbed one of the books on the shelf as if she were taking it down to read. Instead, something clicked and Jennah pushed the entire bookcase aside with ease, revealing a small wooden door.

The vines around it were much more ornate than any she had seen throughout the rest of the house, painted green and inlaid with something white and shimmery. Jennah took a key from her pocket and turned it inside the lock. Something inside clicked five times and once it was done, the door swung open and the two snuck inside.

There was a tiny landing that gave them just enough room

to stand while Jennah closed and locked the door behind her. She reached up to a metal lever and slid it to the right until it clicked, which Mim assumed had put the bookcase back in front of the door. The only light was a small oil lamp that hung on the wall, which Jennah grabbed and took with her as she began to climb the stairs.

They were narrow and steep, and reminded Mim of ones that led up to the attic at the Last Stand. When they reached the top, Jennah stopped and unlocked yet another door that clicked five times before allowing them to enter. As Mim stepped inside, her jaw dropped. What she saw was certainly no attic.

The third floor was one large room with what looked like a tiny water closet at the one end, and far from empty. It was filled wall to wall with grand pieces of furniture, paintings, and tables full of strange trinkets and jewelry. A handful of fancy lamps burned on some the many tables, which gave the room a comfortable light and dry warmth that was hard to come by in the Quilt. It was instantly obvious to Mim that Jennah had taken everything of worth that her great aunt had left in the house and shoved it up on this hidden floor.

As if reading her mind, Jennah chimed in. "When my aunty died, she left me the entire house and all of her estate. Unfortunately for me, most of her fortune was in the house itself and what you see around you, leaving me no cash to pay for the upkeep and fees. I thought about selling off some of the valuables to make money, but I didn't want to attract any attention to myself. If the people of the Quilt knew I had a fortune like this sitting in my house, they would be relentless in trying to steal it. So instead I decided to open a boarding house and let the ladies downstairs do all of the covering for me while I figured out what my next move was."

Jennah led Mim across the room to her bed. "Climb on up," she said, gesturing to the elegant four-poster bed.

Mim tried to pull herself up, but needed Jennah's help before squishing down into the many layers of bedding. As Jennah went to retrieve something from the desk across the room, Mim took a moment to look around.

After a few moments, she was confident that Jennah had enough money in this one room alone to buy the entire Quilt. Mim didn't know quite how much that would be, but she was sure the woman could cover it. Some of the pieces were quite large, most notably a tall mirror that stood to one side but had a sheet draped over most of it. All she could see was a corner of its silver and stone frame. It had the strange vines on it also, and at the corner it wove around in a circle that surrounded what looked like three stars.

Something else that caught her eye was a shiny crystal orb on one of the shelves that looked particularly expensive. The center looked to be filled with a dark fluid that had black whirlpools spinning around in it. It was the first magical thing she had ever seen in her life, and had she been tall enough, she would have grabbed it and tried to figure out how it kept moving.

As she came to the desk on the side of the bed, she saw an old sketch of a lady. But to Mim it was much more lifelike than any sketch or painting she had ever seen. It was of a handsome older woman dressed in many shawls, with a young girl sitting on her lap.

"Who's the woman and girl in that odd painting?" Mim asked.

"That," Jennah said as she walked over to the desk, "is a *picture* of my great aunt and me." She opened the desk drawer just below, and pulled out a small leather book before heading back to the bed.

"You mean that is a real life photo?" Mim exclaimed.

Photographs were a thing of the past and something that only rich lords in palaces now had. At least that was what she had always been told.

"My aunt had books filled with them, and many I still have over in that chest," she said, gesturing towards an old cedar box in one of the jumbled piles of furniture.

"My family line was always very important to my aunt and she spent much of her life doing very extensive research in tracing it back as far as she could."

Jennah showed Mim the journal in her hand, revealing pages upon pages of genealogy written in a fancy cursive writing.

"She traced it back almost 600 years before the records were lost or so fragmented she couldn't make heads or tails of them any longer. But the most interesting part was that she also gathered information on as many of our ancestors as she could, her focus especially being on the women. See, my aunt had noticed very young that she was special, and could do things other people could not."

Mim looked at Jennah, who simply continued on with a serious look on her face. "When she noticed those same abilities in me as a young child, she knew she wasn't alone and decided to start digging through our family history to try and explain them."

Jennah reached over and took a small candle from the side table. She focused her eyes on it and the wick of the candle began to smoke, and within a few seconds had lit on its own. Mim gasped and stared over at her.

"How did you do that?"

Jennah simply shrugged her shoulders. "Beyond the focus and intention I have for whatever I'm doing, I do not know. How did you almost collapse a two hundred year old bridge because you got angry?"

She was right. Mim had no idea why or how she could do what she did, but obviously Jennah had some idea of what her abilities were. "How do you control it like that? Nothing ever happened to me until I got angry and felt threatened, and that only started a day ago."

Jennah closed the book before speaking. "My aunt taught me to harness it. I used to be the same as you when I was young, only having a burst of power when I was angry or in danger. But with help of my aunt, it took me many years to develop the little control over it that I do have, and I certainly would be much farther along if she hadn't passed so suddenly. For example, I can't put out the flame that I just started except by blowing on it like a normal person would. My aunt, however, learned to master that in time as well, along with many other things."

"But I thought your great aunt died of old age," Mim said.

"Oh no," scoffed Jennah. "She might have looked like an older woman, but whatever it is that runs through our blood keeps us younger inside. Had she not fallen as she did, she would have lived decades longer. Not to mention, she might have found out more about our family and why we have these abilities. She was getting very close to something when she died, but never told me what it was. I assume it was a relative linking us to the line of mages of Astolaine in the east. They still have the ability to harness the craft, and can teach others with the ability also, but so far I haven't found anything else."

Mim thought about all of this for a moment before asking her next question. "Jennah, how old are you?"

The woman smiled coyly before answering, and she seemed proud that Mim had put two and two together so quickly. "I'm sixty-one."

Mim's eyes widened in shock. Jennah didn't look a day over thirty-five, and could have passed for much younger when all dolled up. But when Mim looked into those green eyes, she saw age and wisdom reflecting through them, and knew Jennah wasn't lying.

"How do you pull it off? Don't you think people will begin to notice?"

"Eventually they will," she replied. "I never planned on staying long enough for suspicion to arise, and luckily for me I didn't grow up here. Many of my first years in the Quilt I hardly left the house, and for long periods of time I would travel with my aunt. And you'd be surprised what some of the locals don't seem to notice if it's not smacking them in the face," she said.

Jennah had a point. The people of the Quilt were very simple minded and could be oblivious to very obvious things.

"This is also the reason I haven't gone back to the capital to try and see the remaining family I have. See, Mim, my abilities are what led my parents to abandon me to my aunt in the first place, and I don't know what kind of reception I would get."

She looked down into the covers, and for a brief moment Mim saw loneliness creep into her pretty face. The woman, who hours ago she knew only as the owner of a castaway house in the Quilt, now looked like a lost princess that needed a hug from her parents.

"Well, who cares what your family thinks," Mim said, trying to perk her friend up, "it's not like you could distance yourself any further from them at this point. You could at least try and find some answers. Who knows; maybe they need you just as much as you need them."

"Oh, Mim, if they really wanted me, they knew where to find me. But that's not the only issue. My family descends from the royal line of house Toller in Iccobar. Historically, we have had a lot of sway in the capital. At many certain points throughout history we have been in many leadership positions throughout Endmoor, which was the whole reason I was sent away. If I were ever exposed, it could ruin the family name."

"After our neighboring territories outlawed their people from working with the craft and opening themselves up to the Essence, and the Holy Deeds of Pretoria condemned those who disobeyed the law, they feared for my life and couldn't risk one of their children exhibiting behavior from the 'dark days.' Ever since the great war in the north and the Sowing of Sorrow, the world of men has distrusted magic. Only in the far eastern lands is it still practiced openly. Even Alamarayn, the land of tolerance for all, keeps talk of it quiet. It is sad, really. The beautiful craft that once unified all of lands in the glory ages now divides and initiates wars." She turned towards Mim and they locked eyes.

"You are now a part of that danger as well, along with whatever hunts you in the mists. The world is growing darker

Mim, and already it has reached our small corner. What is your next move?" Mim thought for a moment before responding.

"Let's leave," she said.

"What?"

"Let's leave," Mim repeated.

Jennah shook her head slowly in agreement as Mim heaved herself off of the bed and made for the door.

"I have to get out of here regardless, and two is always better than one. I don't have any clue to what I might be getting myself into, but I'll join the Night Runners before getting eaten down here in the Quilt." As she reached the door, the handle wouldn't turn and she had no idea how to get it to open.

"How do you work this damned thing?" When she looked back, Jennah was smiling.

"Well, I'm glad you think that not knowing how to unlock a fancy door is funny, but it still isn't solving the problem of me standing here and needing it to open," she said.

After a moment, Jennah composed herself and got up off the bed. When she got to the door, she leaned down and looked Mim directly in the eye. "I'll go on your adventure with you Mim, but my path leads towards the capital. What about yours?"

"To the Charis Vale," Mim said proudly. "I'm gonna teach some elite kids how to fish."

Jennah laughed. "I do have one condition, though. We must keep our little journey secret and hope it goes as unnoticed as possible. Our biggest obstacle is what lurks out in the mists. Once we leave the house, we will be vulnerable."

"I agree," said Mim. "We keep it quiet. But we have to leave as soon as possible."

Jennah nodded in agreement as she unlocked the door. As they headed down the stairs, the two were already making plans.

"The first thing we need to do is get you healed. Your back should be better within the next few days, and by that time you won't be relying on the comfort elixirs anymore. This will also give me time to work everything out with the house."

"Speaking of medicine," interrupted Mim, "I'm going to need some more when I get to my room. My body is killing me."

And that was an understatement. It felt more as if she had been tossed off of the top of a cliff. All the excitement had made her forget her injuries, but they were returning now with a vengeance.

"I forgot them upstairs in my room. Just stay right here."

As Jennah made her way back up the stairs, Mim leaned against the wall and heaved a sigh of relief.

She now had her coins, a plan, and a friend to boot. Things were starting to come together for her, and it was about time. Just then she heard a ding, like a tiny dinner bell being rung. It was a signal from Warly downstairs and went to every room in the house, save Mim's shed, telling Jennah that someone wanted to come into the house. As she made her way down the stairs, Mim watched her transform. She straightened herself up, let down her curly hair, applied some lip color from a tube in her pocket, and after a few moments of fussing with her dress seemed ready. When she heard the click, the door opened and she poked her head out into the hallway.

"Alright, the coast is clear. I want you to follow me downstairs, but when we reach the front, you will go directly to your room and shut the door. I'll be down shortly."

Mim nodded.

When they got to the bottom of the stairs, a ruckus was coming from the front porch where Warly usually sat guard. There was no door left after the events that had occurred two evenings before, and only one of the old curtains pinned up by nails at the corners now blocked the entry. There were some raised men's voices, and she could hear Warly telling whoever it was that they were not allowed to enter without Lady Jennah's permission.

After a moment there was more commotion followed by a loud thud, and Mim assumed Warly had just gone down. Jennah immediately reached back and grabbed Mim, shoving her inside a set of the moldy crimson curtains just as one of the townsfolk peered inside the doorway. His name was Frent, and although Mim didn't know him well, he had a reputation for having a hot temper and no wits.

"Hello, Frent. How can I help you?"

"The mayors say that troops are on the way, but until then me and some of the other men are taking issues into our own hands. Defend our own, if you know what I mean."

"Well, I think it's a splendid idea," Jennah said. "We can't be too careful after what happened the night before last. I know we will all feel safer with you making rounds."

The gruff gentleman smiled, but it wasn't friendly.

"We know what kind of... *stuff*, you practice here. You can lie and sweet talk your way with the mayors, but witches practice the dark craft and nothin' else. You're being watched, and so are your girls."

Jennah drew herself up to her full height and looked the man directly in the eye, showing no sense of fear or backing down to his threat. But Mim could also see a small blade that had once been tucked up Jennah's sleeve now resting stealthily in her palm. Mim could definitely learn some tricks from this woman.

"Well I can assure you that neither I, nor any of my girls, were involved in such atrocious activity. We were all hiding in the back room from the terrors outside, being gallantly protected by the man you just knocked out on the porch," she said.

"Well, we have heard a rumor that the beast was following young Mim across the Quilt during the killings. Ilanya told us that she saw her runnin' from it, but Collette says she is restin' just fine in the back. Now how do you suppose she escaped, but ten others didn't?"

"Luck and quick feet?" Jennah said.

The man grumbled and spit onto the carpet.

"Well, when Mim wakes up, we wanna have a little chat with her."

He took a step forward and got put his face very close to Jennah's.

"That beast didn't stop at your door for no reason, witch, and if I find out you or your girls had anything to do with this, me and my boys here will burn this place to the ground. With all you in it."

VIII

Through the Veil

IM COULD SEE JENNAH STANDING regally in the doorway, stone faced with her hands on her hips, until the men disappeared into the fog with their torches. As Warly groaned from the ground, Jennah walked over and dipped her hands into a bucket of rainwater and threw it on the man's face. "Get up, Warly! They didn't hit you in the stomach any harder than all that vexor you polished off last night did."

He groaned and began to rise, and Jennah walked over and pulled the bell lever three times before heading towards the curtain and getting Mim. Mim could barely hold up her own weight, and sagged onto Jennah's arms as she tried to stand.

The three dings alerted the other women in the house to come to the front, and within a minute the whole household was crowded around the spiral stair and whispering.

"Alright, ladies, we've got one hour to get this girl ready to travel. I need clothes, boots, and anything else that will fit her. I'll pay you back double for what your belongings are worth. Whatever it was that was out in the mists is looking for Mim, and Frent and his gang won't be leaving us alone for long. She's got to get to the capital. Now move."

It was as if Jennah was commanding a small army and the women of the house immediately broke and began running into their rooms, grabbing the requested supplies. Whether it was the threat of the monster coming back to the house and looking for Mim or loyalty to Jennah, she never knew. But they didn't hesitate for one moment.

Warly was now up on his feet and Jennah instructed him to help Mim back to her room while she ran to grab something. The woman was crazy if she thought Mim was going to be making it anywhere within the hour, and at the moment she didn't even have enough energy to try and fight off Warly as he wrapped his hairy arm around her waist and began to walk her towards the shed.

Within a few minutes, Jennah was propping Mim up and making her drink some terribly bitter-tasting liquid. She sputtered most of it out, but managed to swallow enough. It numbed her throat as it went down, and once it hit her stomach her entire abdomen seemed to freeze. Within moments, her body felt like it had been dipped in an ice bath and her energy and clarity shot through the roof. She felt like she had slept a whole week and just awoken to the fresh start of a new day.

A moment later Jennah had her up on her feet and Mim felt steadier than ever. One of the girls, a sweet younger gal named Purri, came in with food and began ladling stew, bread, and cheese into Mim's mouth while Jennah changed the dressing on her back.

"Your back looks much better than it did earlier. You will

probably need to change the dressing and put the medicine on it only a few more times. You are a fast healer, Mim," she said.

When she looked up at Jennah, the woman winked.

While all of this was happening, another one of the girls, a very round orange-haired woman named Burnda, came hulking into the room and began holding up different traveling clothes. After a few moments she found some that fit pretty well, and took the thread and needle from her mouth and brought in a few seams. As all the people rushed in and out of the room, preparing her for who knew what, time seemed to slow. Were she and Jennah really getting out of here?

When all was said and done, Mim turned towards her shard of mirror. Although still terribly skinny, pale, and a bit bruised, she was dressed up nicer than she ever had been. She had a lovely pair of worn brown leather boots that came up to her knees and fit her perfectly. The woman that had given them up was named Tash, and she had always been kind to Mim when they crossed paths. Under them she had a nice pair of white stockings. They went well with the maroon traveling dress that Burnda seemed to have found in the hodgepodge of clothing. It was like a dress up top, but split at the hips into pants that went down over the tops of the boots.

"It's goin' to be a bit loose around the chest and hips, but ya won't be tha' skinny forever!" she cackled.

"Burnda, tell the girls to secure their rooms and meet at the front door in five minutes, please," Jennah said.

The hefty woman nodded her head and gathered her things. "Aye, Lady Jen," she said as she squeezed out of the door and disappeared into the hallway.

When Mim looked back, Jennah was sitting on the chair, smiling. However, she didn't look like she was ready to travel anywhere.

"Come sit. We have some things to discuss and not much time."

As Mim took her seat on the bed, Jennah reached down and picked up a large brown leather bag and handed it to Mim.

It was extremely soft to the touch, but old and strong. It was heavy, and as Mim opened it up to peer inside she saw a variety of things. Most of the space was taken up by different pieces of wrapped food and a black leather canteen. It was enough to last her at least a week if she rationed it properly. In a side pouch was a rolled up piece of parchment. Mim took it out and opened it up.

"A traveler can't get far without a map to guide them," Jennah said.

As Mim looked it over, she took in the contents of the map. It showed her current position in Endmoor and all of the territories of on the Great Isle. As she looked towards the east, following the trade road, part of another territory named Avaya appeared and was covered in thick forests. To the north it showed the Grey Mountains, which eventually met another great range called the Vellorian, and these stretched across the entire northern coast. And right there, tucked in a valley at the base of the second range, was a dot labeled Charis Vale. Mim's heart skipped a beat as she looked up.

"It's the Vale, Jennah! Look!" Mim's smile stretched from ear to ear. She couldn't believe what she was seeing. She always knew it had to have been real, but seeing it on a map for the first time really solidified it into her mind.

"I found this a few years ago in one of my aunt's trunks. When I remembered it had the Charis on it, I knew exactly who needed to have it."

Jennah leaned forward and traced her finger over a few of the roads. "If you follow the southern highway to Iccobar, you will have plenty of gold to buy passage. But while on the trade road you must stay hidden. Any wagon or footsteps you hear approaching, you immediately duck off to the side and wait for them to pass, is that clear?"

Mim nodded and Jennah went on.

"Iccobar isn't the largest of cities, but it is certainly big enough to blend into. However, this also means it's big enough to get lost in. When you arrive, walk to any street corner that has a green and white flag and wait for a coach. Tell the driver to take you to the sky lounge, and here you will be able to get a clipper ticket. Even if one hasn't landed in the city, you'll be able to find the schedule and hole up somewhere for a few days until one arrives. Then you will be off. If my memory holds true, the school at Charis Vale isn't allowed to turn away anyone that wants to learn, but that won't mean it will be easy getting in. Just be polite and keep your wits about you, and it shouldn't be a problem."

Mim couldn't believe what she was hearing. This was actually going to happen and she was so happy that tears were welling up in her eyes again. But this time they were of joy and excitement.

"The biggest obstacle in your way is to avoid the mobs around town. If they get their hands on you trying to leave, it could be days before you're set free. You should go now, with the storm and fog giving you cover."

Mim knew she was right. If she were going to escape, it had to be now. Even though the idea of being a fugitive was not appealing, it was a ray of sunshine compared to staying in this place. Then something dawned on her: Jennah was talking as if Mim would be traveling alone.

"You aren't coming with me, are you?"

Jennah just looked at her and didn't speak for a moment. "Mim, if I left now I would have to forfeit this house and everything in it, including the girls and their children. I couldn't leave knowing that they would be left in harm's way. I was hoping for a week to get things in order, but it seems that destiny has other plans for me at the moment. But don't worry. I'll be close on your heels," she said.

Mim smiled weakly and sat down. "Alright, but you have to promise me that once all of this trouble dies down in the Quilt and you get everything in order that you will get out of here."

"I promise," Jennah said, putting out her hand, and they shook on it before hugging.

"What else is in here?" she asked as she started digging

through the bag. It helped Mim to look away since she didn't want Jennah to see the tears in her eyes. Inside a large pocket there was a small blade, the matches from the Last Stand, and a compass that looked like another heirloom from Jennah's aunt. Mim noticed that the compass rose on the back matched that of the map, and the two looked to be a pair. In another, she found her medicines, which she promised to use until she was healed. With them was a small glass vial that contained a clear liquid that Mim didn't recognize.

"That is what I put into your tea, and is the only thing keeping you standing right now. It's something my aunt called *elinine*, and it gives your body its life force back when its own has been depleted. I warn you though, the longer you use it and don't get the proper rest you need, the harder you will fall in the end. Never use more than one drop per day, and it has to be taken with water. You have to be kind to your body; it's the only one you've got."

Mim kneeled down and reached under the bed, loosening the floorboard to her hiding spot. She grabbed her coin purse out of it and tucked it into her bag. When she looked up, Jennah was holding out the amulet.

"Forgetting something?"

Mim put her hands up. "No, you have given me more help and friendship than I could ever have asked for. I'm not taking one more thing that is dear to you."

"I have an entire floor of things to protect me, Mim, and that's not including whatever shields this house. You are taking it, but I would keep it in hidden somewhere on you in case your bag gets stolen. Only wear it when you feel the most threatened. Otherwise your eyes will give you away immediately."

Mim placed it inside a little pouch near her thigh and dug into her bag and pulled out five of the endins.

"This should cover the front door." They both laughed for a moment before heading out towards the front of the house. Mim turned around and looked at her small space for a moment. It was strange that she was leaving her tiny sanctuary, and in a way she felt she would miss it. Its four walls had sheltered her through tough times, but in her heart she knew it was time to move on.

When they arrived at the front of the house, every one of the other women stood there, watching Mim intently. Warly was there too, puffing on his stinky pipe as he leaned nonchalantly against the doorframe. As she looked at all of their eyes, she smiled. She reached into her bag and pulled out thirteen of the endins, one for each woman and one for Warly. "I don't have much, but this is all I can give you for now. But I promise I'll be back someday and when I do return, I'm going to get you all out of here."

She walked to each woman and placed one of the silver endins in their hand. Their eyes lit up, and for many of the girls this was at least two days' worth of hard work. And lastly she turned towards Warly.

"You're lucky. If I wouldn't have bitten your hand and felt bad about it, you wouldn't be getting anything."

She winked as she put the coin in his big ugly hand.

"Maybe now you can buy yourself some good looks," she said.

Warly let out a wheezy gurgle and patted Mim on the head. "Good luck, ya little rat."

The scuffling of shoes and stomping of boots came echoing from the street and were moving fast, and outlines began to appear as they neared the house. It seemed Frent and his mob had come back much quicker than expected, or perhaps it was another group. But Mim didn't have time to stick around and find out. Jennah quickly took charge and began issuing orders.

"Warly, find a way that we can barricade this entrance. Girls, back to your rooms and arm yourselves just in case."

She turned to Mim and grabbed her by the arm and began leading her back towards the shed.

"Alright, there's been a change of plans. I was hoping to get you across town but there are too many of them. There is only one way out now that no one will follow."

After a moment Mim realized what Jennah was suggesting.

As they entered Mim's small room, she wheeled around. "You can't be serious."

"It's the only way, Mim. You've got to trust me. The compass will guide you. Just keep going east and north until you hit hard ground. But whatever you do, don't get out of the boat for any reason, no matter what you see. Do you understand me?"

Jennah looked scared for the first time Mim could remember.

"I promise," she said.

Jennah moved directly towards the small window. She took her fist and banged hard twice on the right side, once on the left, and once up top. She grabbed the base and shoved it towards the roof, opening it fully.

"Well, I wish you would have taught me that trick when I was sweating to death in here over the last two summers," Mim said.

A scream echoed from the front of the house. It was Warly again, and apparently a few of the girls had jumped into the argument as well. Jennah turned back quickly. "You've got to hurry."

Something shattered down the hall, and rushed footsteps were coming towards them. Jennah cupped her hand and Mim put her foot in it and was launched out the window. Mim made the tick tick tick sound for Jessel to follow, and the lanky cat jumped quickly onto the windowsill and down into the boat.

Jennah poked her head out for one more piece of advice. "Trade in some of those old coins for Endins as soon as you can. I've never seen anything like them and they will draw unwanted attention. Until we meet again, Mim."

She drew her head back in and hit the window in the same manner and got it halfway closed just as Frent entered the doorway.

Mim hurried and paddled herself against the outside wall, but from there didn't dare to move.

"Give up the girl! We are taking her to the mayors' hall for questioning. Colette says she's fine by now. That little purple-eyed witch is hiding something and we want to know what!"

As Mim heaved the paddle into the water, her muscles were starting to ache again and exhaustion was beginning to creep back into her bones. Once they neared the grey wall, Jessel jumped up onto her lap and stared cautiously ahead. Mim was thinking about what lay beyond and it terrified her.

She shook that out of her head and reached into the pouch on her inner leg and withdrew the amulet. Looking down at it, the purple gem in the middle glimmered slightly, yet there was no sunlight. She felt a warmth from it that radiated through her thin gloves and a desire came over her to put it on. She placed it around her neck, and as soon as the cold metal touched her skin, she could feel her eyes glowing again. The rush of power entered her once more and she closed her eyes, taking in every sweet moment of it. When she looked down at Jessel, her eyes shone brighter too. Mim couldn't tell if it was reflecting the light from hers, but whatever the reason, her cat's green eyes looked like emeralds in the summer sun.

She grabbed the oar and stuck it down into the muck, pushing herself forward. Within two strokes, the tip of the canoe was touching the wall of mist. She closed her eyes. *You have to be brave,* she kept repeating in her head. *You have to be brave.* And with one final stroke of the paddle, Mim held her breath and crossed through the Veil and into the Endless Marshes.

IX

In the House of Lena Moore

A S SHE WENT THROUGH THE thick wall of fog, the temperature dropped. It felt as though she had taken another drink of the elinine, except this time without any of the positive side effects. Her eyes were still closed, and she sat huddled with her head down and her arms around Jessel. But she realized that the air wasn't all that had changed. Strange noises that she didn't recognize now echoed all around her. Hoots and screeches from strange animals rang out and odd smells drifted on the air. After a few long moments she realized she wasn't going to die instantly, and slowly raised her head.

It wasn't nearly as terrible looking as she had expected, and strangely a bit brighter than where she had just come from. While still not near the light of normal day, she could at least see out a good distance in each direction. As she took in her new surroundings, most of it was filled with the creepy shapes of old black trees. Most were so overtaken with draping lichen she wondered if they still lived underneath.

But after a moment she felt they were very much alive, and staring back. Then she realized the entire place felt this way. It was if it were aware of her presence in some fashion, and wondering who the new intruder was that had just come through the Veil. As she turned in her seat to look back at the wall she had just passed through, it had vanished. What was behind her looked exactly like everything else did, leaving no trace from where she had just come. The amulet seemed to heighten her senses as well, which added to the paranoia that she was feeling from her surroundings, so she took it off and hid it back inside of its pouch.

As she began to paddle, bog islands appeared on either side, making navigation tricky. They were covered with deep green mosses, and many had a strange plant with black spiky stalks and sickly red flowers blooming on them. The petals were jagged and poisonous looking, and seemed to twinkle lightly out of the corner of her eye. Every once in a while she would get a smell of sweetness mixed with rot as she passed a large clump of them, and she assumed this was their attempt at giving off an attractive scent. It was a feeble try at best.

The islands also let off a terrible and putrid smell of decay as they moved through the water, and within the first few minutes, Mim had abandoned trying to breathe through her nose. Looking down, she saw Jessel also had her snout buried in Mim's grey cloak. As she started trying to navigate around more of the drifting mounds, she remembered the old compass Jennah had given her and retrieved it from her bag.

She rested it on Jessel's back, who didn't seem to mind, and tried to read it. The compass was spinning around in circles and unable to tell her which direction was which. "Well, that figures," she said. But as she began to put it away, the compass needle settled on **W**, for west.

She shook it bit but it didn't move, so she sat it back down on Jessel and prepared to turn the canoe in the right direction. But the second Mim's hand left the device it began to spin wildly again. *How strange*, she thought. As she picked it back up, a moment later it once again settled on **W**. This was going to be both difficult and annoying, since there was no way she was going to be able to paddle and keep the compass in one of her hands at the same time. But eventually she managed and swung the canoe around towards the northeast, and her destination, and began to paddle.

As the hours wore on she started feeling the effects of the elinine and the comfort elixirs wearing off, which made her mood decline sharply as well. Her back was also starting to burn again, which meant the bandages had to come off soon. She spotted a little island up on her right that looked perfect to try and dock against for a minute.

Once she had paddled up and secured the boat, she slipped her dress down off of her torso and paused, wondering how she was going to manage the bandage change by herself. She looked at Jessel as if the cat had an answer, but she simply stared back. "You're always such a help," she said. Jessel turned and laid her head down on the cloak to fall asleep and Mim gave her a quick scratch behind the ears.

Mim did her best to remove the dressing from her back, which Colette had put on as one big square. Once it was unstuck, she pulled it in front of her to see if she was still bleeding at all. To her surprise, the bandage was clear. As she reached her hand behind and touched her skin, all she felt were the scabs from wounds that seemed to be over a week old.

Mim sighed with relief, thinking that it must have been another affect of the elinine. At least she wouldn't have to keep worrying about infections and trying to change bandages by herself, especially in this forsaken place. She tossed the used dressing onto the small island next to where she was docked and slipped her garments back on.

Her body still ached badly, and whatever had helped her back heal so fast wasn't as speedy on her bruised muscles. She dug around in her bag for a minute until she found the elixirs and needle. She stared down at the long metal injector for a moment, wondering if it was it worth jabbing it into her hip and getting groggy just to get rid of some pain. She was just about to fill the cartridge when she heard a low growl coming from Jessel.

Mim looked around cautiously, but nothing seemed different. Her growl was now getting louder, and her tail had fluffed to twice its normal size. Mim quickly put the meds back in the bag and grabbed the paddle. Although she couldn't see anything, the air around them had definitely changed. As she looked down where she had thrown her bandage on the dark moss, she now saw what had got Jessel's attention.

A patch of the sickly red and black flowers was growing over the bandage as if consuming it. Mim immediately pushed off from the bog and drifted out into the water. She pulled out the elinine and placed one drop on her tongue and followed it with some water from her canteen. As her strength returned, she made herself take a few bites of food and gave Jessel a snack. Then it was time to paddle.

She dipped the oar in and out of the water for hours, rounding the large bogs as quietly as possible and stopping only long enough to drink a sip of water and drop the elinine on her tongue when her body couldn't take it anymore. The light around her remained constant and Mim lost track of time. She had no idea how long she had been awake and paddling, but to the north and east she kept going. Waves of exhaustion began to come over her, and not even the elinine was helping any longer. Her eyes were getting heavier by the moment, and a strange feeling was coming over her.

Oddly, as time went on and the wearier she grew, the more she became used to the world on this side of the Veil. The red flowers began to smell sweeter with each passing grove, and a desire grew inside of her to stop and pick one. A large island loomed up in front of her, and was by far the biggest she had come across. It disappeared off to the side in either direction, blocking her way. But this didn't bother her, because on it was a cluster of the beautiful flowers that was bigger than any she had seen, and they seemed to call to her.

It was a strange sound, just on the edge of hearing, but she swore the twinkling red petals were whispering her name. It was as if each had its own voice, and Mim's desire quickly overcame her logic. From her boat she reached out and plucked one. As the black thorns from the stem pierced her fingers, she took in as much of the sweet smell as she could with each breath.

Things began moving out of the corner of her eyes. Grey shadows moved in the mists, and darker things were beginning to move beneath the water's surface. They never showed themselves fully, and all she caught were brief glimpses of their pale and slimy bodies poking up here and there.

She giggled lightly at this, and could feel the marshes around her breathing in and out just as she did. Mim leaned over and dipped her fingers into the water, swirling them in a figure eight pattern and laughing. Now she understood why people that strayed in never found their way out. Who would want to? It seemed the longer you spent inside the mist, the more you understood it and forgot about the outside world, or that there even was one.

As she fell back into the canoe and looked up at the sky, she smiled at the branches of the dark trees that were tickling her face. She had never felt so relaxed and at ease in her entire life. *This was what living was supposed to feel like,* she thought as she stroked Jessel. The cat's purring now felt like it was coming from inside Mim's own chest, and she smiled at this wonderful sensation.

"Let's rest here a while Jess. We deserve it, don't you think?"

She looked over at her cat and began laughing to herself as if she had just made the funniest joke in the world. And with another large inhale of her flower her gaze drifted up towards the sky.

Tiny lights began popping up in the trees, and they pulsed with a rhythm like fireflies. Their dark blue and purple glows seemed to hum as they twinkled, and their song filled Mim's ears and a desire grew to climb up into the trees and live with them forever. But as their song grew louder, so did the flowers, as if they were competing for Mim's attention. And she relished every moment of it, and the symphony playing in her mind was beautiful.

After a time, the flowers seemed to claim victory, and their song had taken control. As she crawled out of the canoe and laid herself down in the grove. She drew the flowers in and closed her eyes and finally felt at peace. But as the roots of the flowers began to cover Mim and take her down into a mossy grave, another strange song appeared on the air. However, this one came from a person's voice.

She opened her eyes and the flowers began to retreat. A woman appeared in the mist, and she seemed strangely familiar. The song she sang was dark and beautiful, and although Mim couldn't understand the words coming out of her mouth, she knew somehow that she was singing the tale of the marshes themselves. The woman bent down over her and Mim smiled. She was beautiful. Her hair was like silver silk and her face was draped behind a white veil that seemed to be made from the mist. Her eyes were the color of polished steel with a ring of black around their outer edge. They had no iris in the middle, and although Mim found this odd, she thought it only added to the strange woman's beauty.

She helped Mim up and walked her back to her boat, climbing in after. They began to move yet the woman hadn't picked up the paddle. Mim lay there listening to her song as they maneuvered through the bogs with great speed. After a time, the spell that the flowers had draped over her mind began to lessen and she sat up.

"Who are you, my lady? You seem familiar to me but I don't know how or why exactly."

The woman merely smiled and continued singing, and Mim sat back against the edge of the boat and listened.

As they came upon another large piece of land, the woman docked the canoe and got out, offering Mim her pale hand. Without a second thought, she put her bag over her left shoulder and Jessel over her right and grabbed the woman's icy cold fingers. She led them down a path of mossy stones.

The flickering lights were in the dark trees all around her. The dangerous red flowers dotted the sides of the paths here and there but were now intertwined by strange clumps of green ivy with tiny black and maroon flowers on them. The light was a bit brighter, and the lichen that had draped the trees was replaced by more and more leaves. The two rounded a corner and an old stone house, which looked very much like the Inn, stood in front of them.

It looked as if it had been built yesterday, and its white limestone and masonry work were flawless all the way up to the polished tin roof. Around the house sat four ancient willow trees bigger than Mim had ever seen, and their long branches tickled the ground in the breeze. The strange lights twinkled from inside their massive branches, and blue daisies dotted the grass that lead up to the steps of the front porch. As they drew nearer to the house, Mim could see the faces of other children and adults looking out from the windows. They smiled and beckoned too her, like she was a lost daughter who had finally returned home from a long journey.

The woman led her up the front porch steps and walked into the entryway, and Mim smelled a fire inside. She walked down the main hallway, and as she peeked into each room, she saw all sorts of lovely wooden tables and comfy furniture. The wood floors gleamed brightly in the electric light that lit the whole house, and the walls were clean and shiny and decorated with intricate carvings. Mim didn't think that even the hall of the mayors back in Slaidburn was nicer than this home, and it was definitely the most wonderful she had ever set foot in.

At the back of the house, the woman led Mim into a large room that seemed to be the master study. It had a large fire in the stone fireplace, and its light danced off the polished wooden furniture and finely woven maroon rugs that filled the inside. It was warm and comfortable, and as the woman laid Mim down on a comfy day bed against the window, she began to grow weary.

"Rest now, my dear," the woman said, and rest she did.

Mim wasn't sure how long she slept, but when she woke up the light outside hadn't changed and the warm fire still crackled. Her cloak and bag were sitting on a small side table next to her. As she rose and went to the window, she looked out and saw children swinging merrily on a wooden swing that was tethered to one of the massive branches of the largest willow. After a minute or so, the strange woman came in through the door and smiled at Mim.

She was so familiar, but the veil she wore blocked just enough of her face that she couldn't quite make out all of her features.

"I see you have finally regained your strength, my brave traveler. Not many people that go beyond the Veil are lucky enough to find me." Her voice was trying to comfort but was cold, as if she spoke from some deep and forgotten well.

"I can't thank you enough for helping me," Mim said. "I fear I would have been dinner for those flowers if you hadn't gotten to me in time. Actually, I have a gift for you for being so kind."

She walked over to her bag and fetched out her coin purse and grabbed one of the ancient coins and went to put into the woman's hand, but she recoiled.

"I do not have need of coin, child. Not any longer."

"But surely you must need to pay for all of these expensive things and food for all of the other people that live here with you. You even have electricity!"

Mim smiled, but the woman stared back seriously, and Mim noticed the corner of her mouth had started twitching. The stare started making Mim feel uncomfortable and she decided it would be best not to push the issue any further.

"Alright, then! I was just offering to help since you've been so nice and all," she said as she went back and put the coin into its purse. As she did so, she grabbed the small blade Jennah had put into the bag and slipped it into the pocket next to the amulet. Mim put on a smile before she turned around and did her best to imitate Jennah's girlish speech. "Where exactly are we? Everyone that I've ever heard speak of the old counties say the swamp swallowed all of the homes and towns years ago. How do you get food and electric light all the way out here anyway? Am I closer to the capital than I realized?"

The woman once again stared, and after a moment turned and walked out of the room, locking the door behind her. Mim became fearful and needed to figure out what was going on. As she looked around the room, she took in some of her surroundings. On the far side of the room was an old hand-painted family tree that stemmed back generations upon generations. It took up the entire wall, floor to ceiling, and at the base of its trunk read:

The Ancient House of Moore

The name rang a bell, but she couldn't think why. As she surveyed it for a while, she looked at some of the names and followed the branches back and forth. It amazed her that someone had taken the time to do all of this. It was especially inspiring to Mim, since she had no idea who her parents even were, let alone this many generations of relatives. Maybe someday she would be able to trace her origins back this far, and figure out if she had anyone out there in the world she could call aunt or grandfather, or maybe even mother. With a bit of a frown, she abandoned this dream and moved towards the mantle. It was lined with at least thirty real photographs, and all of them sat in ornate wooden or silver frames. They were even nicer than the ones Jennah had in her treasure trove on the third floor of the Inn.

They all depicted what Mim assumed were important members of the family. As she went down the row, she came to one on the far right that was of a young girl of maybe twelve years in age. She had a happy smile and beautiful dark brown hair, and was draped in an expensive looking dress. After a moment, she realized it was a younger picture of the woman who had rescued her from the swamp. Although her hair was different now and she had some age in her face, it was definitely her.

But this picture triggered something else. Mim thought she had recognized the woman when she first saw her and dismissed it, perhaps due to the strange veil that muted her features. But now it made it even more obvious that Mim knew her. She took the picture off the mantle and turned it over in her hand to see if there was a name on the back, and sure enough there was. In the same fine script that had written all those names on the tree, the name Lena Moore was written.

As she read, she froze. As the reality sunk in, Mim gingerly put the picture back on the mantle as if it were dangerous. Turning around, she ran back towards the tree and began searching vigorously for Lena's name. *It can't be! It can't be her, it's not possible!*

The newest of the generations were too high up for her to see, so she grabbed an old wooden chair from the desk in the corner and stood on her tippy toes as she surveyed the top most branches, searching for the woman's name. Finally she found it, etched in the tiny corner. But it had been changed in a vicious manner, and as soon as Mim saw it she froze in terror. It read:

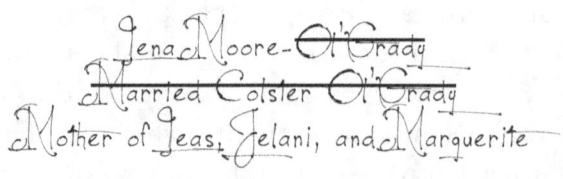

She must have read it ten times over and over in her head, until she finally came to the realization that what was in front of her had to be true. The woman she had recognized was Lena Ol'Grady, wife of the clockmaker from the Quilt, who had disappeared almost two years ago and had never been heard from again.

But how did she end up in this house with all this money? Mim thought.

From what Lena had told Mim and everyone else in town at least a hundred times, her family had abandoned their estate when she was a child. When the swamp overtook the remaining towns and rift gas pumps, they left everything behind and moved north to Slaidburn. They fell on hard times along with everyone else and had lost their fortune.

How had she made her way back here, to a place that time seemed to forget? Had this been her plan all along?

A noise from the hall made Mim jump down and replace the chair. Just as the woman unlocked the door and re-entered the room, Mim had nonchalantly placed herself back on the day bed and pretended to stare out the window as if nothing had happened.

The woman entered and surveyed the room slowly before her cold eyes turned directly on her. She smiled now through her veil but it didn't touch her eyes, and when she spoke again it was strained. "Lunch is ready."

Lena turned slowly around in the doorway and glided out into the hall. Mim thought she had no choice but to follow, not wanting to risk angering her further, and grabbed her bag and slowly exited the room. As she got to the doorway and looked down, a puddle of water was on the floor where Lena had stood. The woman left watery footprints on the wood as she went. But she no longer moved in the dignified manner of the woman that had glided to her rescue, but limped and sagged as if weighed down by an unseen force.

Mim began to cautiously follow, and soon realized that Jessel was nowhere to be found. As she crept along the hallway, she quietly began *tick tick ticking* in the hopes that her cat would hear. As she rounded the corner, still following the watery footprints, Lena disappeared behind a swinging door. She crept forward, and as she got to the door she heard a distant echoing chatter as if the other members of the house were inside the room as well.

As the smell of mildew met her nose, she looked around and saw mold was beginning to grow up the walls from the floor, and the air had become damp. As she pushed through the door, she looked upon a room that seemed to be a large dining area and kitchen all in one. On the right hand side was the cooking area, and near the stoves and the cooling box stood Lena with her face turned away from Mim's. She was looking out of the great bay windows that lined the entire back wall of the room.

On the left was a huge wooden table that held at least twenty seats. It was set with fine dishes and huge, lit candelabras, and in each spot someone sat, except at the chair at the head of the table. Some of them were children, and some older in years towards the age of grandparents, but all were in fine suits and dresses that Mim knew hadn't been in style for decades.

But besides their garb, there was something else strange about them. As Mim surveyed each of the guests, she saw they were all strangely pale and stared blankly straight ahead at one another, none of them moving a muscle. Two of the three Ol'Grady children were there as well, looking not a day older since Mim had last seen them two years before. All of their eyes were silver and ringed with black, just like Lena's.

Mim was frightened, and as she backed towards the door, Lena spoke again. "Please sit. We've saved you a seat at the head of the table. You are our guest of honor."

Her voice now sounded like it bubbled up from a deep and icy pool and sent chills through Mim's veins. She cleared her throat anxiously.

"No thank you. I'm really not that hungry at the moment. I just came in to say thanks so much for your generosity, but that I really must get going."

As Mim backed up against the door, Lena turned. "You misunderstood me, child. You will not be enjoying our company for lunch. We will be enjoying you." She smiled terribly and slowly raised her hands and lifted her veil.

Underneath was not the face of a woman, but of a decomposing corpse. Her sockets had no eyes and were filled with mold, while her skin was a shade of greying green. As Mim looked towards the table, the others looked the same as Lena, but were now staring at her with their rusting knives and forks upright in their hands. Lena's head dropped toward one of her shoulders, and her rotten dislocated jaw dropped three times as low as it should have; and a terrible sound escaped. Mim knew she was looking directly into the mouth of death.

When she turned around to bust back through the kitchen door, it was already gone. The only part of it that was left were the corroded hinges that had once held it up. As if coming out of a dream, Mim finally saw the house around her for what it really was.

Mold and mildew had long ago eaten all the plaster walls away, and knee-deep black water now took the place of the fine wooden floors that had been there a second before. As she began to slosh through and head towards the front door, pale dead figures began to appear in the rooms on either side of her. Mim knew the family wasn't going to be letting their guest of honor escape without a fight. The mist walkers were hungry.

As she neared the front door, the water became a bit shallower and Mim could get better footing. Old and gnarled tree roots had taken the place of some of the decayed flooring and she was moving with much greater speed. Just as she was about to exit the house, the ghastly corpse of Lena rose from the waters to block the doorway and Mim froze in her tracks.

The woman's strange melody began to echo throughout the house and Mim felt herself losing focus again. The song of the Sirens of Endmoor floated through the dead and empty halls, telling the tale of all who entered here and never left.

Mim couldn't concentrate and her movements were jumbled, her limbs now barely being able to hold up her weight.

When she looked up, Lena was gliding towards her with her pale green hands outstretched towards her throat. Mim reached into her pocket and retrieved her amulet, and when she put it on, purple light blazed from her eyes. The siren paused, but not for long, and as she edged forward again Mim's fear seemed amplified through the amulet. She regained some of her focus and felt power trickling into her like a pitcher pouring water.

From her right, another pair of hands clasped her shoulder. Her fright triggered something, just like it had on the bridge, and a burst of energy radiated outward from her and blasted the sirens backwards. But her power was stronger now, and took out part of the wall and most of the old banister that led up the stairwell to her left. Another screech pierced the air and a streak of brown flashed from somewhere on Mim's right.

When she looked up, Jessel was latched onto Lena's face. It gave her just enough time to gather her wits and make a run for it. As she bolted by her, she grabbed Jessel by the scruff of the neck and yanked, taking her cat and half of the woman's face with her.

Mim barreled down the steps and out into the muddy water that had long ago overtaken the lawn, and turned back towards the house. The broken and rotten windows were hollow and in them stood the corpse bodies of the Moore family. And there in the front doorway, stood the terrible form of Lena Moore Ol'Grady.

The sirens slowly began to float toward her, and as fast as she could she ran back in the direction of her canoe, trudging down the muddy path with Jessel on her shoulder.

As she sloshed through the black water, on the right hand side of her path she noticed tiny raised piles of earth. She looked down at them as she ran, realizing they were small piles of rock that denoted shallow graves. There seemed to be at least fifty of them, some almost completely swallowed by the marsh, others resting just above the water line on tiny rises.

The running had quickly exhausted her tired body, and she stopped to catch her breath for a moment. To her right were three of the graves, but these looked newer than the rest and closer to the path. They were marked with the names of Lena's three children. Mim felt so terrible for them, having lost their lives in this terrible place. It seemed Lena had finally regained her fortune, but Mim didn't think all of the gold, silver, and gems in the world were worth the price she and her children had paid.

The smallest of the piles was on the left and was made for Marguerite, which saddened her the most. Mim had known her well and remembered sneaking her food from the alley door behind the Last Stand. Once, when she was sick, Mim had even given her a few coins from her stash to get some medicine from the apothecary. As she straightened up the stones on her grave, she realized that Marguerite had been the one missing from the table at the sirens' banquet.

Hopefully she has moved on to the Halls of Luna and isn't stuck here, she thought.

As she looked around Mim realized she had no idea where she was, or how she would ever get out of there without her canoe. The thought of swimming the black water seemed like suicide, and she barely entertained the idea, which left her completely stuck. But behind her she could hear the sirens' song again and it was growing closer, and after a lonely moment of despair and a tiny prayer for the girl, she rose with tears in her eyes and began to try and find her way through the mist.

Within a few steps on the path, a pale light appeared a few yards ahead. As Mim drew closer to it, she realized it was Marguerite, or a shade of what Marguerite had once been. Mim was about to run, fearing Lena not far behind, but when she looked into the young girl's eyes they weren't like the others at the house. They were normal, iris and all, and still held the kindness the girl always had when she was alive.

"Are you going to hurt me?" Mim asked.

The young girl didn't speak, but raised her finger to her

mouth to tell Mim to be quiet. She looked around apprehensively, and waved her hand, beckoning for Mim to follow. Mim didn't feel that the girl meant her harm, and although she had grown distrusting of everything in this hellish place, what choice did she have?

She followed the misty figure as she drifted between trees and bogs, never leading Mim near the water. The sirens' songs behind her grew and fell, and at times Mim swore she could feel the breath of the dead upon her neck. But as quietly as possible, she ran after the girl. She needed answers, but no matter how close she seemed to get, the translucent shade of young Marguerite remained just out of reach. After a time, the girl stopped and turned towards Mim. Her pale wispy dress blew gently in a breeze that did not exist. The songs were louder again now and approaching quickly.

"Where have you led me to?" Mim whispered.

The girl slowly turned and extended her white finger forward in earnest. She was pointing Mim towards a large clump of dark trees. As Mim began to run, she turned for a moment. "Thank you," she said. And with a small smile, Marguerite glided off and disappeared into the grey.

X

Hitching a Ride

S MIM RAN FORWARD, THE trees became denser and she kept snagging her cloak on the branches, but she began to notice a difference in her surroundings. She passed less and less of the sickly flowers now, and any time Mim saw one she covered her nose and mouth as best she could. Finally, the air around her was becoming less thick and the ground less soggy. A few moments later, and seeming to appear out of thin air, the grey wall of the Veil rose up in front of her and she sighed with relief.

She had made it back to the wall of the living and dared not take her eyes off it, worrying it might disappear somehow and leave her stranded. Without pause, she trudged through and emerged back into a world that seemed familiar to her. It was raining lightly and the temperature rose, and the clouds were thicker. Jessel jumped down and began walking at her side.

Mim stopped for a moment and sighed with relief. She was starving and imagined Jessel was also. She reached into her bag and got the food container and canteen, but when she opened it she almost became sick. The food inside was rotten and moldy and looked as though it had sat in her sack for a month. The canteen was also bone dry and smelled of mildew. Whatever dark presence loomed within the marshes seemed to have affected it, or maybe she had been lost for much longer than she had thought.

"Sorry Jess, we're going to have to wait a bit longer for a snack."

Within a few steps, the two walked out into a large clearing and Mim felt hard packed earth beneath her feet. As she looked around it took her a moment to realize where she was, until it finally dawned on her that she had reached the southern highway. She knelt down and kissed the earth, never so happy to feel solid dirt in her entire life. She was exhausted as she knelt there on the road, but alive. She reached over and snagged Jessel and launched her into the air and caught her on the way down before spinning in a big circle.

"You were brilliant back there, you know?" she said, smiling at her green-eyed friend. But Mim didn't need to tell Jessel that; she was sure her cat already knew. She took off the amulet and shoved it back into her bag as she looked around.

She wondered how much progress she had made on her way to the capital. She hoped she was nearing the halfway point since she now had no food, but at least she knew where to get water. She made her way over to the edge of the road and began siphoning rain water from the large leaves of an old maple tree, trying to fill her canteen. But then her worries took a darker turn as a hand reached around her mouth and dragged her back into the trees. She fought furiously, but it didn't affect the stranger's grip. After a moment, another figure stood in front of her, and the thud of his gloved hand across her face immediately stopped her from moving.

"You keep quiet, girl," he said. His raspy voice sounded like wood on sandpaper, and she could smell vexor oozing from his skin. A twig snapping to her right made her turn, and in the fog she saw many more shapes of ragged men hiding near the ground.

"Trell, tie her to that tree and gag her. We'll figure out what to do with her after our job is done. But keep her quiet!"

A bitter-tasting gag was shoved into her mouth and she was tied to the trunk of an old tree. She couldn't see much of the man that had done the tying, but he crept forward and crouched down low in front of her.

Mim was panicking, but she had to keep her wits about her if she were going to remain alive. And the thought of what these men would do with her after completing whatever they planned sounded like it would be mostly one sided. *But what are they doing out here in the middle of nowhere?* she thought.

Her answer soon came with the clopping sounds of hooves upon the road and a rumbling in the distance. As she drew her knees up to her chest, she heard the *tink* of metal on metal, and realized the amulet was hitting the small metal blade she had stuffed in her pocket back at the house. Relief flooded in as she quietly strained towards her legs. Her finger tips finally pinched the small blade and she drew it up into her hands where she immediately began to saw at her bonds. A loud crack came from the approaching wagon on the road, and a man's voice called through the air. It slowed and came to a halt almost directly in front of where she and the others were hiding.

———✦———

As his coach lumbered along the southern highway on the third day, Éolan had his bag open with papers strewn about on the seat. He had been through all of them for what seemed like the tenth time, and now his gaze lingered out of the window. His welcoming address to the members of the Hall and students was complete and memorized, and with Chessa asleep on the large velvet-clad sleeper seat across from him, he had only his thoughts and the lack of scenery keeping him company.

As the coach hit a large hole in the road, Chessa jerked upwards with a fright, letting out a few choice curse words in her native tongue as she straightened her gown and hair.

"Sorry, my Lord!" said Master Gill from the box seat. "We cannot see but ten feet in front of us, and that last hole might have done some damage."

A moment later, they crept to a halt and Éolan could hear Captain Selar barking orders as he dismounted and set up a perimeter around the coach. Alrik jumped down and opened the door and Éolan stepped outside with Chessa.

It was like they had walked into a cloud. The air was so thick and warm it was like breathing in steam. The blue shaded lanterns that stood at the four corners of the coach barely lit a foot around their flames, with their bluish light making the scene all the more eerie.

On the journey so far, they had passed only two other souls on the road since they crossed the border into Endmoor; one was a farmer with his cart and oxen while the other was an old woman clad in grey. The forward guard had almost not seen her, but luckily the horses had sensed her coming and veered off. Éolan had seen her smile through the pale veil in the flickering lamplight as they passed, and it had sent chills up his spine.

He looked around, remembering a time when Endmoor had bustled with activity and prospered greatly from its rich supply of rift gas. Its counties had boasted some of the best hospitality and cuisine in the south of the Great Isle, and heavy trade had once come through here. But once the swamps had started moving north and the Veil had descended, all that had changed. In the last hundred years, it had become little more than a forgotten name on a map, and he pitied the people that lived here. It saddened him at how far Endmoor had fallen.

The driver was on the ground and shining his lamp beneath the wagon and mumbling to himself.

"Anything wrong, Master Gill?" Éolan asked.

"Aye," he said, standing and brushing himself off. "That last hole we hit cracked a tress."

"Where are we on our journey, Captain Selar? Any nearer to lands where the sun still shines?"

"Aye, milord. Only about six hours outside of Iccobar, depending on our speed of course. We are sitting right on the junction that leads down to Slaidburn in the south."

As he looked over to his right, Éolan could see the outline of an old rotten sign. A carved finger pointed to their right, and under it read: Slaidburn, South. ¼ Jaunt. Master Gill spoke again. "Last I knew there was a smith in practice there, if you care to spend the time. But the tress is still strong and should hold to the capital if we keep a slow pace."

"Well, we certainly do not have the time," said Éolan. He stretched his back and yawned. "We are too close to Iccobar to spend a half day to travel down and back, not to mention repair time. If you say it will hold, I suggest we continue on."

"Yes, milord," said Master Gill.

"Captain, I'm stepping off for a moment," Éolan said.

But before he rounded the wagon, Chessa grabbed his arm and stopped him.

"We need to be quick. I do not feel safe in this place," she said.

Éolan trusted her judgment and felt the same. "I will be quick. Get yourself back into the coach and we will be off shortly."

He marched a few paces towards an old tree and stopped for a moment as he unbuttoned his fly. But the sound of approaching armor made him stop. He turned around to see Alrik standing there with his back to him, hand on his sword hilt, and peering cautiously out into the fog. "*A man cannot even take a loo in peace anymore,*" he thought. But as the loud scream of a girl came from the woods along the other side of the road, he was thrown face first into the wet dirt.

———⚬⚭⚬———

From Mim's precarious position in the trees, she sawed at her bound hands as fast as she could without raising suspicion. A coach had stopped on the road and she could hear men's voices just a few paces ahead, but she didn't care. She had to get away from the bandits. But the large man that had struck her now came over and kneeled down, talking to the man that watched her, and the others now huddled around the tree to listen in as well.

"There are five guards and what looks like a higher proper. Could be a captain. We have to move quick and surprise em'. We only have one chance, so you kill fast and get whatever's worth takin'. We move on my mark, and not before. Three hoots. Listen for em'."

He crept off and the others moved in a rehearsed pattern to their positions.

"You stay quiet," said her watcher. He moved off and joined the others, giving Mim more time to free herself. She finally cut the bonds lose, but she kept still, hoping to escape in the ruckus that was about to start. But as she listened to the gentleman from the coach speak, she realized a very important detail. She was still very far from the capital. Six hours by horse would take her twelve or more on foot, and this could be the luck she needed.

She crept quickly down the tree line away from the men, and just onto the edge of the road. As she heard the first hoot, she readied herself, on the second she took a deep breath, and on the third she let out a piercing scream, alerting the travelers of their peril.

As the bandits jumped out from the trees, the split second she had given the guards seemed to have helped. The sounds of swords unsheathing rang out, and she bolted to the opposite side of the road. In the lamplight of the coach she could see at least fifteen men in dark cloaks fighting with the guards, and although trained and in armor, they were outnumbered. But one stood taller than the rest and was quickly cutting down the bandits as they ran forward.

On the other side of the coach, four of the attackers bore down upon two figures. The shorter was in armor, but the other rising from the ground was only in a leather hauberk and trying to draw his sword, and Mim could tell he wouldn't have it out in time. She ran forward and just as one of the thieves was about to strike a deadly blow, she jumped onto his back and drove her knife deep into his shoulder.

Éolan stood as quickly as he could and reached for his sword. Alrik had taken care of two assailants, but another rose from the shadows and was about thrust his sword into Éolan's chest. But just as he was about to strike, a small cloaked figure jumped onto his back and sank a blade into his right shoulder.

As he fell backwards, his bulk landed on a small girl with a thud. Two more men circled the coach, and with his sword hand free, Éolan unleashed his blade. With a quick attack, his Alamarayn steel sliced the forward attacker's hand off at the wrist. The blade fell with the hand still grasping the hilt, and with a graceful flick of Éolan's wrist his neck was cut. As the second advanced, Éolan feinted left and with a quick toss to his opposite hand, thrust his blade into his opponent's heart.

As his last adversary went down, Éolan nimbly hopped over their corpses and ran over to the girl. He yanked the injured man off and threw him to the side of the road, reaching down to help her up. As his blue eyes met her violet ones, he realized it was the face of the girl from his dreams and the shock made him pause. *How could this be?*

But the man that the girl had injured was not dead, and

lunged from the shadows. As he raised his short sword over his head to strike a death blow, a small throwing dagger whizzed past Éolan's ear. With great accuracy it pierced the center of the assailant's throat, and he fell to the ground. Looking back, there stood Chessa with one arm outstretched from the throw and not a hair out of place.

Alrik was at his side now, sword in hand and covered in blood. Chessa had moved in too and still held a throwing dagger in her other hand, which she held at the ready.

The captain called, "Lord Éolan!"

"Here, Captain!" said Alrik.

He came running around the back side of the coach with his lieutenant in tow, and their shiny armor was now scarlet instead of silver.

"We've lost two of the guard. Are you injured, my Lord?" he asked.

"No worse for wear. And although he did very well, we are going to have to work with Alrik on the protocol of how to address my safety without shoving me into the dirt," he said.

As he brushed off some of the mud and examined his hand, he looked back up. "However, thanks to you and these three I'm standing and alive," he said.

"Three sir?" asked the Captain.

He looked at Alrik and Chessa, before resting his eyes on the short girl standing off to the side.

"Yes," said Éolan. "I could have had a sword buried in me if it wasn't for their handiwork. And I have a feeling that we all might have had this young girl not alerted us with her scream. That was you, if I'm not mistaken?"

"Yes, my Lord", she said, attempting a very poor curtsy.

Even in the aftermath of what had just occurred and the danger he could still be in, Éolan couldn't take his eyes off of her. The mysterious girl, which he thought lived only in his subconscious, was alive and standing right before his very eyes. But there was something else about her, a familiarity beyond that of the dreams that he couldn't put his finger on. A scuffling then came from beneath the wagon, and as everyone turned and drew their blades, Master Gill came scooting out from beneath.

"Coward," mumbled Alrik.

"There is nothing cowardly about it, young man," said Master Gill. "I was loosening the bolts to the horse pulls so they couldn't make off with the coach and anyone in it."

Alrik lowered his head a bit, but kept his gaze forward.

"Thank you, Master Gill," said the captain. "Now, if you can tighten them up quickly. There could be more bandits in the woods."

"Or worse," said Chessa, looking out into the fog. "There are rumors of a terror that dwells between da feet of da Grey Mountains and da sea. I can feel it in my bones. We must move."

"I agree," said Éolan. "But we have not addressed the issue of our young heroine. What is your name, young lady?"

All eyes then turned to the girl. "My name is Mim, my Lord. Umm, well, Mikky Hart in full, but everyone calls me Mim," she stammered.

"Well, Miss Hart, I am Lord Éolan of Alamarayn, Steward of Nausica. May I inquire to why you were on the road with the group of bandits that killed two of my men?" he asked.

"I am from Slaidburn, my Lord. My destination is the capital and then hopefully onto the Charis Vale. I was taken by those men just minutes before they attacked your coach. I was lucky you happened by when you did, or I don't know what would have become of me."

"Very lucky," said Chessa. Éolan noticed her brown eyes sizing the girl up and down, and the tone in her voice was suspicious.

The captain cleared his throat, giving the signal it was very urgent for them to be leaving, and Éolan spoke again. "Well, Mim, it seems we are headed to the same location, and by the looks of things I am assuming you are on foot. Would you like to join us for the last leg of the journey?"

He noticed she let out a small sigh of relief. "If that would please you, my Lord," she said.

Chessa let out a boisterous "Oh-Ho!" But before she could continue on, Éolan stopped her.

"For my safety, and those of the others, we will have to search you and your bags before you come on board."

"Of course, my Lord," said Mim, turning over her bag to the large captain as he stepped forward. The woman then came over and patted her down quickly. "She is clear, except for this."

Chessa's plump hands grasped the amulet and handed it over to Éolan. He could tell the girl was nervous and as it touched his hand, he shifted slightly and then understood why. A tingle went up his arm, and he felt an old and familiar power trickle into him. One which he hadn't in many years. He tried to nonchalantly place it over into his gloved hand, but he thought the girl noticed. As the tingle disappeared, he looked at her inquisitively.

"This is a very old piece of jewelry, Miss Hart. Where did you come by it?"

"My grandmother, sir. I mean, my Lord. She gave it to my mother before she died, and now it is mine. It is very special to me."

Éolan could see that she desperately wanted it back, and for now he would oblige. The captain had rifled through her bag and come up with nothing. "Nothing dangerous as far as I can tell. A map and an old compass that doesn't work properly. Some moldy food," he said.

"Well, it seems you are approved. And here is your heirloom," Éolan said.

As he handed it back, he noticed she was sure to grab it with her sleeve. And although he doubted that the young girl realized the power of what she carried, this definitely showed she knew it was much more than just a necklace. As he handed over her bag, Éolan gestured to the open door. Chessa was first in, but before they followed it seemed the girl had one last issue to clear up.

"Excuse me, my Lord. But I am not traveling alone." She made a ticking sound and within a few seconds a thin cat came out of the mist. But instead of jumping onto Mim's shoulder, it sauntered right up the steps and into the coach, perching herself comfortably on the seat across from Chessa.

Éolan saw Mim flush.

"If it doesn't please his lordship..."

But before Mim could get it out, he raised his hand to stop her. "Your companion is also welcome to ride along, Miss Hart."

He smiled at Mim as she stepped in and sat down next to Jessel. He settled in the seat across from her, next to Chessa. As the guards outside strapped the bodies of their fallen comrades onto the back, the three of them sat in silence. It was obvious to him that Mim had no idea what to say next, and Chessa was making no attempt at conversation. And as the coach lurched forward the silence continued. *This is going to be a long six hours,* he thought.

XI

Painting a Picture

AS THE COACH RUMBLED ALONG, the three of them sat in silence for a while longer. The lord finished tucking his papers away in the embossed leather bags he carried, while the woman kept a watchful eye in her direction. She was polite, but no less than twenty minutes before Mim had seen what she could do with a throwing dagger.

The Lord named Éolan spoke first.

"Now all of that unpleasantness is behind us, I think some formal introductions are in order. Miss Hart, as I said before, my name is Éolan. I am the Steward of Nausica, and a High Lord of Alamarayn. And this is my first assistant, Chessa."

Mim nodded politely, as did the woman named Chessa, but neither said a word.

"And how shall I address your traveling companion?" he asked, shifting his gaze up towards Jessel.

"Oh, I beg your pardon, my Lord. This is Jessel. She's my closest friend," Mim said. She reached over and scratched Jessel's head and she began to purr loudly. But before Mim could stop her, she dug her sharp nails deep into the plush velvet cushion and began to rip at the fabric. Mim reached up and quickly detached her, and with a curt "Bad girl" shoved her down into her lap. Jessel didn't seem to mind the reprimand, and daintily began cleaning her paws while looking over at Éolan and Chessa. Mim smiled weakly.

Lord Éolan let out a laugh and reached over and gave her a quick scratch on the head. "Well, luckily for you, Mim, I have always been fond of cats. I have two just like her back at my estate in Nausica."

"And it seems they make me sneeze here as much as there," Chessa said.

Mim could see her eyes were beginning to get puffy, and with a quick flourish she pulled a handkerchief out from her cover-up and sneezed loudly into it.

"Be well", Mim said politely after the sneeze.

"Many thanks, dear," said Chessa. She blew hard through her nose, and the loud noise made Jessel's eyes widen and ears go back slightly.

Éolan cleared his throat.

"If I had not made it clear before, I thank you greatly for your assistance back there on the road. That was very brave of you. But I must ask why you would so freely risk yourself for someone you have never met?"

Mim thought about the question, but worried about the answer she would give. She decided to be honest. "I suppose it was to gain your trust. Without food or water, I don't think I would have made it without hitching a ride somehow," she said.

"How long has it been since you've eaten, child?" asked Chessa.

"Well, perhaps a few days, give or take," Mim replied. She honestly didn't know how long she had been beyond the Veil or in the house of the sirens, but she shivered and didn't dwell on it for too long.

Chessa reached under the seat and pulled out a large wicker basket and opened it. Inside were dozens of different foods wrapped in fancy paper, and Mim's mouth began to water. The woman pulled out five different types of cold sandwiches and handed them over to her, along with a large canteen of water. Mim went for the water first, and her dry throat welcomed the cool liquid. She had to make herself quit chugging before it ran out completely.

Smelling the food, Jessel perked up as well, and looked eagerly from the wrapped packages to Mim and back again. Mim ripped one open, and took some of the salted pork and placed it on the paper for Jessel before shoving the rest into her mouth as fast as she could. She had never tasted better meat, but after the first two sandwiches she realized how unladylike she was being.

When she looked up, Chessa had her pudgy arm outstretched with another handkerchief in her fingers. Mim gingerly set the sandwich down and took it, wiping her mouth and trying not to blush. Lord Éolan was the most handsome man she had ever seen, and here she was eating like a winter beast.

"What was it that made you leave for the capital? That is a long journey to take alone at your age," Éolan said.

Mim could tell he was smart, but she was no dummy. She could easily read people just like Miss Barley could, and his blue eyes bored into her like she was a riddle that needed solving. So she chose her answers carefully as she swallowed more of the food.

"I desired a change of scenery, my Lord," she said.

"I see," he said with a smile. "You also said you were looking north towards the Charis. Are you familiar with the Vale?" he asked.

"I have heard stories, but little more than that. I was told that they can't turn away those who wish to learn, and so I thought it would be a good place to start," she said.

The lord let out a boyish smiles. "Yes. That it is." And with a sideways glance towards Chessa, he continued. "I have spent a lot of time at Charis in the past and am quite familiar with how the institution is run. However, I am concerned with your timing. The term starts in only nine days."

Mim bit her lip. She hadn't thought of that. But the Lord continued on. "It is quite prestigious, and most of the students have been registered for months, some even years. Many of those who attend have special talents in certain areas. Is there anything special that you think the deans will find interesting about you?"

The two locked eyes again, and although he was trying to be nonchalant, Mim could tell he was fishing again. *Certainly he can't know anything about what happened in Slaidburn*, she thought. But as she looked into his crystal blue eyes, she felt that it was possible he did somehow.

"I'm an extremely good worker," she said quickly, "and have years of experience in kitchen service. I'm also a decent baker, and very skilled at fishing."

She hoped to not raise any suspicion, but her hopes had now sunk even lower. The only thing interesting about her had been the revelations within the last few days, and no one knew about those besides her, Talula, and Jennah. Other than that, she didn't know what skills she had to offer that were special. And if that was a qualification for getting in, she was in more trouble than she realized.

Éolan said, "Well, we can worry about that once we arrive at the River Palace. I'm assuming you do not have any lodging in the city?"

"No, my lord," she said.

Mim didn't want to say it out loud in case it made her look

like a fool, but she hadn't planned that far ahead yet. Worst case scenario, she assumed there would be a dry barn somewhere.

"Well, we can work on those arrangements as well," Éolan said.

———— ❦ ————

As the coach rolled on, the group went silent while the girl and her cat finished the food. Éolan was becoming more intrigued by her with each passing moment, and although he had enough of a sense of propriety not to stare, he almost couldn't help himself.

After finally speaking with her, he now knew for certain that she was the girl from his dreams. She was guarded, yes, but that was easily deciphered by reading her body language and demeanor. But it was her eyes that spoke the untold story. It could be random, but he hadn't seen a maiden with golden hair and purple eyes in many years. Nor, did he think, had anyone else on Aldaya.

As the coach rounded a bend, it slowed once more, passing a large company of foot soldiers that were heading south. As they came out from beneath the lichen draped trees, sunlight beamed down for the first time from a break in the clouds. They had finally cleared the fog, and as Chessa lowered the window to let in some fresh air, another small opening appeared in the wall of the coach behind her.

"We are nearing the capital, Lord Éolan. We should be approaching the gates within the hour," said Alrik.

"Thank you," said Éolan, also lowering his window slightly. The worst part of his journey was now over, and the sun and breeze were welcomed by everyone in the coach. But he noticed Mim particularly enjoyed it.

She was plastered against the window and staring out at the fields that stretched northward towards the distant Grey Mountains. In the light of day, he also noticed how pale she really was, and he could see the remains of old bruises on her face. But she closed her eyes and smiled as fresh air filled her lungs, and he smiled also.

The rest of the ride passed quickly, and as they approached the city he could see Mim's awe had intensified. She obviously hadn't ventured to any place larger than Slaidburn in her life, and although the River Palace was small compared to most of the royal capitals, he imagined it would be quite the sight for a newcomer.

A great wall of timber and stone surrounded it, standing at five stories in height, and as they fell under its shadow, Mim withdrew back into her seat.

As they approached the iron clad wooden gate, Éolan could hear the voice of the captain out front speaking with one of the city guards. He sounded frustrated, and after a moment appeared at the window with the member of the guard in tow.

"My Lord, this is Gratham of the city guard. His orders insist that all persons entering the city must be subject to search. Even *royal* coaches."

He could hear the disdain in the captain's voice, and Chessa shifted in a dissatisfied manner, but Éolan was not going to contest the instructions. "If those are the orders of the king, then we will do as instructed."

As the group exited the coach, the soldier began to read from the parchment in his hand. But before he had finished his first sentence, a deep booming voice roared from somewhere off to the left. "Fog be damned! Something must be afoot if Éolan of Nausica is standing in Iccobar!"

Although he was short and a little round in the midsection, the man walked with a fierce dignity and pride. He was stout but not fat, and light on his feet. His hair was greying at the temples and looked to be somewhere in his fifties, but his large arms easily filled out the polished silver armor. His short green cloak had white and green rivers on it, which were the symbol of Endmoor, and he wore two strange silver earrings that looped around the upper curve of each of his ears. His smile was bright, but his face had been hardened by years in service to the king.

"Hello, Commander Friedan, it's been too long a time," said Éolan. "We were just allowing a brief search before entering the city."

"Gratham!" the man boomed as he addressed the guard. "This is a coach on a diplomatic errand from Alamarayn. It carries the flags. You and your men don't search a royal coach without a commander present."

The guard looked embarrassed, but Éolan stepped in before the berating continued.

"Commander, he was only doing his duty. Strange things are afoot in the mist lands and diligence is what will keep your city safe."

"Aye," he said, dismissing the guard. "Open the gate!" he shouted. "If it suits you, my Lord, may I accompany you through the city?" he asked.

"That would be acceptable indeed, Commander," Éolan said.

As the group climbed back into the coach, Chessa sat down next to the commander, which left Mim next to Éolan.

As the coach lurched forward, Commander Friedan pulled out a small pipe from beneath his armor and lit it, producing a plume of smoke from his nostrils.

"We passed a squad of ground troops about an hour out of the city. Were they on training?" asked Éolan.

"No," said the commander, slowly exhaling his pipe smoke out of the window with a sigh.

"Unfortunately they were headed south to Slaidburn. If you haven't heard, it's a terrible story, that one. Not three nights past something the mayors describe as a 'beast' attacked over twenty people in one outing. The king sent a squadron of troops down to hopefully make the folks feel a bit safer, but the reports were gruesome, my lord. They say that body parts are the only things left of some of the victims. And of most of them, they've found nothing at all." He shook his head slowly. "As if those poor people down there needed anything else to dampen their spirits."

Éolan noticed Mim had not raised her gaze from her lap as the two had begun talking, and now that the terrors of Slaidburn had come into the conversation, her knuckles had gone white.

"I had not heard, but the severity of it is alarming. We were ambushed on the road by bandits and lost two men at the junction leading down, but obviously what attacked the town was not human. Nor have I have never seen the fog so thick, even in those parts. And I sensed something else lingered inside of it besides cloud."

At this the stout commander looked over at Éolan and stared for a moment but said nothing, and after a long silence Éolan decided to quit beating around the bush.

"It was fear, Commander."

The stout man was looking out of the window now, seeming to weigh whether he should speak openly or not in his current company. But after a moment he came to his decision and started again in a low speech.

"Tales have been reaching the ear of the king of late, Slaidburn only being the newest, albeit far worse than the others. I also feel as if something dark is brewing in the lands that stretch between the Grey Mountains and the Marshland. We sent inquisitors to the towns of Burke and Dane that lie north of the highway, and the mayors there report that more people have gone missing in the last two months than in the past thirty years combined. The king dispatches troops, but I believe even he is at a loss of what else can be done, save finding the Esmë themselves."

For a moment they all sat in silence, and Éolan mulled over what he had just heard. The territories of Aldaya had all been prone to the normal ups and downs of society over the years, but large-scale murder and disappearances of this nature were almost unheard of. They had been commonplace in the years when the shadow had loomed in the north upon Atlan, but it had been ten centuries since that time.

But Éolan knew very well what lay entombed near the center of the sphere, and also of those that had escaped imprisonment. Whatever was hunting the Riverlands was certainly real, and perhaps a few years ago he would have rested on the conclusion that it was some hungry beast that had come down from the high fells of the Grey Mountains. But the world had taken a darker turn of late, and this was no longer a viable explanation.

Within the last week a puzzle had been forming in his mind. He supposed he had begun to sense it much longer ago than he realized, but after Callan's cryptic message of something afoot in the east, he had started to wonder at the state of Aldaya as a whole.

The eastern territories were much more quarrelsome than usual, and only six months ago had the prince of these lands lost his life in a simple skirmish while traveling through them. This had nearly destabilized the entire region, had Alamarayn not intervened. That fact made Éolan think of the vagabonds that had attacked them. What was the likelihood of bandits encamped on a road rarely traveled, and mostly by farmers with their produce and little in the way of coin? He had to consider that the attack was an attempt at assassination, though he honestly couldn't think of a political power that might wish him dead.

And then there was Bronwyn, the Queen of the Wanderers, whose network of informers and powers of perception were unrivaled in the modern world. She was a close confidant to Éolan, and he trusted her judgment. She sensed the dissent as well, and was now moving her people away from the central lands. It was an old saying in the south: "Your fortune will be well if you follow the Wanderers."

Then his thoughts drifted to his dreams. Next to him sat the very girl that wandered in them, with her extraordinary eyes that clearly held mysteries that she was not divulging. And then there was the amulet she carried. It was worth more in currency than the town of Slaidburn as a whole, and he could feel the power within it without even trying. She did as well, and revealed that by purposefully avoiding it touching her skin. Had he known what it was, he would not have made the mistake of handling it in front of her. But its strange appearance solidified that her flight from the south was for much more than a change of scenery. She was on the run.

He wondered if the massacre was what had initially driven her out, but as the image of the veiled woman they passed in the fog came to his mind, he couldn't help the chill creeping up his spine. Something much more sinister was at work in there, and now he was sure of it.

"I will speak with the king and we shall see what we can do to set things right in the south once more, Commander," he said.

The commander smiled back half-heartedly and "Aye" was all he said.

The coach slowed to a halt as it pulled up to the gates of the palace. Commander Friedan hurriedly put his pipe away and got out, instantly regaining his booming tone and ordering the troops to make way for Éolan. But before giving the all clear, he poked his head in through the window for one last word.

"You've got an escort through the grounds to the palace and the king should already be aware of your arrival. I will also see to the proper transport of your fallen men back to the Sea Palace. Keep me informed, if you would."

Éolan nodded. "As always, Commander."

After the men's bodies were removed from the back of the coach, the wagon once again took off and glided up the smooth grey road to the River Palace. After a few minutes it came to a halt and the door opened, allowing Éolan to step out while leaving Mim and Chessa inside. He turned to them briefly.

"Chessa, please accompany Miss Hart. I will alert the king that we have an extra guest."

He turned towards the high manors and stretched his back. The main building was five stories in height and its walls were made of thick and durable grey limestone. It had high windows of stained glass and the trim around each sill and door was painted in green and white, the signature colors of the nation. The roofs were made with many colored tiles, but their vibrancy had become a bit muted due to the mosses and lichens that thrived in the moist climate. The five main buildings that made up the capital moved off to both sides and back at an angle, forming a pentagon around the grassy hill that rose in the center.

In its middle were fair gardens with tall spruce, maple, and hemlock trees, and the strange white *vintalia* flowers that bloomed all year long dotted the grass. They were shaped like stars with bright yellow buds in the middle, and they got thicker as they rose towards the top of the low hill. Here they wrapped around the base the largest sycamore tree that graced Aldaya. It stood nearly two hundred feet high, and its crown was so large that it almost shaded the entire estate on its own.

The people called her *Teela'Moori*, Crown of the Mists in the common tongue, and she had stood on this knoll since the Esmë had graced the lands. Éolan loved that tree, and had always liked Iccobar as well. Although it wasn't the most lavish, it was certainly comfortable and much more to his liking than the cold castles in the east.

Alrik and Captain Selar were at his side now, and as the large wooden front door opened an elderly man walked out. He was flanked by guards and a few banner men, and strode over to Éolan. He was nearing seventy, and besides being a little hunched in his old age and white of hair, there were no other signs of aging. He was tall and proud, and had been on the throne longer than any other ruler in the territories of men. As he approached, Éolan bowed low with one hand on his stomach and the other appropriately placed on his back.

"It is my pleasure to be in the company of Jehrym, King of the Riverlands and Steward of Endmoor. I come with council and news if he would have me."

As the king walked up and stopped, Éolan kept his bow until he spoke.

"The King of the Riverlands welcomes High Lord Éolan of

Nausica, Ambassador of Alamarayn," he said. "And from what I see before me, it seems the journey has been quite eventful," he said. Éolan could seem him staring at the dried blood on the guard's armor, the bandage around Éolan's hand, and the gash marks on the side of his coach.

Éolan turned around and took in the scene. Perhaps he hadn't fully realized the state of his entourage. He turned back and smiled slightly, as did the King.

Jehrym was one of his favorite leaders, and Callan held him among the closest of all political allies to Alamarayn. He also had a sense of humor, which Éolan thought was one of the most important qualities to have as a person, especially in a ruler.

The king slapped a firm hand on Éolan's shoulder and smiled as he spoke. "I figured we would be seeing you sooner or later. You have a knack of showing up right when things start going south. I fear if you weren't so good at turning them north again, no one in their right mind would have you!"

The two chuckled for a moment before Éolan took a somber tone. "Before we go any further, I wanted to give you my personal condolences on the loss of your son. I regretted not being able to attend his services. I was still with Callan in Puruma, negotiating with King Eron at the time."

The old king nodded. "And I give my thanks to Alamarayn for putting out another brush fire to avoid further blood being spilt. Had Callan not intervened, I would have put that bastard king's head on a pike. And that surely would have brought the Sansorian army down upon us, which I assure you would have been quite a messy affair."

He put his arm around Éolan's shoulder, turning to walk him inside. "But what's done is done. The River Palace and the royal house of Toller are always open to friends. Now come. You need to get cleaned up and properly situated. We have much to discuss."

XII

A Girl Named Bette

EOLAN STRODE OFF TOWARDS THE doors with the king, and Mim and Chessa remained inside as the coach took off towards the back of the large buildings. Mim was still plastered to the window, pretending to take in the beautiful structure. She had never seen anything like it, but her mind was sidetracked by what the king had just said. He was of house Toller, and so was Jennah. And while Mim didn't know if the king had any other kin, it seemed that Jennah's presence might actually be needed here.

With all of the jumble in her head, she wasn't sure what to do next. Although she seemed to have come into the lord's favor and had appreciated the ride, she wasn't sure if she was happy about it or not.

She didn't like the idea of being trapped, and Lord Éolan assuming that she would be staying in the palace under his watch made her uncomfortable. But she was resourceful and, at the moment, planned on keeping her options open and her eyes peeled for a way out.

As the coach stopped, Chessa leaned over and patted her hand. "Don't be nervous, young Mim. You will sleep well tonight and be safe in da River Palace. However, da *Coachise* of da king is a very unfavorable woman. I would suggest you refrain from chatter and let me do da talking for now," she said.

Mim nodded quickly as the coach stopped, and she appreciated the advice, but Chessa's warning had done the opposite and made her more on edge. Mim knew how to behave herself in front of the Mayors back in Slaidburn, but she had never been somewhere that had a real Coachise. As the door opened, Mim stood up and threw Jessel over her shoulder and followed Chessa outside.

The commotion and unloading had begun, and the sun peeked from behind the spotty cloud cover as it neared the horizon. From the base of the manors, an elderly looking woman strode out of a small door and walked towards them. She looked like an ancient and gaunt bird with her white hair pulled into a tight bun on the top of her head.

"I am Griselda Plarn, Coachise of the River Palace," she said. Her tone was curt, and nothing close to friendly.

"I am Chessa, first assistant to Lord Éolan of Nausica. And this is Mikky Hart, an acquaintance."

"Welcome back to the royal house of Toller," she said to Chessa. "And I have been made aware of the situation with the girl. Now, if you will follow me," she said, not bothering to spare a glance towards Mim.

She led them inside and through a number of dark

passageways before coming to a large cloth tapestry. "Miss Hart, you will remain here while I show the premiere's assistant to her rooms."

The two disappeared, leaving Mim alone for a short while. She took the moment to try and catch up with her thoughts, but her insatiable curiosity took over and she peeked out from behind the tapestry. She enjoyed watching the palace servants bustling back and forth, and could see large pieces of painted and cloth art along the hallway walls. Just as she was about to risk a bit more of a peek, a small beady black eye appeared in front of her, making her jump back with a curse.

Griselda had returned, and without a word led her back down the dark passages until coming to a small set of steep stairs that Mim could tell were used for service workers. The old woman marched steadily up the many flights with Mim in tow until they reached the top floor. They came out into the hall and up to a small door.

"This is the best I can do with such short notice. You will remain here until called for. And you are not to wander about." She opened the door and gestured for Mim to enter. As she turned around to ask the woman about a washroom and food, the door closed, leaving her standing alone in the dark. She fumbled in her bag and pulled out the matches and lit the small lamp on the wall above the bed.

She could tell she was directly under the roof due to the slant of the ceiling, but it was much better than what she was used to. Although it was a bit drafty, it was dry and the two beds along the wall looked cozy. She stretched and sat down on the one closest to her and took off her bag, cloak, and boots. Exhaustion flooded her body instantly and, as her head hit the pillow, Jessel curled up next to her as she quickly fell asleep.

Inside the manor, Éolan had been brought to his room where he unpacked and bathed. Chessa had come up and had just finished bandaging his hand properly when the gong sounded twice, signaling dinner in fifteen minutes. She laid out his outfit, and was just about to head down for her supper before Éolan caught her.

"Do you know where Miss Plarn has put Mim?"

"No, meh Lord. But I can inquire and will see that she is well taken care of," she said.

"Please do, and make sure she is fed. And Chessa, I plan on taking her with us to the Vale, so do your best in making sure she does not disappear."

Chessa shook her head slightly. "I trust your judgment, but I do not understand your interest with da young girl. You are keeping something from me, and you know I will get it out of you eventually," she said.

Éolan smiled as he pulled on the last few pieces of his outfit and took in his reflection from the large oak framed mirror.

"I have often told you of my dreaming, and of late an old and recurring one has become more frequent and intense. The girl in it is Mim, yet we hadn't met until today. And if I'm not mistaken she has been swirling around my subconscious since before she was born. Something brought us together, and I must figure out why," he said.

Chessa nodded slowly and seemed lost in thought for a moment as she looked out of the window. "You are wise to listen to da messages that da spirit gives when your mind is idle. On da islands this time is called *o'uheva*, and is when da clutter around you falls away and you truly begin to listen. And if young Mim has a bigger part in da puzzle that is forming, then we must keep her close."

She chuckled a bit before walking behind him and lacing up the rear of his shirt and brushing the lint from his back.

"And as you know, my lord, I have raised eight *ihi's* of my own. And young Mim reminds me of my third oldest, who is named Geva. The moment I laid eyes upon her I saw it, and you can bet two coconuts and a cart full of kuva beans that mischief follows her like a shark to blood. Both of my eyes will stay on her," she said.

She finished clasping his cloak around his neck and gave him a once over before making her way towards the door. She stopped at a small bowl of interesting looking sweets that had been placed near it and rifled through for a moment. She took a few choice pieces and tucked them inside a knapsack before turning around. "I think I will take some of these up to young Mim," she said.

When the gong for dinner sounded, Éolan made his way out and down to the hall, but he walked slowly and took in the beauty of the River Manors. Its hallways wound just like rivers did, with gently curved walls that would eventually lead all the way around its circular estate and back again. The stained glass windows shone in the sunset and filled the hall with many colors, and Éolan stood for a moment by one of the open ones and looked down and out upon the city.

Most of the structures in town were circular in shape and had domed tops. All of them were made from the same grey limestone as the manors, with most of their roofs being made of the same many colored tiles. Some were thatched in the less affluent areas near the wall, but were all well kempt. There was only one main road, and it looped around the city in eight great circles as it made its way up to the crest of the hill and the gates of the manor. Its people were content and enjoyed being out of the way. And it gave Éolan hope that the capital seemed to be untouched by the threats of the mists for the moment, whatever they or it may be.

A flustered looking red-headed service girl came running down the hall, muttering to herself about being late. As she caught her foot on a slightly raised stone, she fell face first and smashed against the hard floor. Éolan smiled a bit but quickly composed himself and walked over to her.

"It is interesting how trying to move too quickly can sometimes slow us down, is it not?" he asked kindly. But when the girl finally raised herself off the floor and looked up, wiping blood away from her crunched nose, she met Éolan's eyes and all color drained from her face. For a moment she just stared blankly as the blood ran towards her chin.

He pulled out a blue silken handkerchief and gave it to her to help stop the bleeding, and it seemed to rouse her from her stupor.

"I'm sorry to appear in such a state my Lord, please forgive me," she said. She took the handkerchief and tried to catch the bleeding, but ended up smearing most of it across her cheek. Éolan felt sorry to see her in such a state, but also found the girl to be sweet and endearing.

"I'm sorry, but I did not catch your name," Éolan said.

"It is Lisbet Brooke, my Lord, but everyone in the palace knows me as Bette," she said.

"Well, Bette, I am heading down to join the king for the evening meal and I don't want to keep him waiting. Are you well enough to continue on?" he asked.

As she nodded, her auburn curls bounced up and down, and she curtsied. "Thank you, my Lord."

Éolan turned and walked towards the main hall, smiling to himself while the girl named Bette bustled off.

———————

A few floors above, Mim was dreaming again. It started the same, but her usual waking point had come and gone, and for the first time in her life it continued. After the initial tremor, the walls shook again. From outside screams began echoing in through the tall open windows and the tolling of bells filled the night air. Mim was sitting up again, and saw the woman rush to the window and look out just as another tremor shook the room.

Another woman appeared in the doorway, her dark brown hair piled beautifully on top of her head, and the long golden dress she wore glittered in the lamplight. The two seemed to be arguing about something, and as another tremor shook the palace, the blond woman ran towards the bureau and once again took out the magic mirror. She spoke into it hurriedly, but this time it began glowing so brightly that Mim had to shield her eyes. After a moment it was over, and the mirror was locked back into its box and Mim was hoisted over her shoulder and the three began to run.

As they fled through the corridors of the palace and down stairs upon stairs, the tremors grew steadily worse. All above them windows were shattering and dust began falling from the ceiling where the structure was beginning to collapse. Strange dark eyes began appearing in the shadows around the three, but the two women kept them at bay. The blond woman unleashed rays of white light from her free hand, while the other kept a shimmering golden aura around them, acting as a shield.

As they reached a small stone door, they entered and the air began to grow colder and the marble walls had changed to stone. They were moving faster now, and the torches on the wall blurred as they ran past.

Mim was laid down in something soft, and she could hear the two women arguing again. Then the purple eyes of the golden-haired woman looked down and were filled with fear and urgency.

Something cold was pressed into Mim's hand and she was kissed on the forehead before the woman in the golden dress carried her away. Bright lights started flashing behind them and the sound of a scream came to her ears. A pair of bright blue eyes flashed in front of her and then all went dark.

Mim bolted up in her bed, drenched in a cold sweat, with her hand touching the spot on her forehead where the woman in the dream had kissed her. She was still groggy, but before she got her bearings she heard a clank and a rustle of clothes. Within moments a young auburn haired girl was standing in front of her and holding a small candle snuffer.

She was wielding it like a sword, and Mim thought it was quite humorous for a moment. But the blood that was smeared across her face, and her wide-eyed look made Mim a little uncomfortable. But as the girl reached over with her free hand and turned up the oil lamp on the wall, Mim got a better glimpse of her and she knew this girl didn't have the grit to hurt her in the slightest.

"Listen, just please put that down and I'll explain. I arrived with Lord Éolan and that Plarn lady brought me here and told me to stay put. I was so tired from traveling that I didn't realize this was somebody's room when she first brought me in. My name is Mikky Hart, but everyone calls me Mim. That brown fur ball that ran under the bed is my cat Jessel. We're alone in the world and from Slaidburn in the south, trying to make our way to the Charis Vale," she said.

The anger and fear that had fueled the girl seemed to wither as fast as it had sprung up, and she turned red with embarrassment as she put the snuffer back on its hook near the door. She moved towards the other bed and sat down.

She was very pretty, even behind the layer of dried blood on her face. Although it wasn't to her liking, her clean and tailored green and white silken livery complimented her auburn hair and green eyes. However, she seemed miserable and Mim could tell her day had obviously been a long one.

"Are you alright?" Mim asked.

The girl jumped and became extremely high pitched and fidgety. "I'm as dandy as a poxy in a pumpkin patch, thank you very much!" she said. She smoothed her dress and wiped a few tears away from her eyes with her bloody handkerchief, which smeared more, and turned away from Mim.

"Well, even so, that bloody hanky isn't doing you any favors. Come over here and let me help you get cleaned up," she said. The girl turned back and looked at Mim suspiciously for a moment, but quickly caved and sat down on the bed. Mim grabbed a small dish of water from the washbasin, but was confused about what she could use to get the blood cleaned up.

"Do you have any old rags?" she asked.

"Yes," said the girl. "Bottom shelf to the right."

Mim bent down and picked up a bright yellow cloth, and

although it had a few stains here and there, it was so soft she couldn't believe it was a rag. But she took it over, dipped it in the water, and began helping the girl clean herself up.

She was trying to tuck some of her dark red curls behind her ears but having no luck without a mirror, and with a curt look from Mim, gave up and put both hands on her lap and smiled weakly. Mim had never found silence to be awkward, especially when she was getting down to a task at hand, but the girl in front of her seemed to feel the need to talk.

"It figures Miss Plarn would put you up here. We have plenty of room for guests of status, but obviously that's not us," she said. As the words came out of the girls' mouth, Mim saw her flush. She tried to retract her statement quickly, but stumbled over herself. "Oh I'm sorry. You-you know what I meant, right? I wasn't trying to be insulting," she said nervously.

Mim smiled coyly as she looked down and wiped the last traces of blood from the girl's cheek. "You're all done," Mim said. "And yes I do know what you mean. I'm sorry about invading your room," she said.

As a bell rang form somewhere within the manors, the girl ran to the bureau and quickly pinned her hair up and straitened her uniform. "Oh, don't be! It'll be nice to have some company for once. I don't really have many friends here in the palace. But right now I have to head downstairs. I am on the serving detail tonight for Lord Éolan and the King, but I will be done within a few hours. I'll bring us up some food before bed," she said.

She was smiling brightly, and it made Mim happy. As she neared the door Mim stopped her. "I didn't catch your name," she said.

"Oh how silly of me. My name is Lisbet Brooke, but everyone calls me Bette." She smiled again and walked out of the door.

Mim smiled and sat back on the bed. She could tell that she and this girl were going to be quick friends.

XIII

Being Watched

AS BETTE MADE HER WAY to the kitchen to start on the dinner service, she was smiling. She couldn't wait to get back to her room and talk with Mim. She herself had never been outside of the capital city, and although the thought of traveling made her nervous, she admired how Mim had decided to pack up her life and start somewhere new.

As dinner finally ended, Bette gathered a large tray of extras that the kitchens couldn't keep to serve again and headed back up the stairs. When she walked back into her room, Mim was asleep and this time her brown cat was lying next to her. It made Bette happy that she hadn't run under the bed this time, but when she set the tray down and snuck over to pet her, a low growl made her recoil. It also made Mim come to with a large yawn and stretch of the back.

"Oh, hi Bette. What's that delicious smell?" she asked.

As she sat up and saw the tray, Bette brought it over to her and she began to dig in. Bette had kept a little something for herself, but the way Mim was devouring into the food, Bette decided she needed it more and was happy enough with her bread and stew. After all, those in service at the manors were used to eating three meals a day, and by the gaunt look Mim had, Bette knew she hadn't been as lucky.

"So how long have you been on the road? And I'm interested in how you got on board a royal coach, *especially* with Lord Éolan; I mean, isn't he a vision? And didn't you say you were from Slaidburn? I've heard some dark talk in the halls about people disappearing outside of the capital. Is it true what they are saying?" Bette asked.

Mim looked over at her and smiled. "Which question would you like me to answer first?" she said through a full mouth.

Bette smiled back.

"Sorry. I can be a little bit of a chatterbug," she said.

"Nothing wrong with that," Mim said. "I can be a bit of the opposite, but I think that's because I have never really had anyone to talk to. But my story is going to take some explaining. You up for it?" she asked.

Bette nodded and crossed her legs on the bed nonchalantly as she began, but after Mim finished she sat clutching her knees to her chest. All Mim could see of her face were her large green eyes flickering over the tops of her kneecaps in the lamp light. A light rain was now falling on the roof, and a moderate wind was blowing through the manor, making the old timbers moan and creak slightly.

"That sounds like a tale from the old world," Bette said

quietly. "I spend most of my spare nights reading in the library, thanks to the grace of the king, and am always digging around for tales with magic in them. But nothing I've found even compares to what you've seen. And jumping into a battle to save a Lord! I couldn't imagine," Bette said, trailing off with a shake of her head.

Mim contemplated what she had said for a moment. Until now she hadn't stopped to think about how much she had been through in a relatively short span of time. Within the last few days her world had been turned upside down, but it felt strangely good to tell someone about her adventure.

It wasn't that she didn't trust Éolan and Chessa, but talking to them felt like being interrogated. But when she talked with Bette, it felt more like confiding in a sister. The only part she had left out was due to Jennah's advice, and for the moment Mim felt safer with keeping the amulet and what had happened on the bridge quiet. After all, she had only known her new friend for a few hours. But Bette quickly moved past the terrors of the swamps and became particularly interested in the part about the king having a sister.

"Well, that would be huge news for the kingdom. The Queen passed away the year I was born, and his only son and heir died last year in an ambush. He was traveling back from Omoniro with a small company and the Sansori king thought they were a camp of Ring Riders," she said. Mim looked confused, so Bette elaborated.

"They are a group of outlaws that live in the plains and ride big horses and steal from the farming towns. Anyway, apparently a nasty group of them had been spotted near the capital, so King Eron took a company out to ambush their camp in the night. By the time he realized his mistake, the prince had been killed. From what I hear, King Jehrym still thinks it was on purpose. It is no secret that he is not well liked by some of the other dynasties, and killing his only heir would be a great way to ruin his house," Bette said.

It amazed Mim how much she knew. It must have been since she worked here in the palace, but Mim had never heard of Ring Riders or a land named Omoniro. She got out her map and traced her fingers across, finally finding it bordering the ocean in the east.

"Well, we've obviously got to tell the king about Jennah. Everyone down there is in danger with that creature lurking about. Don't you agree?" Mim asked.

She saw Bette shiver at the mention of her but quickly moved on. "Most definitely. King Jehrym is a great man, and so was the prince. If it weren't for their generosity I would most likely be on the streets or working at one of the taverns. And it won't be difficult to get him a message. Just send a note to Lord Éolan and he could arrange for you to tell him before you all leave," Bette said.

Her words hung in the air and the girls looked at each other. Mim felt sad at the thought of leaving Bette behind. For these last short hours it felt as though she had a confidant, and that was something she never had before.

"Hmm. Well can you help me write a note that I can send? I'm pretty lousy at writing, especially something to give to a king," Mim said.

She dumped her rucksack onto the bed and began rifling through to find a scrap of paper, but stopped as the bag of old coins dropped onto the covers, spilling its contents.

When Bette saw them, she looked from the coins to Mim's face and back a few times before Mim tossed one of the coins to her. "Have you ever seen one of these?"

Bette shook her head as she turned the coin over in her hands, but still looked at Mim strangely. "Where did you get them? They look like some sort of royal currency."

Mim realized what she was getting at, and quickly dispelled it. "If you are asking if I stole them, the answer is no. That creature left them at the Last Stand for me as a 'thank you' for my services."

A quick knock at the door made Bette toss the coin back to Mim, who scooped them back into her bag. Bette straightened her livery and hair before going over to answer.

When it opened there stood Chessa with another tray of food and drink. Bette curtsied low and stood off to the side, and Mim awkwardly got up off of her bed. She hadn't realized the need for such formality with Chessa, but she did her best to follow Bette's lead.

Chessa set down the tray and picked up the empty one.

"Hello, young Mim. I see that you already have gotten some food, eh?" she asked.

"Yes, Bette here works in service for the king and I am sharing her room. She brought me up some supper," she said.

"Hello Bette, I am Chessa and am da premier's first assistant. Thank you kindly for bringing up a meal."

As she looked around the room and down at the two beds she pursed her lips slightly.

"And I see that Miss Plarn has gone to da trouble of finding you a space with someone already occupying da other half. She sure has some nerve, that one. But worry not. I will find other arrangements for you when I get back down to da mains," she said.

"No!" both of the girls said in unison. They looked at each other and smiled, and Chessa gave them a sideways glance.

"I see. Well, you two just stay up here in da room, and outta trouble. This message is for you Mim. It is from Lord Éolan and I'm thinking it says something along the same lines," she said.

As Bette began to close the door behind her, Chessa stopped. "I almost forgot. These are for da two of you, and quite tasty." She pulled the bag of candies from somewhere within her wrap and tossed them to Mim, but not before pulling one out for herself and dropping it on her tongue. "Have a peaceful rest," she said before pulling the door closed.

Mim looked at the bag of strange sweets for a moment and

then over too Bette. She took out a candy and put it on her tongue. As it began to fizz and bubble she quickly spit it out and tossed them to Bette. "They're all yours," she said.

"You don't know what you're missing!" said Bette, unwrapping a small blue circular candy. As it fizzled on her tongue she laughed a bit, and then dropped a purple one on as well.

Mim smiled as slowly undid the fancy blue wave seal on her parchment and read the note from Éolan.

> Miss Hart,
>
> I hope your accommodations are adequate. Please stay where you are for the night and I will be in touch with you by tomorrow morning before I meet with the King. The clipper we are taking will be ascending tomorrow afternoon towards Charis. Please do not leave the palace. If anything is needed, please find either myself or Chessa.
>
> ~Éolan

"Well, it looks like I'll be leaving tomorrow afternoon for The Vale. But Lord Éolan will be meeting with the king for mid meal. Could we get him a note before then?" she asked Bette.

"Oh sure, let's write it real quick and I can run it down to Chessa's room. She'll be sure to get it to him. And after that, I want to know all about what you plan to focus your studies on when you get to Charis," Bette said.

Mim bit her lip and looked over at Bette. "What do you mean, 'focus'?"

Bette took a deep breath in and raised her brow. "Let's just get the note finished first."

Morra Losis was draped in deep black robes that blended seamlessly with the shadow of the trees outside of Iccobar. She was alone, and her children were off hunting for her meal. The sky was beginning to clear after the rain, and as she looked up at the twinkling stars above and the glowing moons, she spat onto the ground. She couldn't wait to see Rayna, Selna, the *Tari*, and all others like them drown in the shadow of her master. But it was not time for that yet.

She sniffed the night air. It reeked of humans, but mingled within was the bag she had given the girl. Her plan had worked, and she had tracked her this far. Had she regained more of her power, she would have ripped the stone walls to pieces and torn the city apart to get to her. But her instructions were to move quietly, remaining in the unseen for now. And so she was stuck with using tact and stealth, which she had plenty of but hated wasting the energy on.

But something else in the city also eluded her and made her act cautiously. She sensed a power within, but it was masked somehow, just as the girl's smell had been. It was old, much older than the girl, and much more powerful. But as she regained more of her powers every day, these issues would soon be no more.

A rustle in the forest to her right made her turn. It was a large pair of grey does, and they had the audacity to stare at her. One had a white stripe down its back, and the other's was dark purple, and they were radiant as they basked in the moonlight. It angered her that they dared to come so close. In the days of her wrath, her presence alone would have scared off every living creature within miles. *What hideous designs of the Esmë,* she thought, growling at them.

As her children glided up silently behind her, she turned to see each one bearing a succulent human. One was a tall muscular man, and the other was his soft skinned wife. *Perfect,* she thought.

After she was done she took their hearts and devoured them, leaving the remains for her spawn. As the strength of their spirit coursed through her, she looked back into the forest with blood dripping from her mouth, but the does remained. "You will all burn!" she snarled. As a cloud drifted past the moon, they turned and ran into the shadows. She was so angry she could not contain it. She turned and punched her hand through the core of an ancient maple tree before staring back at the moons once more.

"You will all burn."

XIV

A Note for the King

CHESSA WOKE ÉOLAN AT ELEVEN the next morning. Although it was nowhere near cold, her dark purple sheet was thicker now, and extended from high on her neck down to her ankles and wrists. He tried not to entertain the thought, but she reminded him of a giant *poppleberry*. The flowers in her hair were the white and yellow ones from the knoll outside, and woven into the braided bun on top of her head. She had a parchment scroll in her hand, and Éolan could tell by the green river seal that it was from the king. It read

I do not know how they do things in Nausica, my young lordling, but here in Iccobar we try and discuss our matters of importance while the sun still shines. I expect you promptly at noon in the hall for luncheon and a discussion on matters of importance. If not, I promise you Cmdr. Friedan will be at your door by 12:01 with the company horns.

Most Sincerely,
The King

Éolan chuckled to himself. "Chessa, will you please write back to the king, telling him that he can send his horns, but that I will not be rushed around his halls like cattle."

Chessa smiled, and scribbled the note, but insisted on serving Éolan the small snack that had been sent up and preparing his bath before leaving. The food on the breakfast cart was cold by now, and besides a few pieces of fruit, Éolan left the rest for Chessa. Lunch was close enough.

It seemed that the same storm-delayed clipper that should have taken him north to Iccobar and then north again to Charis Vale almost a week prior had arrived, and right when he needed it. It would be the last direct flight to that region for over two weeks. King Jehrym had assured him that they could cover everything that was needed in this afternoon's meeting, and wouldn't hear of keeping him when he was needed elsewhere.

Éolan was torn by this, since a part of him longed to stay. But it seemed that the universe, for a reason all its own, was drawing him north. That was where Mim was headed as well, and he already had his plan laid out on how to approach her on board the clipper. He needed to address some very important issues with her before they landed, and wanted answers before she became too enamored with the Vale.

He pondered all of this during a very quick bath until the large grandfather clock reached twenty minutes from the top of the hour. He quickly dried and dressed and started his walk down to the hall. He feared the king would uphold his threat and send the company trumpets up to his room, and from experience Éolan knew better than to put it past him.

As he entered the great stone hall, he once again admired its many tapestries and vaulted wooden `beamed ceilings. The four fireplaces had all been lit and had taken the dampness out of the air, and the massive stained glass windows remained shut to keep out the steady rain that was falling.

The long banquet table from the night before was now gone, and in its place stood a smaller one laden with food and drink with three cushioned chairs pulled up near it. One was for him and two for the gentlemen that stood in front of the central hearth, speaking with bowed heads. As he shut the door, the king started in immediately.

"Good afternoon, Lord Éolan. I trust you slept well?"

"Very well indeed," he said. As he neared the table, Éolan smiled and bid them both good morning. They sat down and filled their plates, wasting no time with pleasantries and getting right down to business. The king had not been exaggerating when he said there was much to discuss. Éolan barely touched the food. The information that Jehrym had from the summit in Volaris was more filling than anything he could have eaten, and it only added to the deepening mysteries and troubles of Aldaya.

"I have never seen it so bad," the King said. "You could barely get a word in edgewise, and the moment one person was given the floor, another would interrupt and begin shouting. The tension between the dynasties was so thick it could be sliced with a sword. And without protection from the magi, Queen Delane most certainly wouldn't have been safe enough to attend. She had six within her escort, not including the Sovereign herself," he said.

Éolan raised his brow out of surprise. "If she convinced Melrose to attend a summit then her needs must be dire."

The king nodded in agreement. "Every Visconti and

Courisaunt has a knife up their sleeve with her name on it. Sansori and Kaiair are pitted against Omoniro and Astolaine, with the Five Holy Deeds fueling the tensions with their new faith and pressing the ban on the use of the craft. I swore lighting was going to rain down from the sky by the look on Melrose's face at the mention of it."

"The Dwarven barons weren't even present, nor were the Giant Margraves, and the sea traders literally stood up and walked out on the second day during a ranting from the Visconti's about ludicrous trade taxes on shipping. All proper decorum was completely abandoned. Chancellor Denautra barely holds control over the senate any longer, and I fear his days are numbered. And mark my words: if he is deposed, Volaris will fall, which leads to the end of the Trade Consortium and the last barrier to war is then removed. To me it almost seems a bit calculated, don't you agree?" he asked.

Éolan nodded. It seemed calculated indeed, and masterfully so. It was no secret that the five territories which had once formed the Empire of Men now detested one another. Omoniro, Kaiair, Sansori, Endmoor, and Astolaine had been squabbling since the first treaty was signed just after the disappearance of the Esmë. The severity usually depended on who occupied the thrones at the time, but Éolan had not realized how quickly things had fallen. The chancellor had always been one of the most powerful and influential persons on the Great Isle. This was especially true in the realms of men, who held most of the resources that were widely traded throughout Aldaya. But the news of power slipping from him added an entirely new threat, and as Jehrym had just said, it was clearly planned.

"Tell me: who was the main antagonist in the senate?" asked Éolan.

King Jehrym smiled over the rim of his cup before finishing the rum inside. "It was young King Eron. He seemed pumped full of grand ideas, and kept spouting wildfire phrases like 'death to the old ways'. The little snark," the king grumbled.

"I find that all the more strange," said Éolan. "Usually the hostility is between Omoniro and Kaiair, or focused on the Mages from Astolaine for their use of the craft. But for Sansori to take such a bold stance is most definitely unprecedented. Especially coming from a king as young as Eron."

"Indeed," said the king. "But he is little more than a puppet, with the Holy Deeds are pulling the strings."

They were briefly interrupted by Chessa, who came to the table to deliver Éolan a small note.

"Pardon my intrusion, but I just received this in my room. I have no idea how long ago she left it." She handed Éolan the small roll of parchment. On the outside it read:

> To Lord Éolan and Chessa. Please read and pass
> on to King Jehrym. –Mim

Éolan read and passed on the note as instructed, and as the king began to read his eyes grew wider.

> King Jehrym,
>
> My name is Mim, and I arrived here yesterday in the company of Lord Éolan. I am a refugee from Slaidburn, where I lived as a tenant in a home owned by a woman named Jennah. It has come to my attention that this same woman is also your sister, whom you thought deceased. She is alive, and was sent by your parents to live in the south with your aunt. After the recent massacre in Slaidburn, and the news of the death of your son, I thought this would be of interest to you. I feel you might need her as much as she needs you. I would suggest evacuating her and everyone else out of Slaidburn and into the capital. I know firsthand what is happening there, and it needs your attention. Your sister resides at a place called The Inn. It is at the end of

Eppalong Wynd in the Quilt. If you cross paths, tell her I'm well on my way. I beg your pardon for my letter being so short and informal.

Warmly,
Mim Hart

The king folded up the small piece of paper and leaned back in his chair.

"Atlan be damned," he muttered. "After all this time..."

A few moments later he finally turned towards his guests. "Well, Lord Éolan, it seems your traveling companion has piqued my interest." He handed over the letter to Commander Friedan.

"My King, I never knew your sister still lived!" he said.

Jehrym poured himself a generous shot of brandy before answering, "Nor did me, Commander. I was told many long years ago that she had passed away when staying with my aunt. We were close as children, and I remember being very sad when she left and even more so when I learned of her passing. I asked questions about her death but my parents never seemed interested in talking of her, so I eventually dropped it and moved on. It seems I should have pressed the issue," he said.

Éolan could see he was lost in thought for a moment as he stared into the flames that danced in the fireplace.

"This could solidify your family's hold on the throne. We need to escort your sister out of Slaidburn and get her to the palace as quickly as possible," said the Commander.

The king still stared over at the fire as if contemplating his next move. "Aye. I suppose we should."

The Commander seemed anxious and confused. "Please forgive me your highness, but she is our last chance for a direct male heir. Shouldn't we move as quickly as possible?"

The king looked over at his loyal confidant. "Commander, there are issues at work here that you are not privy to, and this has to be handled with great delicacy. As a child, my sister was gifted in a way that I cannot and will not address here, which was the reason for her departure from the capital. She has obviously made a point not to be involved in her lineage or the dynasty. And this all depends on the young girl's assumption that the woman in Slaidburn is who she really claims to be."

The commander nodded obediently.

"But I think I am going to take young Mim's other suggestion to heart, for I have been contemplating it often over the last few weeks. And it will kill two birds with one stone."

He turned towards Éolan. "I will be writing Premiere Callan this very evening to suggest the closure of the Southern Highway through Endmoor. I am also writing to the mayors of Slaidburn, Burke, and Dane, telling them that they are to evacuate their people to Iccobar. We have room here and jobs that need doing, and until we figure out what is going on I want my people inside the walls."

He stood and turned towards the commander. "We need to prepare for everyone. You and I are in charge of that, Commander."

He saluted, and with a brief, "Yes, my King," took his leave.

"And Chessa, could you fetch Miss Hart for me please. I would very much like to talk with her."

Tucked away in Bette's room on the fifth floor, the two girls had been up nearly all night sharing stories. Bette was alone now, just as Mim was. She had never known her father, and her mother had passed away from a blood cough two years prior, which was just around the time she had started working in the manors. She owned an old horse that had belonged to her mother, and the yardmaster allowed her to keep her in the outer stable as long as he could use her for pulling carts.

Mim was also intrigued by what Bette had told her of the clipper that was moored at the edge of the city. She had seen a few of the airships before as they glided over the Quilt on clearer days, and the thought of actually flying above the ground excited her.

A knock came at the door, and once again Bette strode over and opened to see Chessa. But she was in much more of a rush today than she had been the night before.

"Young Mim, da King wishes for you to attend him immediately. Is this all you have for garments?" she asked.

"Yes, this is all I have," she said. But her nerves were jumping higher by the second.

"I assume this means that he got my note. Why does he want to talk with me? I told everything I needed to," she said earnestly.

"Oh-ho! Young Mim, we have some learnin' to do on da ways you approach royalty. I'm not thinking you realize the implications that the news of his sister will have on da realm. But we can save that chat for later. Up with you. We can't keep him waiting," she said.

Mim grabbed Bette's hand and drug her out into the hall with her, and shot her a nervous glare. Chessa saw and chimed in before Bette had a chance.

"Do not be nervous, young Mim. When dealing with the elites, remember these three things and you will hopefully not start a war." Mim's color drained from her face as Chessa smirked and continued on.

"Da first is to only speak when spoken to. Da second is to answer fully and directly. No fluff. No tripping on words. And da third is to stand properly, which is upright with your hands neatly in front of you. No slouching. Oh, and address him as 'your highness'. However, since you are a native of Endmoor, 'my king' will also suffice," she finished.

As they neared the doors to the hall Bette leaned over and straightened Mim's hair the best she could. "You'll do fine. I'll be waiting out here for you. Chessa is smart and knows what she's doing. Just follow her lead."

Chessa opened the door and they walked over to where the King and Lord Éolan sat. Both men stood as they entered, and when they got to the table the king gestured for Mim to have a seat.

"Have you eaten today?" asked the king.

"Yes. Well no, my King. But I'm not hungry. Thank you very much for the offer though," she said.

She looked over at Chessa to see how she was doing, and Chessa simply stared back with her lips pursed. Éolan had a bit of a smile lifting the corners of his mouth, as did the king.

"Well, if you desire anything, I am sure you will not hesitate to ask," he said. "Now, I called you down here to ask about this lovely note you left for me this morning. It says that you know of my sister, Jennah?"

Mim swallowed hard, and briefly told the king about living in the house with her, and assuming they were siblings after hearing what he told Éolan by the coach. When she was finished, the king kept his eyes on her for a moment before pushing his chair back and standing up. "Could you follow me, please?" he asked.

The two of them walked across the hall to a very ornate piece of wooden furniture larger than Mim had ever seen. The king unlocked and opened one of the large doors, and after rifling through a number of aged books, pulled one from a shelf. It was old and leather bound, and Mim could smell a bit of dampness coming from the paper as he opened it. It reminded her of Miss Barley's ledgers from the Last Stand, and for a moment she felt a bit homesick.

As he rifled through the pages and mumbled to himself about dates, Mim could see the old photographs inside were all of royalty doing fancy things like sitting on thrones, dancing at balls, or standing at joining ceremonies. Finally the king stopped and pointed to a picture of two young children.

The boy was older, maybe Bette's age, while the girl was no older than twelve. But suddenly Mim understood, and could see the resemblance in the faces. "My king, is this you and your sister?" Mim asked.

"I was about to ask you that same question. This is the most recent picture I have of her, and I know it is a long shot, but is this the woman you know?" he asked.

"It is very much her, my King. I once saw a photo of her as a young girl and sitting on the lap of your aunt. They are the same," Mim said.

The King closed the book and put it back in its place and closed the door. He looked down kindly upon Mim and surveyed her for a moment with a sad smile upon his face. He pushed a bit of her hair back behind her ear.

"I do not know how to thank you, Miss Hart. You have returned my sister, who is now the heir to this throne, back into my life. You have done a great service to the kingdom; a kingdom that I'm afraid has let many of its people slip through the cracks of poverty and fear. I assure you that will be no more, and I hope it pleases you to know that I am taking your advice and bringing everyone here to the capital."

Mim welled up with joy for a moment, and was relieved to think of Miss Barley, Talula, and everyone else from the Quilt being safe here behind the walls of the city. "Thank you, your highness," she said proudly.

The king stared at her expectantly for a moment before continuing. "Is there nothing you would ask of me? The reward for returning a lost member of a royal family is not trivial," he said.

Mim was stunned and couldn't think of what to say next. But Chessa had told her that she had to answer any questions, so she cleared her throat.

"Well, if you insist. Let's see. If you could make sure that Miss Tella Barley and Talula Ashlar, along with her family, are well taken care of when they arrive I would be very grateful. They are excellent workers and would do well here at the palace. Miss Plarn permitting of course," she finished quickly.

The King chuckled lowly. "I will make sure they are well. But what about you? Surely there is something that you will need on your journey that I could help with."

Mim pondered this for a moment and went over her supplies

in her head. After mentally checking off what she had in her bag, including her coins, and remembering Éolan's help along the way, she really couldn't think of anything else she needed. Then it hit her like a willow reed.

"Actually, there is something," she said.

———————————

After being dismissed by the king, she walked out of the doors with Chessa and found Bette sitting in a small wooden chair across the hall.

"How did it go?" she asked as Mim walked up.

"You two have one hour," Chessa said as she walked by, quickly disappearing towards her room.

Bette seemed confused, so Mim took her by the arm and began leading her towards the stairs.

"It went marvelously. But the king kept asking me if I needed anything for my journey. So I asked if I could take you with me, and he said yes! I was so excited. But obviously if you don't—"

Bette grabbed her hand and pulled Mim towards the stairs even faster.

"What's wrong?" Mim asked.

"We've only got one hour to pack!" she said.

———————————

Bette got her items together quickly, as did Mim, and now they were rushing towards the stables where the horses were kept. It was taking all of Mim's effort to keep Jessel tucked down in the bag, but upon seeing the four large white horses that pulled Éolan's coach being tethered and tied into their bridles, she settled down a bit. Mim hadn't properly seen them when she had first met Éolan on the road, but in the sunlight they were magnificent. They each stood over nine feet tall and, while Mim was preparing to give them a wide berth, Bette stopped to pet one.

Mim slowly crept towards it while Bette patted its large head and snout. "They're beautiful, aren't they?" she asked. Mim agreed, but was still nervous to be around a creature so large.

"Why are they so much larger than the others?" she asked.

"These are Cavalla Whites, the horses of the gods," Bette answered.

"They are nearly extinct now, but once ran in great herds across the central and southern lands of Aldaya. My mother told me that in the old stories the Esmë Queen, Maia, and the High Ladies of the Seasons rode them into battle during the war in the north. Wouldn't have that been something to see?" she asked.

Mim nodded for an answer and gently put her hand up and touched the horse. Even though she had never seen a caricature of them, she imagined the Esmë goddesses charging into the ranks of darkness upon the valiant steeds and excitement welled up inside of her. As her hand touched the cavalla's glossy white fur its eyes locked on hers, and she could feel the amulet in her pocket grow warm once more. And although the stable boys came to take the horse away, the images continued to dance around in her mind.

As they continued on inside, the two rushed by a salty looking strawberry roan that Mim liked, but Bette led her right past and on towards the last stall. Inside was an old blue dun named Carmen.

"She's all I have left of my mother besides my locket," Bette said.

She reached towards the small chain around her neck for a moment, but quickly unlocked the wooden gate and led the old horse out. Bette put her head against its large snout, and Carmen closed her eyes. Mim could feel the sadness inside of her, and could tell she was far too old to be pulling heavy carts. She also had many scars on her hindquarters, but after Bette saddled her and lead her out of the barn and towards the front gate, her slow walk got a bit faster.

As they neared the front, the girls followed the coach around towards the gates and waited for Éolan and Chessa to come out. With them strode the king, Commander Friedan, Captain Selar, and the young man she had heard them call Alrik. As the King bid farewell to Mim and thanked her again, he knelt down and pulled her close. "You are always welcome in the Manors of House Toller. The name Hart will always be remembered as that of a friend," he said.

He also gave Bette his blessing on her travels and thanked her for her service to him. She was much more elegant in her curtsy than Mim, although hers was slowly improving. After the pleasantries, she watched Bette lead Carmen around to the back of the coach and gracefully hop up onto her back, while Alrik held the door open for Chessa, Mim, and Éolan to enter.

As Éolan climbed in, he turned to the King and Mim heard him say, "I don't think I need to lecture you on keeping your eyes open. I also have a strong feeling that this issue with your sister is important to follow up on. She has a large part to play in your future and the future of this kingdom, and getting her out of Slaidburn must be your top priority. We must keep in contact with any news. I will be at the Charis Vale for a time, so please send any correspondences there until I give word of travel."

The king smiled. "I knew it the second I saw you get out of that damned coach. When the winds blow from the east and the sun sets in the north, Éolan of Nausica will come knocking on your door." The two of them smiled for a second at one another before Éolan climbed in and the coach took off toward the city gates.

XV

The Ourana

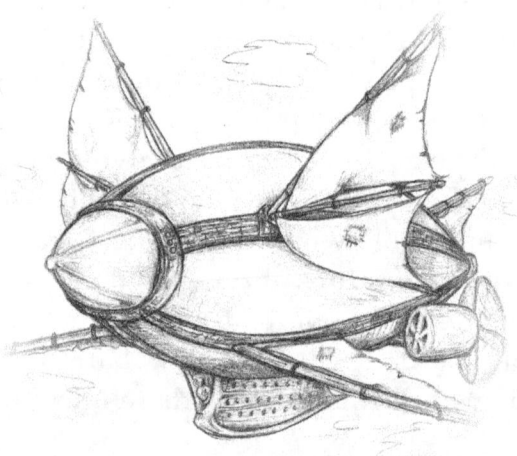

A S THE COACH AMBLED DOWN the road and toward the edge of the city, Mim realized that the large domed building looming up in front of her was not a building at all. It was an airship, and the grey colored balloon was so huge that Mim wondered how it could possibly fly.

It had four large propellers on the back of the three-storied gondola section, and inside she could see passengers were already in most of the seats. The blades were currently spinning, but very slowly, and looked to be warming up for the journey ahead. On the side of the balloon section, Mim could also see the giant bat-like wings folded neatly along the sides. That was what had fooled her at first, because the few she had seen flying above her in the sky always had their wings out, catching the winds.

Huge docking lines were hanging down from all over the bulky balloon section, and attendants were starting to unhook the smaller ones in preparation for flight. A hose was attached to the side, which ran to a large tank a few paces away. Mim could hear the whirring of pumps and hear liquid moving as it sloshed through the tube and into underbelly of the clipper. As they drew nearer, the coach stopped and Mim got out with the others.

"Just follow Chessa and take these tickets to the ramp over there. I'll meet you on board," Éolan said.

The girls smiled in return and led Carmen over to the dark wooden ramp that led up to the clipper. Two young men were there and dressed in matching attire. Jessel was getting restless in the bag and was squirming again now, and Mim had no idea if they would let her ride where the humans did, so she gave the side of it a gentle slap. "Stay put, or you'll be riding with Carmen," Mim whispered.

"Good evening, ladies, and welcome aboard the Ourana. Brom will take your mount, so if you would please head inside we will be on our way shortly," he said.

As the girls walked to the right and up the ramp, they were in even more awe when they emerged inside. An aisle with cushy dark carpets ran up the middle of the room, and on each side were rows that held three seats each and angled to look out of the large, clear glass windows. The seats themselves were all made of cream-colored leather, and small electric lights glowed dimly above each of them. The air was cool and dry, and she could smell wonderful food being cooked somewhere.

Chessa led them towards the back of the cabin and with each row they passed, Mim noticed the wealthy-looking people in the seats. All of them wore expensive robes and clothing of all different styles, and their jewelry and belongings were nicer than she had ever seen. A few caught her staring and pulled their things closer, so she finally decided to look straight ahead and not make eye contact with anyone else.

When they got to the back, Chessa led them up two flights of stairs and into a luxurious cabin that was empty of people but full of comfort. It reminded her of an overstuffed and overly plush great room from a manor.

The carpets were deep blue and soft, and there were huge cushy brown pieces of furniture that dotted the room. Along with them was a dining table that could hold at least fifteen and was made out of sturdy hard wood, with the light glistening off of the mother of pearl that filled the intricate carvings along its legs and surface. Lamps of all kinds hung and stood in every corner and gave the room a comfortable glow, and where the sidewalls should have stood in a normal room, huge glass windows took their place and allowed the passengers to look out upon the landscape as they traveled. Suddenly, the whole room shifted and Mim's stomach seemed to lift into her throat. She and Bette were experiencing flying for the first time, and they ran to look out the window. They watched the city of Iccobar slowly grow smaller and the geography of Endmoor slowly unfold beneath them. The rivers began to look like lines on a canvas and the troubles of the world below seemed distant now as they lifted away. The two looked at each other for a moment in silence before hugging and breaking into fits of uncontrollable laughter as they jumped around. They had finally made it.

A door behind them opened and Lord Éolan strode through, smiling brightly at the two of them. "I was hoping to make it up before we ascended, but I was taking care of some arrangements downstairs," he said.

The clipper was steadily rising hundreds of feet higher off of the ground, and Mim finally let go of Bette's hand and crept carefully towards the window. He palms were a bit sweaty as she looked down, and she quickly withdrew back as the airship shuddered slightly while rising through some low clouds.

"How does this thing even work?" she asked. It was more of an internal question, but Éolan gladly chimed in with an answer.

"Etherium," he said. "It is an opaque substance that is found in pockets throughout the different layers of rock under Aldaya. As a liquid, it can be processed into a lubricant, but it is also flammable. And when burned, it turns to a gas that is much lighter than air. This is what they fill the large balloon above us with, allowing us to float," he explained.

"It is concentrated more in the east and south, and Endmoor once produced more than any other kingdom. It brought great wealth to the region until the swamps swallowed a majority of the infrastructure."

"Oh, you mean rift gas," Mim said.

"Yes, exactly. Etherium is its technical term," Éolan said, looking down towards his feet. Jessel had escaped Mim's bag and was now rubbing the side of her face along the buckles of his tall leather boots. He reached down and picked her up, scratching her belly as she purred louder and louder.

Mim was surprised at her behavior, but she remembered Éolan saying in the coach that he had always been fond of cats, and they of him. But as he was about to put Jessel down, Bette awkwardly chimed in. "Lord Éolan, may I get you something to drink or eat?" she asked.

Mim looked at Bette as if she were crazy, and Éolan smiled.

"Get me something? Miss Brooke, you and Miss Hart are passengers on this vessel and requested guests of mine. You are no longer in service to anyone, which makes the more appropriate question to be, might I get *you* something?" he asked.

Bette smiled lightly, and with a polite "I couldn't say, my Lord," lowered herself onto the couch.

As if on cue, Chessa came in through the doorway pushing a small cart. Bette immediately got up and walked over to help her, and Chessa seemed grateful. Mim felt awkward for not knowing if she should help or not, but Éolan gestured for her to remain seated. Chessa and Bette brought everything over that they needed, and as the four drank in silence, the clipper finally ascended through the grey blanket that covered the capital. The captain's voice crackled over a hidden voice box somewhere in the room. "If everyone could please return to their seats, we are about to enter the air stream," he said.

Mim didn't know what that meant, but she held tightly to the side of the armrest. She noticed Bette did the same, but Éolan and Chessa sat comfortably and made no effort to brace themselves. The engines of the clipper roared louder as the large wings along the side of the balloon slowly opened. They looked to her like giant white sails, and as they fully extended the clipper entered the upper winds and lurched forward with great speed.

It was now skirting along the cloud tops and Mim could see the distant peaks of the Grey Mountains poking up through them in the west. After a few moments, the sun went low enough on the horizon to make the puffy cotton blanket below them suddenly turn from white and yellow to a fiery shade of pinkish orange. It was an amazing sight, and more beautiful than anything she had ever seen.

As a flock of white birds flew by the window, Mim smiled. She had always wondered what it would be like flying up where the birds were and where the sun shined, but never thought she would actually do it. It was gorgeous here on the top of the world, especially since her only vantage point had been from below and within a life of never-ending gray. Bette was transfixed by the experience also, and Mim could see tears in her eyes.

She glanced over at Éolan, and in the light of the setting sun his level of attractiveness was far greater than any man she had ever been in the company of. Even Jessel, who detested most men, was purring loudly as he scratched in between her big brown ears. *Traitor*, thought Mim.

The brilliant sunset quickly went violet, and Bette was trying to wipe a few tears away from her cheek without anyone noticing. Luckily for her, Chessa suddenly stole the attention.

She had begun snoring in her chair, with her empty teacup and plate perfectly balanced on her belly.

Mim stifled a smile and turned back to her friend. "Are you alright?" she asked.

"Yes. Sorry, it's just that my mother always told me I reminded her of Ourana, the goddess of the setting sun. I've never seen a sunset like this before today, so I never knew what she was talking about," she said.

"That is quite a compliment Bette, and I would have to agree," Éolan said.

Bette flushed and managed to get out a weak "Thank you" before getting up and walking towards the washroom. She was only gone for a few moments before a big commotion came from outside the door, and Chessa came to with a large grunt. Alrik entered with Bette's arm clasped firmly in his large hand and walked her forward.

"Let me go, you oaf! I told you I am a *guest* of Lord Éolan." Bette squawked.

But Alrik marched right up and stood proudly in front of them. "I found this girl lurking in the back washroom as I was doing my check. She claims to be familiar with you, but by her look I hardly believe it. Nor was I informed of her presence, my Lord," he said.

Chessa was laughing to herself as she stood up from her chair and letting a few spare crumbs fall to the floor. "Let her go, Master Alrik. She is telling you da truth," she said.

Alrik gave her a stiff bow. "Yes, ma'am. I am sorry for the intrusion, Lord Éolan," he said.

"It is fine, Alrik. I should have made sure to inform you of my guest. The fault was mine. Please excuse the mix up as well, Bette."

Alrik let her go and she straightened her clothing and fussed with her hair with as much dignity as she could muster. But her face was the color of a brick and she glared sideways at the young officer as he moved back towards the door.

As he left, a tall and lovely brunette came gliding through.

She beckoned to Mim and Bette, and with a nod from Chessa, they followed her. She led the girls to a large and plush room with mirrors and puffy lounge chairs.

"Please feel free to use anything you like. Once you are undressed, please put your clothes inside the white basket, along with anything else, and we will launder them for you before dinner. Within the hour, Lord Éolan would like you to join him back in the main car for the evening meal." She smiled and stepped out, leaving the girls standing there.

"I guess they are trying to tell us we're dirty." Mim said.

"Well, we don't need to be told the obvious. We are dirty. You especially," Bette said.

Mim went into her stall and put her rucksack on the hook, taking the amulet out of her pocket before undressing and throwing the worn clothes over the door and into the white basket. After soaking in the tub and asking Bette all sorts of questions through the wall about what cream and soap did what, the two were dry and clean.

When they came out, their clothes were pressed, stitched, and folded neatly on the counter. Mim couldn't believe the efficiency, and when she slipped into her old outfit, it felt and looked like new. Bette owned many more clothes than Mim, and picked out a lovely brown dress and threw a silky green shawl around her shoulders. They both looked like new women when they strode out into the dining area, and their stomachs growled as they saw and smelled the grand meal that now sprawled across the table.

There was some sort of large roasted bird in the middle with four wings, which Bette called a *darly*, and all around it were different colored baked vegetables. There were two pots of steaming soup in fancy silver servers, which were accompanied by huge loaves of purple bread and scoops of something orange that seemed to be an approximation of butter. There were also various cheeses, fruits, and dips scattered in between. Bette knew much more than she did, having been in service to the King, but Mim had never seen or smelled delicacies like this.

Just as they were sitting down, Chessa and Alrik entered, followed by one of the clipper's service workers. As they sat down, Alrik looked over at Bette and flushed. She and Mim looked much prettier now, and it seemed to shock him. At the same time, he was also much more handsome now that he was clad in his dinner attire, and his face was particularly attractive. Mim noticed Bette's cheeks had become a bit rosy as well, but Éolan's appearance distracted all of them.

"Usually I would host a more proper evening meal, but under the circumstances I concluded that we could use a more relaxed supper. All of us have had quite an eventful few days. So please, serve yourselves and eat to your hearts' content."

He let Mim go first, and after she had filled her plate to the brim, the others much more elegantly gathered their food and began to eat.

It was quiet again, so Mim tried to break the ice. "Lord Éolan. Why aren't you eating any of this wonderful darly? It's the best thing I've ever tasted!" She said, taking another large bite.

"Well," Éolan said, "That's because I do not eat fauna."

Mim laughed out loud for a second and it took an elbow to the ribs from Bette before realizing he wasn't kidding. Mim was flabbergasted. Even if she had not liked meat, there would never have been enough vegetables in the Quilt to live off of.

"You only eat vegetables?" she asked.

"No, no, no," said Éolan, "I eat everything you do, like breads cheeses, fruits and grains; just no animals."

"That's, *interesting*," Mim said. She shrugged her shoulders and took another bite of the succulent bird. *Well it's his loss,* she thought. The rest continued to eat in silence and look out the windows until they had their fill. Mim had thought about trying to start more conversation, but since her last attempt hadn't gone as well as she planned she decided to keep quiet. Éolan seemed lost in thought, and she came to the conclusion that it would have been easier gutting a spike fish with one hand than to try and get Bette and Alrik to say anything. So she kept quiet until Chessa brought in a beverage cart. She could see the top shelf held more pitchers of water and sun brew. But the bottom contained strange glass bottles of different colored liquids. "What are in those?" she whispered to Bette.

"Different types of fancy vexor," she whispered back.

Mim knew what vexor was, but had never tried it after seeing what it did to people like Mr. Ol'Grady back in the Quilt. But the stuff there was murky brown and nothing like these. As the plates were cleared, Alrik politely dismissed himself and left before having to make eye contact again with Bette. Chessa was now rooting through the bottles on the lower shelf, and pulled a small one from the center. Its contents were a vibrant blue and she poured a small glass and handed it to Éolan before he gestured for Mim to join him back by the large windows.

"Mim, as I'm sure you have noticed, I have taken quite a fondness to you. I find your courage and strength very refreshing in a world that is becoming increasingly stagnant and unaware. However, I must admit that my generosity is, in part, stemming from selfish motives. The moment I saw you on the road, when we first met, was not truly the first time. Well, on my part, that is. I have seen you before, though you may not have seen me."

Mim was confused, but it made sense to her when she thought back to the wagon ride and how he had become so interested in her so quickly. She had seemed to recognize him as well, but the harder she thought on it she still couldn't think of why.

"You seemed familiar to me as well, but I can't think of how. I've never been outside of the Quilt, and if you had visited the Last Stand I surely would have remembered you. The whole town would have, a southern proper like yourself," she said.

Éolan took a small sip of the vexor and set his cup down on the table next to him.

"I agree that we haven't met in our waking lives," he said cryptically.

"What could you mean by that?" Mim asked.

"For quite a number of years I have been having strange dreams and, although I am asleep, they feel more like lost memories than actual dreaming; yet I have never experienced the situations in my waking life. Most of them revolve around trying to aid a young girl who always remains just out of my reach. The scenery constantly changes, but the girl remains the same. The night before I departed on my journey north I was finally able to reach her, and then not four days later she saves my life during an ambush. She is you, Mim," he said.

She was stunned. Not only did these dreams sound realistic like hers, but she finally knew why Éolan had seemed familiar somehow. The bright blue eyes that flashed at the end of her dream were his. She quickly explained her repeating dreams to him as well, including his eyes, and they both sat in silence for a moment. Bette had been helping Chessa but listening closely, and quickly abandoned her duties and used Éolan's empty vexor cup as an excuse to come over to take a seat.

"But what does this mean?" she asked, refilling it with quick precision before sitting. "Is it some sort of ancient craft? How would you two dream of one another when you had never met?"

Chessa now sat down next to the window and chimed in.

"In the early days of my people, there were a very select few of our elders that had achieved da skill to walk in their dreams. We called them *tar'luci*, and even in their sleeping states they could remain aware of what was happening around them. Some stories even tell that they could stay in the land of sleep for as long as their earthly bodies would allow, and create paradises around them that they could return to. But I have never heard tell of them seeing the future," she said.

"There is also another explanation," said Éolan. "During the time that the Esmë graced the sphere, there was a group among them called the Tari. They were divine spirits as well, but wished to remain in their natural states, having no desire to exist within the corporeal confines of the airs. And so they chose to remain in the *outersphere*, which to you is the land of stars."

"What do you mean 'natural states'?" Bette asked.

"The divine, whom in the common tongue you call the Esmë, did not originally exist in the state of flesh and blood as we do.

Their true form is of light and energy, which they called *Nu*, but they feared that the radiance and power they exuded in this state would make the five free races fearful of them when they awoke. So their solution to this problem was to take on a form that resembled the peoples. This is how they came into the descriptions that our histories remember, bodies which look generally like ours, which they called their *Taar*.

However, the transition back and forth from the two proved to be much more difficult than any had guessed. Once they were on the surface for a long period, only the most powerful of them could do so unaided and of their own free will, and many remained in their Taar forms almost permanently," he continued.

Mim took a big breath in and looked to Bette. She was on the edge of her seat, with her chin in her hands, and wasn't taking her eyes from Éolan. But Mim understood, because she too was amazed at how much Éolan knew of the Esmë. She, along with all the other children on Aldaya, had learned stories of them as children, but they had always seemed so distant and unbelievable. But when Éolan spoke of them, they seemed tangible and real, and it gave her a wonderful chill up her spine to think how amazing they must have been.

Chessa seemed to notice Éolan's drift from the true topic at hand and said, "But what does this have to do with da dreaming, my Lord?" she asked.

"Ah yes, sorry," he continued. "So, obviously when the Esmë decided to remain here in their Taar state, they no longer had access to the outersphere, and it muted their connection to the deep tones of the void. This left them feeling empty and cut off, if you will. So some decided to remain outside of the sphere, but still desired to take part in its guidance. These spirits were called the Tari, and many of them formed the guiding star constellations that are shining above us now. Rayna and Selna, the sisters of the moon and guardians of the mortal spirit, were counted amongst them also; as were Aurora and Ourana, the goddesses of the rising and setting sun."

"But, on occasion, a few could take form and visit the sphere on special occasions, like the mingling of the seasons, for example, and would delight in all of the strange creations and unique beauty here on the surface. But while on the sphere, their astral powers were so strong that they would unknowingly project their thoughts and desires into other people's minds. Now usually that would not have any bearing on a topic amongst humans, but one curious trait that all of the Tari shared were purple eyes," he said.

Mim sunk back slowly into the plush chair and looked out of the window and up at the clear night sky. The moons were bright and full, and Rayna's brighter light bounced brilliantly off the tops of the clouds while Selna's purplish orange glowed strangely behind. The stars were also more luminous this high in the atmosphere and since Mim had only seen a few in her lifetime, so many of them twinkling right outside of the window made her feel elated. But there was also another strange sensation as she looked at a cluster of five that stood close together and twinkled brighter than the rest.

A longing burned inside of her as she looked at them. Mim thought of the woman from her visions and was now certain that this was a memory and not a dream. But then questions began building up with every passing beat of her heart. If the woman was one of these Tari, did that mean she was as well? Did they have the same powers she did, and more importantly, did they know how to use them? And if the woman had been her mother, why would she abandon her child to grow up miserably in a place like the Quilt? But then the loneliness returned when she remembered how long it had been since the Tari, and all the Esmë, had disappeared.

"Now that he mentions it, I have never noticed how purple your eyes are," said Bette.

Mim was a bit surprised.

"Usually that's the first thing anyone notices, especially since they've now gone more purple than blue," she said, still staring out the window.

175

"Well, I noticed," said Bette. "But they seem extra so right now. I've never met anyone with eyes like yours."

"They are interesting indeed," said Éolan. "Many people in the northern deserts have eyes of pale yellow and orange, and the Elves have deep greens or light grey if you're ever lucky enough to see them. But most men and other free folk tend to be brown or sometimes blue. Does it run in your family?" he asked.

"I don't have any family. Well, family I know of, that is. I was found by a passing cart driver on the banks of a small stream near Slaidburn, wrapped in a blanket and in some funny wicker carrier. I don't know anything other than that," she said.

Then another curious question came to her mind. "What about people with black eyes? Have you seen any of them around?" Éolan looked up at her and stopped his glass mid raise to his mouth. "What do you mean by black?"

"Before I left the Quilt, the night of the massacre, a strange woman came to the Last Stand where I worked. Well I assume she was a woman, but if I know the old stories at all she was something much worse. Her eyes were black, and I think she was behind the murders," she said.

It felt strangely nice to get it off of her chest, but the look on Éolan's face was serious now.

"Why did you not tell me of this before?" he asked. His voice was stern, and for the first time Mim could see a powerful lord coming through in his demeanor.

"I was afraid, my Lord. I had never been so terrified in my life and, to be honest, I didn't think anyone would believe me. It was like she had walked out of a nightmare. And she said she would be back for me, so I ran."

"Did she say anything else? Anything strange?" he asked.

"It's all kind of fuzzy, the details I mean. But when I came into the dining area I seemed to surprise her. She said something odd about not being able to *smell* me. And my two coworkers were just standing there, like they were frozen. I know I was scared stiff as well, but the way they looked was like they were in some sort of trance."

"Or spellcraft, perhaps," Bette said in a hushed voice.

After everything she had just learned and revealed, Mim's hands were a bit shaky and Bette reached over to help steady them. Chessa looked at Éolan. He said nothing for a few moments, and stared pensively out of the window before turning back towards the girls.

"In a darker age, when the Esmë and the free peoples waged war with the emptiness that was vying for power in the north, those who were in the service of Izman mimicked him and turned their eyes to black. And although most of them were imprisoned or destroyed afterwards, a select few did escape. In my limited way, I could sense something beyond the work of thieves in the mists of Endmoor, and now I know for certain that my instinct was correct. You have not had any contact with this woman since you fled the south, have you?" he asked.

"Oh no," said Mim. "And I have a terrible feeling that if I had, I wouldn't be sitting here talking with you now," she said.

Éolan's eyes probed hers for a moment.

"Well, I am glad you told me of this, and you are wise to sense the urgency and danger of this creature. Although I do not know her origins, anything that escaped the wrath of the Esmë and hid this long would have to be cunning and very powerful. With what you have described, it is very likely she is of dark design, or at least making a good impersonation of something that is," he said.

"But I thought practicing the craft was heresy in the central lands?" asked Bette.

"It is. But there are many corners of the Great Isle where it is still practiced and embraced. You must remember, the Holy Deeds of Pretoria City may hold sway over the kings and queens of men, but beyond that they and their new canons of embracement law have very little clout. The Mages, Dwarves, Elves, and what are left of the lost races all practice the craft in whatever ways they see fit. Even Alamarayn allows it, as long as it does nothing to harm one another."

Mim let out a small sigh. She had a lot to learn about the world around her. Some of what Éolan and Bette thought of as common knowledge she had absolutely no clue about. But this just made her eager to learn more.

"To be honest, I don't think anyone could impersonate something like her. The way she looked at me was just—" she said, trailing off and looking back out of the window.

Éolan leaned in and grasped her hand for a moment.

"Do not worry, Mim. It will take some digging, but we will find out the identity of our foe. Not only for your safety, but it could also be an important part of a much larger threat to Aldaya as a whole. Yet another piece of the puzzle, if you will."

Mim shifted in her seat and heard the jingling of coins within her rucksack. For a moment she questioned whether handing them over to Éolan was smart. In her entire life she had never owned this much coin, and if the Vale didn't work as planned, she and Bette would need it to start over somewhere. But as she looked at him staring out of the window, something deep down urged her to trust him. She reached down and pulled out the bag of coins, leaving five in the bottom of her purse, and set them on the table.

"She gave me these before she left. Other than that, I know nothing else of her, and I don't think I ever want to," she said. She opened the bag carefully and dumped the coins out onto the table, tossing the bag off to the side.

Éolan picked one up and slowly examined it.

"I know them, but to my knowledge they have not been seen in these lands for over a thousand years. It was once the royal currency of Laurasia, which was the capital city of Atlan. The people that had bartered with them during those days were only of the highest and most prestigious ranks, each one of these being worth hundreds in the modern currencies, especially to a collector," he said.

Mim's eyes widened. *Hundreds!* she thought. She moved uncomfortably around a little in her chair.

"I will keep these for you, if you wish. And undoubtedly it will be much safer than in your bag," he said.

Mim supposed he was right and thanked him. But she was so fuzzy and clogged with information that the coins were now only another item on the list growing in her head. As she stifled a yawn, Chessa stood up and clasped her hands.

"We have talked about quite a bit tonight, and I think we all have plenty to lay on until tomorrow, eh?" she asked.

Mim was tired, and although her eyes were heavy she had so many questions. But Éolan seemed to agree with her.

"You are right, Chessa. And we will have plenty of time and resources to aide us upon reaching the Vale. But do not worry; you are safe above the clouds, and no terror from the swamps can reach you here. Now, tomorrow is a big day for you both and I suggest you get some rest. We will have a lot to discuss in the morning if we hope to get you into the Charis. Chessa, will you show them to their room?" he asked.

"Yes, my Lord. This way ladies," Chessa said.

As they stood up, Mim smiled at him, as did Bette. And although they didn't need it, Chessa led them to their room and turned down the bed before bidding them a good rest. Although they were both exhausted, the girls just lay there staring at the ceiling. But where Mim seemed overwhelmed and anxious, Bette was a mix of awestruck and determined.

"This is so exciting and terrifying at the same time, Mim. I always dreamed of being on an adventure, and I can't wait to get my hands on some of those books in the Charis libraries. They are bound to help us figure out some of what's going on, and I love a good mystery, don't you agree?" she asked.

Mim admired her friend and did her best to seem just as excited. "You bet," she said. And as Bette clapped her hands excitedly, she rolled over and almost immediately began to breathe deeply in her sleep. But Mim still lay there, with her eyes open and her hand wrapped around the amulet that sat hidden in her pocket.

———⋙⋘———

When Chessa reentered the parlor car, Éolan barely noticed her as she cleaned up the last remaining cups and brought him his pipe before bidding him goodnight. He had a lot on his mind, especially after the conversation he had just finished with the girls. He had already spent plenty of time pondering the origins of Mim's strange eyes, and as of now he had no explanation. To his knowledge, none of the Tari had been on the sphere in over 1,000 years. But Mim's encounter with the creature from the swamps had shaken him deeper than any of the others realized. As did the realization that had occurred shortly after the girls had left the room.

The coins were a bit suspicious, especially with all the mystery that already surrounded Mim and her journey, and with all things considered it could have just been a relic from the past. But he had a knack for detail, and he noticed something that was very small in size but could be very serious and sinister in its implication, which was the bag.

The fine black cloth was extremely old but very well preserved, and on it was a thin and meticulously woven spidery writing. Éolan knew these symbols were not just decoration, but were reminiscent of a script that very few today would have recognized. The writing looked like that of an ancient dialect once used by the Esmë. But during the Great War, Izman and his foul children had twisted it into a dark and secretive speech.

Although Éolan didn't have the ability to translate the runes and was not positive of their origin, if he were correct in his assumption this little bag could indicate a much larger problem. And the description Mim had given also triggered a memory. It was one of an ancient horror that was used to terrible effect by Izman during the wars on Atlan. She had been one of his most powerful generals, and her cunning had kept her out of the subterranean prisons where her master still dwelt. But the thought of her being loose in the world terrified him, and if she felt it safe enough to wander out from the lightless places, the world was in much more danger than war starting within the kingdoms of men.

Once again he was faced with another mystery that needed unraveling, but this took precedence over everything else. He needed the runes translated, which would certainly tell him his answer. And luckily for him, the Ourana was headed in the direction of someone that could help.

XVI

The Charis Vale

HE NEXT MORNING, MIM WAS dreaming of a glorious breakfast being cooked somewhere. The smells had entered her dreams first, and she imagined rooms filled with food and all the people from the Quilt eating to their hearts' desire. The children were full and content and laughed as their parents wiped their faces clean.

Talula was there, and laughing heartily with Jennah, Candy, and Miss Barley at large table across the room. Mim had never seen them look so healthy and happy, and joy filled her for a moment. But suddenly the mood shifted, the feasting and laughter stopped, and everyone stared at her. Mim's gaze was drawn down to the table in front of her, and on it sat the familiar hand mirror. It was the same one used by the blond haired woman from her dreams. As her hand wrapped around the cold crystal handle and raised it to her face, the frame began to glow. Her reflection was staring back in all the same ways she recognized in real life, except her eyes were black pools like the creatures had been at the Last Stand.

The mirror dropped from her hands and shattered on the floor. Mim stared down at the broken pieces and was afraid. Suddenly, the shards of glass turned to liquid and flowed back into the undamaged frame, becoming whole again. Mim hesitantly picked it back up. A copy of her was staring out of the mirror, another version that seemed to know things she didn't. Then, somewhere off to the right, there was a loud clamoring and crashing. As she began to go investigate, her reflection spoke, "Tsk-tsk-tsk. Remember, curiosity killed the cat, Mim."

Her reflection inside the mirror now had Jessel over her shoulder and was scratching under the cat's neck. Mim wanted to scream, but for some reason no words would come out, and the fear she felt before now mixed with anxiety and was beginning to make her heart race and palms sweat. A loud BOOM echoed throughout the room, and the large stained glass windows that lined the walls shattered inward, sending shrapnel flying all over the people from the Quilt.

"Psst! Down here. Hurry!" Her reflection was beckoning to her now, and as she leaned in towards the mirror, her copycat's face suddenly turned into the grotesque form of the demon woman. Her cold and bony hand reached out of the mirror and clasped around Mim's jaw, pulling her downwards.

"You can run, but I will find you, piglet. Nothing can hide from me."

She opened her mouth, revealing her two rows of terribly jagged teeth. The closer Mim got, the bigger the woman's mouth became, as if she could unhinge her jaw to make room for larger prey. The smell was more horrific than anything Mim had ever been exposed to, and just as her blond locks began bouncing off the first row of the cracked white razors, she bolted up in bed.

After a few moments of confusion, she remembered where she was and took a deep breath. She always hated when good dreams went sour, and she tried her best to keep the happy images of her friends in her head. But Mim was not one to ignore the truth, no matter how bitter it tasted.

As she rose and went to the lavatory, she found her clothes neatly pressed and laundered again. She rinsed off in the lavish tub, remembering Bette's advice on how important first impressions would be for the deans. As she finished and got dressed, she sat in front of the mirror and brushed her hair for a few minutes until Bette came billowing in, all in a dither.

"Mim! Why didn't you wake me up? We land in three hours and I haven't even gotten into the tub!" And with a flash of auburn, the door to Bette's washroom slammed shut.

Mim didn't understand the rush, especially since they did, in fact, have three full hours until they landed. Mim got up without a word and headed out into the bedroom. It was still a bit dark with the shades drawn, and after a minute of trying to figure out the electric switch to make them rise, she gave up and headed out into the main area.

Éolan was already there, looking over a pile of papers and scribbling things down in a large dark leather journal he had resting on his lap.

When Mim entered, he looked up from his business and smiled. "Feel better after a good night's sleep? I was about to send Chessa in to wake you. First meal is over there by the window. It is all self-serve, so feel free to dig in."

Mim smiled before walking over to dish herself out some breakfast. She ate alone at the table while Éolan finished with his papers and scrolls, along with two visits from Chessa about various arrangements once they landed. Just as she finished her third helping and pushed the plate away, Bette came barreling out of the door from their room.

"First meal is laid out for you, Bette," said Éolan. "And you have plenty of time to get ready. There's no need to rush."

"Thank you, my Lord," she said, but obviously ignoring the last part. She was furiously dishing food onto her plate, and seemed to have forgotten about the comb that remained in her hair, mid brush.

Mim got up and finished the brushing and was putting it into a lovely braid while Éolan told the two his plan upon arrival.

"When we land we will not quite be at Charis yet. The clipper is far too large to land its bulk on the cliffs within the Vale, so it sets down in the small town of Far Darron that sits just outside the gorge. It is a lovely little place, and I am sure you will visit it on your free days."

Bette choked and dropped her toasted bread as she began to ask questions. "Free days? What are they? How often? Are they chaperoned? Will Mim and I get to share a room? What about—?"

Éolan raised his hand and Bette stopped. "All those questions will be addressed during orientation, I promise. But before that I have to make sure you are admitted at all." That last part had made Mim nervous, but she listened intently as he continued.

"When we reach Far Darron, we will get a coach that will take us into the ravine and up to the castle. When we arrive, we will be greeted by at least one of the deans, maybe more. Many are dear friends of mine and have been expecting me."

"However, they will not be expecting the two of you since I had no time to write ahead. This is where you both need to be on your best behavior, especially you, Mim."

Bette laughed until Mim gave a yank on her braid. "Only because Bette has had formal training with nobility, and you have not. For now, just keep your answers short and direct and only speak when spoken too," he said.

"Once inside, I will ask them to meet with me while the two

of you wait outside. Hopefully after a few short minutes, I will come out with good news."

"But what if the news isn't good?" Bette asked.

"In that case, you will stay with me in the castle until I leave and then travel back to Nausica if you wish. Do not worry, Bette, you will not be abandoned, I promise you."

Mim finished Bette's braid, and Bette jumped up with a chipper, "Your turn." She was done much more quickly than Bette, and after a few more simple instructions from Éolan they returned to their room to gather what few things they had.

When Mim walked into the washroom to grab her bag, she looked into the mirror and was astounded. Bette seemed to have transformed her in mere minutes. Her hair was smoothed and interwoven with tiny braids all the way until it reached a lovely bun that sat neatly on the upper back of her head. Bette had also left two strands that hung down at her temples which Mim thought pulled it all together nicely. When Bette entered behind her, Mim began to apologize for the simple style she had given her, but Bette had already changed it. She now had a gorgeous side braid that came down past her right ear and sat on her chest.

"Where did you learn how to do hair like this?" Mim asked, as Bette got dressed.

"My mom taught me," she said.

Mim spun a full circle in front of the mirror as she answered. "I actually think it's possible to fool those deans with hair like this."

Bette smiled as she pulled on the rest of her nicest clothing. Mim then went to the laundry basket, grabbed out the linen bag, and walked into her washroom where she made a clean sweep of the different products that lined the shelves.

"That's stealing!" Bette said.

Mim gave Bette a confused look as she made her way into the other stall and did the same thing. "Captain Fancy Pants isn't going to be giving the next rich lord our used soap. They probably throw it away, and I'm not one to waste," Mim said.

"You look like a vagabond, you know," she said with her arms crossed.

Suddenly, a large squelch came from the voice box above Mim's head, and she dropped the bag out of fright.

"Good morning. If you will all return to your seats, we will be coming out of the air stream shortly and beginning our drop into Far Darron. We should be stationary within the next thirty minutes," he said.

The girls walked back to the overlook and sat down as the Ourana approached the small town. It turned west before adjusting into its final landing position, and for the first time the girls laid eyes upon the massive snowcapped peaks of the tallest mountains they had ever seen. Their jaws dropped, and Éolan chimed in.

"Those are the Vellorian Mountains. They are the largest and most expansive range on all of the Great Isle. They run along almost all the northern coast of Aldaya, shielding the central lands from the violent tempests that ravage the Sea of Storms beyond. The tallest is Mt. Windom, which lies to the east and stands over seven miles high." The girls stood in amazement as the clipper landed and the mooring lines were cast and connected to the ground.

"The view gets better outside," Éolan said with a smile as he led the girls from the clipper. They disembarked, and the bright sun hit their eyes and a crisp breeze filled their lungs. Alrik was immediately at Éolan's side and dressed in his armor once again. He fell back behind Mim and Bette, shadowing them as they walked on.

The temperature was mild, but the breeze blowing down from the range and into the small town was quite cool. It was dry and smelled of snow and pine trees and Mim felt invigorated. It was a stark contrast from the muggy and damp air of Endmoor. Jessel made a hasty escape from Mim's shoulder, but walked by her side and made no attempt to run, so Mim let her stretch her legs a bit.

It was still summer, so flower boxes full of red, white, and violet dotted the fronts of the buildings they were approaching. Éolan led them towards the coach that Chessa had already procured. She had squeezed herself inside a giant puffy overcoat with large orange and white flowers embroidered on it. It made her look twice her normal size and completely out of place. Éolan gestured for them to head over to her before quickly walking across the square with Alrik and into a very upscale-looking establishment. Once they got inside the coach, they slid the windows down and took in the air while they waited, and within ten minutes they were back.

Jessel perched above Mim and Bette's head and settled in for the ride. Mim gave her a scratch and peered out of the window and began taking in her surroundings. She could tell that the people of Far Darron were good-natured, with a touch of red on their cheeks, true smiles, and hearty laughs. Most of them had blond hair and blue eyes, and many raised a friendly hand to her as they drove by, which she gladly returned.

As they went through the heart of town, Mim noticed many lovely shops and clothing stores along with some pricy looking inns and taverns. As the coach stopped to yield to a group of chatting women crossing the lane, a young boy ran up to the coach and handed Mim a small purple flower and kissed her hand. As she leaned her head back in the window, she looked over to Éolan. "What a lovely town!"

Éolan smiled back at Mim as he turned from his window. "Yes, it is very lovely. They especially adore those that attend term at Charis and welcome them gladly, for they are how the town survives. The local businesses depend on them and their visiting families, since the deans allow no one but students and invited guests to stay within the Vale itself."

Mim smiled and kept her head out the window on the left side, and Bette did the same on the right. By the time they reached the outskirts of town, each of them had three flowers apiece and their mood was definitely elevated. Chessa didn't seem amused and kept trying to tighten her coat around her neck in an attempt to keep the cold out.

The coach headed uphill and straight towards the base of a large mountain, yet Mim could see no castle. The higher they climbed the cooler it became, and as she closed her window she wondered if there would be any places to get warm clothes once they arrived. On and on they continued towards the range, and just as the coach seemed like it would run into the base of the mountain ahead, it slowed and turned left, disappearing into a small ravine.

It was just wide enough for the coach to fit through, and had the driver not known the way, they surely would have gone right by. Very slowly and cautiously the coach made its way down a narrow and steep incline and into a tunnel. For a minute or two they were in almost complete darkness, with only the low oil lamps hanging outside to guide them. Then sunlight hit their eyes once again and the coach turned right and crossed over a large stone bridge that spanned a deep gorge. Bette moved towards Mim's side, since the right facing windows looked only at a sheer grey wall and the left looked out across a wide valley that held a deep ravine in the middle.

The tips of the tallest pines that grew within barely reached the road, which had only room for one coach to travel at a time. Mim wondered how they managed to deal with passing one another, but quickly got her answer. Far across the valley she saw the small figure of another coach heading out towards the bridge on a similar one-way road. As they slowly wound along the treacherous path, they looked out and down into the progressively deepening ravine.

"How did anyone build this road?" asked Bette. She had backed away from the window as the coach veered dangerously close to the edge.

"The ancient Kasano Dwarves of the Blue Mountains on Atlan carved its track," he said.

This piqued her interest, and she could tell Éolan noticed. "The past of the Charis Vale is long and filled with much lore and magic, which you will undoubtedly learn about if admitted, but I can give you a brief summary if you wish."

Bette immediately assumed an attentive position on the edge of her seat and prodded Éolan to go on. The second he had spoken the word magic it had gotten their attention. Anything that had to do with the mysterious force had always intrigued her, and even more so now. The talk onboard the clipper had given both her and Bette enough to chew on, but it hadn't given her the explanation she needed for what had happened to her back in Slaidburn or about her strange amulet. Although part of her wanted to tell Bette and Éolan, she still held Jennah's advice close to her hear and kept her ability and the affect the amulet had on her quiet for now.

"The original structure and design was brought forth by a powerful and very wise group of the Esmë that were known as the Graces. They were great spirits of intellect and learning in all forms, and desired a safe place of study and introspection where anyone could come to enlighten the mind. They believed, above all else, that their true purpose and that of the free peoples was to learn and further their minds no matter what personal stage of development. But for many years they searched far and wide to find the perfect location for such a place to no avail."

"But one day, the beautiful Janette, who was the Grace of love and healing in all of its forms, wandered into this hidden vale while following an injured fawn. After hours of chase, the young deer led Janette through a small crack at the base of the two mountains that lie ahead. Here, it laid itself down upon a field of fresh spring grass and allowed her to approach. As she surveyed it, she found the fawn had no wound at all, and pondered the creature's strange behavior and wondered why it had brought her into the hidden valley."

"As she stood and took in her surroundings, Janette realized that the vale would be the perfect location for the endeavors of the Graces. Turning back, she saw that the fawn on the grass had vanished. And so, as legends go, if one sees the fawn amongst the grounds, they are to follow it. It is said to still bring messages from the Graces to those in need. And those should not be lightly tossed aside."

The girls said nothing, only wanting to hear more, and so Éolan continued. "And so, Janette told her brothers and sisters of her find, and a plan was set forth. So in year one of the Third Age, the Graces passed into the hidden vale with a great host. Among them came several of the other Esmë spirits that were steeped in the lore of stone and metalworking, along with any others who desired to help. They were accompanied by many of the greatest Dwarven and Elven smiths ever to grace the sphere, and with their combined talents a marvelous realm unfolded inside."

"They created a magnificent fortress that was hewn out of the rock face itself, and the Dwarven smiths carved deep into the inside of the mountain's stone heart. Magnificent vaulted chambers came to life in its depths and were adorned with gems from the great crystal caves of Maia, the eldest and most powerful among the Esmë. The Elves then crafted many winding passageways that led up to dizzying star towers on the peaks of the mountains, and to the high green plateaus and hidden valleys that bloom in spring.

Within a few short years, all was completed and the Graces opened its doors. In its splendor it sat for thousands of years in peace. Then Izman, the Lord of Nothing, fell back into his old ways and the Great War came swiftly down from the north," he said.

"But I thought none of the shadow legions ever crossed onto Aldaya from Atlan," Bette said.

Éolan nodded. "You are correct, Bette, but the repercussions of their actions were felt in every corner of the sphere. Shortly after the conflict and imprisonment of Izman, the Esmë and all of the other Elder spirits disappeared from Aldaya, including the Graces. But before they left, they entrusted the care of the Vale to the deans, who were the greatest of their pupils among the free races at the time. But without the power that the spirits of Grace took with them upon leaving, the institution has periodically found itself on very hard times. This was also exacerbated by a general regression in society during the years of rebuilding after the war."

"What does that mean?" Mim asked.

"Well, Mim, when hard-working families and dignitaries became stuck between the choices of higher learning or keeping their stores filled with food and their people protected, education naturally fell by the wayside. But it is interesting to me, because as far as protection, you couldn't ask to be in a safer place."

Mim looked out of the window and chewed at her nails excitedly. She wanted to learn more about the Graces and what powers they had. She wondered if they were powerful among the Esmë, or if their specialty was in learning only. Did they fight in the wars? Did they have unexplained bursts of power, or feel like something possessed them when they got angry?

These questions reeled around in her head until she noticed the ravine below her was steadily getting narrower. She looked across the valley and saw that the exit route was getting much closer and that she could have hit one of the departing coaches easily with a stone. As she slid her window back down and looked up, she noticed the sunlight was only entering through a very skinny area between the two meeting peaks of the mountains above. The road continued to narrow until it reached a pass, one that must have been carved out by the Esmë and Dwarf lords.

Where the feet of the mountains met, there was a grandly decorated and fluted archway with arrays of vines and flowers. On its right side was a large stone statuesque figure of a faceless woman with her arms outstretched in a welcoming manner, while the left was a man with his hands and fingers intertwined in a strange but elegant formation that he held at chest height.

"Those are the guardians," Éolan chimed in. "She was built in the likeness of Janette and welcomes all people to enter. He was built in the likeness of the Grace called Taurin, who was of logic and known to many as the Philosopher. He bids you a fair welcome as well, but his hands are formed in an ancient symbol that warns to do so in peace only."

Mim suddenly got the chills and felt as though she were being watched, and a tingly feeling crept up her spine. As Bette began trying to mimic the man's design with her own hands, the coach fell under the tall shadow of the statues and entered into another large dark tunnel. This one was much longer than the first, and Mim began to feel claustrophobic after a time. The weight of two entire mountains stood above her, and by some ancient skill it still remained open, but that didn't help her building anxiety.

Just as she was about to tell Bette she was starting to panic, the coach came out on the other side and revealed the fair valley of which Éolan had spoken. But his story had done nothing to prepare them for the sight.

It was much lusher than the one they had just come through, and the girls rushed to lower their windows. Even Chessa unbuttoned her large coat and stared out with a smile. The temperature had risen at least ten degrees and a sweet smell now replaced that of the rugged pines from before.

The lovely songs of birds met their ears, and the brilliant blue sky above made her smile. "It seems to me that the Graces didn't take everything with them," Mim said to Bette with a little nudge in the ribs.

Bette smiled and gave Mim a nudge back.

Looking out, they saw that the vibrant green hillsides were lined with rows of variously sized and sturdily-built stone and wooden cottages. These all sat just off to the side of tiny lanes that switch-backed here and there and meandered haphazardly around the glens. Among the cottages, huge linden trees draped and shaded the lanes, which Éolan said gave off the sweet fragrant smell of honey in the valley.

There were other trees as well. Large tulips, maples, oaks, and willows were chief among them, with tons of flowering varieties interspersed here and there. Under all their eaves sat scores of the largest lilac and butterfly bushes Mim had ever seen, which also added to the pleasant aroma. The other various flowers, vines, and herb gardens that lingered in the tiny cottage lawns also helped, and Mim could see what she assumed were other students working the soil and taking care of the beds.

They were grabbing buckets of fresh spring water from the tiny brooks that wove in between the gardens and the trees. They bubbled merrily along in their tiny channels until meeting the large rushing stream that ran the length of the valley floor.

The clear waters rushed towards the feet of the mountains from where the coach had just come and disappeared underground. A fine mist floated upward from the falls, creating many vibrant rainbows. The distraction of their beautiful surroundings had taken the girl's gaze away from the most prominent feature in the entire vale, which sat majestically at the head of the valley, and this was the great castle of the Graces.

It was larger than any structure Mim had ever seen and obviously very old, and while it gave off a sense of power and strength, it also radiated beauty in both form and design. The sheer walls of the castle were hewn out of the face of the mountain itself, with no bricks or mortar present. It had four towers that rose at its corners, and in the center of its seven-story main complex were two more that reached hundreds of feet into the air.

They were not like the large, battle-worn and turret-encased towers seen in books from the east, but graceful and elegant in the way they rose. On all of them were fluted balconies that looked out and down upon the valley.

All along the castle walls and towers were thick trellised vines that flowered in whites, greens, and purples; and with what Mim thought were roses also. The windows were small and set two feet back into their stone frames and the roofs were all set at steep angles. There were also hundreds of chimneys that dotted the rooflines, but all were smokeless at the moment. In all regards, the aesthetics of this place were beyond what Mim and Bette had ever dreamed. And if what Éolan said was true and much of its bulk lay within the mountain, its full size was massive beyond imagination.

The coach slowed and rounded a final bend before coming up in front of the giant gates that lead inside the castle. They were large and made out of something that Mim assumed to be metal but much shinier. All along them was the same strange vine script that covered her amulet and the entrances of the Inn in Slaidburn. This piqued her interest yet again, and she felt her amulet grow warm inside its hidden pocket. But she kept her composure as Éolan reminded the two of them about the importance of being on their best behavior.

A smaller door down and to the right of the main gate opened and five figures came out. Éolan said, "Oh dear" before turning back to them. "Well, it seems more of them than I expected have turned out to greet me. Just smile and curtsy. I'll do the rest."

The first was a gentleman with graying hair, dressed in green and brown robes. He wore spectacles and had a very content look upon his older face. The next two seemed to be sisters and had a similar look about them. They were tall, thin, and beautiful, and Mim thought they seemed to be somewhere in their forties if she had to place an age to them. They both had long raven black hair that came to their waists and framed their gentle smiles and bright eyes. Their demeanor was queenly, and they each wore a lovely flowing silk gown, with the taller sister in emerald green and the shorter in deep purple.

The last two both appeared to be in their seventies or perhaps eighties. The first was a wiry looking woman who was shorter in stature, had short black hair, and very thin. She was dressed in cream-colored shawls and a light blue pencil dress, and carried nothing with her but a wry smile. The last was taller than the other but not by much, and carried a bit more weight on her frame. She wore a finely woven rose-colored gown that went from the neck to down below the knee. She wore a pin also, which was of a golden rose, and it matched her golden earrings. She had a low bun of graying hair and had a curved cane in her right hand. Her face was kind, but the way the woman moved was with a purpose, and her demeanor commanded power and respect.

After a moment, Alrik opened the door and they stepped down, and out into the sun. All of the deans kept their smiles, except the fifth, who dropped hers to a skeptical smirk.

Éolan left the two standing there and approached the woman in the emerald green dress who immediately wrapped her arms around him and said nothing while embracing him, her large emerald ring glowing in the sun.

As she pulled away, Éolan smiled and said, "Hello, mother! It's so good to see you. And of course you as well, father." He gave the man a hug, which was returned with a great pat on the back.

This took the girls aback for a moment, and Mim realized how much Éolan looked like his parents. He then went down the line and hugged each of the other women, who seemed equally happy to see him, before walking back towards his mother. The kind woman then looked at the girls and back to Éolan. "Aren't you going to introduce us to your acquaintances, dear?"

Éolan let out a little laugh, and doubled back while apologizing a few times for forgetting his manners.

"This is Chessa, my first assistant and second to the premiere. Some of you may remember her from the palace."

Chessa bowed, and the deans returned it with a slight bend at the waist.

"This is Miss Lisbet Brooke of Iccobar, who until recently was in service to King Jehrym of the River Palace," he said.

As Bette moved back, Mim stepped forward. "This is Miss Mikky Hart of Slaidburn, a small village in the south of Endmoor," he said, gesturing towards Mim. She produced her best curtsy and then stepped back next to Bette. Each of the deans gave a polite nod.

"Mim and Bette, I would like to introduce my father, Lord Davian, Dean of Logic."

The man at the head of the column lowered his head with a smile and spoke. "It is a pleasure."

"Next is my mother, Lady Lisle, Dean of Medicine."

The tall woman in emerald glided forward and came up to each and gave them a hug, and Mim felt something strange when the woman embraced her. It was a warm tingly feeling, and she immediately loved this woman but she had no idea why.

The second woman in the deep purple dress was indeed the sister to the first, and her name was Lady Cody. She was the Dean of Grammar, and was quiet but very beautiful and gentle in the way she spoke.

The first of the elderly women was Lady Lee'shan. She was the Chair of the Hall, and the coordinator of all the deans, students, and curriculum at Charis. She smiled at both of the girls, but lingered on Mim's purple eyes a little longer than the rest had. Lastly came Lady Caralaine, whose title was Grand Marchioness of the Vale, and as Mim had already guessed, was in charge.

As Éolan ended the introductions, he stepped back by the girls and smiled as nonchalantly as he could, but one of the deans wasn't fooled. "Well Éolan, we didn't realize you'd be bringing guests. How long will they be with us?" Lady Lee'shan asked.

"That is a matter I thought we could discuss inside. My journey here has been interesting, to say the least. In fact, I feared the details would not be safe to put on paper. I come with news and council for the hall of deans, as well as a favor to ask."

Lady Lee'shan cast a friendly but suspicious look in his direction.

The other deans said nothing, but after a moment Lady Caralaine spoke for the first time. Her friendly tone was neutral and regal, but to the point. "If we are in need of privacy, let us adjourn to the proper setting," she said.

She strode forward and took Éolan's arm before heading back into the gate, and one by one the other deans turned and followed suit. Mim quickly turned and dodged around Alrik, running back to the coach and retrieving her large leather bag from the floor. She ripped Jessel off the top of the seat, taking some of the upholstery with her, and shoved her inside. "You stay put and be quiet, got it?" Another low growl was all she got for an answer.

As she caught back up she darted back in front of Alrik and fell in line with Bette as they followed Chessa into the grounds of the castle.

Gracemere

MIM PASSED THROUGH THE DOORWAY and into the main courtyard. The smooth walkways and sheer walls that surrounded her, along with the intricate flowerbeds and pruned greenery, were breathtaking. Not one single stone or evidence of masonry was visible from the smooth walls of the tall towers to the small and delicate flowers etched into the railings surrounding the garden beds. Each detail had been meticulously hand crafted with the utmost care, and she assumed this was also why the castle had stood for so long. Mim picked up some conversation from the group as they walked. It seemed Lady Caralaine was updating Éolan on recent events.

"...the castle is quite full at the moment. During the spring thaw there was a substantial landslide in the surrounding mountains that triggered a quake. We had some moderate structural cracks appear underneath the western part of the castle. We have a contingent of Dwarven masons from Khalamet staying there while they work on repairs. However, in the usual Dwarven fashion, they prefer not to be bothered so we have given them charge of the entire western wing. But they assure me that all of the necessary repairs will be completed by the time winter takes her seat and we close down the cottages..."

Mim was immediately anxious with excitement. She had never met anyone from another race, and she was determined she would see a Dwarf before they were finished. *They must be mighty grand if they helped with the construction of this place.*

As she looked past the buildings and beds, she began to see the inhabitants of the Charis popping up here and there. Finely dressed students and deans were strolling to and fro, and seemed to be in no hurry but not wasting time either. Mim thought it was nice to see people who moved with a purpose. In one green space she spotted a large group of students that seemed to be contorting themselves into strange positions while keeping their eyes closed. What was even stranger was that they seemed to be enjoying it, but then she remembered some of the strange classes Miss Barley, Talula, and Jennah had told her about.

Looking ahead, Mim noticed they were approaching the entrance to the main structure but just as they were nearing the open doors to the large hall, a voice came drifting across the courtyard. Mim's eyes immediately closed as she took in a deep breath. It was the most beautiful voice she had ever heard, and an image formed in her mind to accompany the sound. It was a nightingale sitting on a bed of lush green grass singing its song, coaxing open a rose on the first dawn of spring. In its melodic tone, the bird in her mind sang one name, and that was Éolan's.

As everyone turned, a young woman came sprinting across the courtyard. She had wavy dark brown hair flowing behind her. She was in a grey and lilac dress, and Éolan beamed as he saw her, and opened his arms as she jumped into his.

"Hello Christiane!" he said.

"I thought you wouldn't make it!" she said in her beautiful voice.

"The opening ceremonies are tonight. I hope you aren't too exhausted to attend?" she asked.

"Of course I will be there. I did not travel this far just to miss the main event. And I must thank you later, for it seems the universe had destined me to come on this trip."

As Lady Christiane looked at him with a bit of confusion, he turned and spoke. "I would like you to meet my two acquaintances, Miss Mikky Hart and Miss Lisbet Brooke of Endmoor."

The girls curtsied politely and still kept their silence.

"Girls, this is Lady Christiane and she is the Dean of Music and Performing Arts."

Lady Christiane bowed and welcomed them graciously before turning back to Éolan.

Just as she was about to excuse herself, Éolan cut in. "I know you are terribly busy with preparation, but would you have a few short minutes to meet with us? It is important."

She nodded. "I can spare a few minutes."

With their new addition, they made their way through the huge entry hall. It was a monstrous rectangular room with eight extremely large fireplaces anchoring the three interior walls. Huge tapestries hung here and there, some so big Mim thought they could have wrapped up the Inn back in Slaidburn like a solstice gift. The ceiling had hundreds of wooden beams, some of them so big that they were the size of whole trees. Inside of their crisscrossed network sat hundreds of lamps with that filled the room with plenty of light.

The floor space was set up like a commons room, with many different sitting areas, full of cushy seats and low tables on strangely decorated carpets. It wasn't particularly busy, but Mim could tell that hundreds of people could easily fit if need be, maybe more. On each side of the hall was a massive staircase that anchored the room. They were identical, and both curved gracefully upwards towards the ceiling and out of sight as they ascended into the towers. Lady Caralaine led them towards the one on the right and just as they approached the base of the stairs, a group of girls came around the bend.

They were dressed very nicely and Mim could tell they came from money. She wondered what the girls would wear to a fancy ball if this were the way they were dressed for a normal day at school. Each of their gowns was hand woven and hooped out at the waist, and as they ascended side by side the three of them nearly took up the entire stairwell. Lady Caralaine stopped to address the girls.

"Good afternoon, ladies," she said.

In unison, the three girls produced curtsied and said, "Good afternoon, Lady Caralaine." They made no eye contact with anyone but the sitter, and Mim admired their focus and etiquette.

She could definitely learn something from these three. The head dean then turned towards Mim and Bette for a brief introduction. "Girls, this is Sesame Lexar, Deidre Comfrey, and Moya Canon. They are among our most gifted students. Ladies, this is Mikky Hart and Lisbet Brooke. They are friends of Lord Éolan and are petitioning for residency. If passed, I assume you would be willing to acquaint them with our protocols," she said.

It was more of an order than a request, but the girls elegantly curtsied and assured Lady Caralaine they would be more than happy to oblige. Mim and Bette curtsied back, and as they rose a great clamor was heard from above, and the sound of rapidly approaching footsteps coming down the stairs. The eyes of the three girls widened as another with dirty blond hair tripped as she came hobbling around the bend behind them. She was having considerable trouble managing her bags and the crutch that was filling in for her injured leg. The other students that were traversing the stairs were diving out of her way as she hurled by them, and she was shouting apologies to all those that she could.

"'S'cuse me! Sorry Penn! Oh Evelyn your hair is lovely today! Whoa Bernadette!" she yelled.

As she nearly impaled a small girl around the age of twelve, she looked up and saw the large group of deans, including Lady Caralaine and Lee'shan, and tried to stop, but it was too late. With a sudden lurch and thud, down the girl went, with her books flying up over her head.

As she slowly began to roll down each of the large steps with a thud, thud, and thud, the three other girls stepped back and out of the way. But Mim and Bette dove and grabbed her, helping her slowly get up and get herself put back in order. "Thanks," she whispered before joining the other three girls.

"Please pardon my klutziness Lady Caralaine. I missed a step," she said. The other three girls were doing their best to keep composed, but Mim and Bette were smiling ear to ear.

"I would say you missed more than one, Miss Hornsby," Lady Lee'shan said with a smile. She turned towards Mim and Bette. "Ladies, this is Hazel Hornsby. She is one of the best equestrians here in the Vale, even when she disobeys orders and rides before dawn with a snapped shinbone," she said.

Hazel flushed as they quickly introduced themselves, and as Lady Caralaine led the group forward Hazel winked and smiled at them. Mim liked her already.

As their group rose up the stairs they came to a landing with many bench seats. Bette called it a dobo, and as each of the group paired off into sets of three, they sat down and the bench glided smoothly upwards in its track along the side of the stairs. They passed floor after floor until reaching what Mim assumed must be near the top. They entered a large wooden carved door and seemed to be in a very stately, yet cozy, anteroom. The girls were told to wait where they were and have a seat while the deans proceeded into the next room to decide their fate. Mim picked a comfortable and large red leather chair and footstool as her seat, while Bette slowly settled into her high backed blue leather choice.

They said nothing until the door opened again. Only Lady Caralaine, Lady Lee'shan, and Éolan exited the room while the others remained within. It was Lady Caralaine that spoke, and Éolan stood off to the side and was completely silent.

"Girls, as Lord Éolan has explained to you on your journey here, the Charis Vale has historically been open to all who have the willingness and ability to learn. However, it is also prestigious and admittance is not to be taken lightly. We, along with our predecessors, have spent hundreds of years molding our curriculum and charter into something to be proud of and cherished. Without the desire, dedication, and the responsibility that come along with that, you will surely not be suitable candidates."

Mim's heart sank to her toes as she looked at Éolan, but the dean had not finished. "While we usually do extensive interviews for new candidates, not to mention bypassing the fact that you two have no previous formal education beyond childhood level, we *have* taken into account your situation and the extraordinary measures you took to get here. That kind of risk and commitment for the chance to learn shows quality. So, with that being said, we have decided to grant you entry."

Mim and Bette grasped hands and squeezed, both doing their best not to jump out of joy, but Mim's smile spread from ear to ear and she made no attempt to hide it.

Lady Lee'shan cleared her throat. "Yes, girls, you may be relieved. However, there are some conditions that you must abide by."

"Of course, my Lady," said Mim and Bette in unison.

Lady Lee'shan let out a low and soft laugh before continuing. "Well, well! It seems we are not mute after all. And you will address me as Lady Lee'shan, not 'my Lady'. I am not your employer, nor do you serve me," she said.

Mim and Bette both curtsied and waited for her to continue.

"Both of your admittances here will be a bit different than

the other students, at least at first. With the help of the staff, we will do our best to catch you up in hopes to reach the proper level at which you should be for your ages. Our goal here is to prepare you for the lives you want to live, of which I believe everyone should be given the chance."

In the brief pause Bette interjected, "You are too kind, Lady Lee'shan."

Out of the corner of her eye, Mim saw Éolan smile from the corner and give them a wink, which let her know they were doing well. Lee'shan continued, apparently without noticing. Yet Mim thought this highly unlikely, since she was sure this woman noticed *everything*.

"And please remember that being given the chance to attend term at Charis is a privilege . So let us not regret our decision?"

"Yes, Lady Lee'shan, and we will do our utmost best to be worthy of your gracious admittance to The Charis. It has been my lifelong dream to study here, as it has been hers, and we will not idly throw that dream away. Thank you both." Mim said.

With a slight nod of her head, Lady Caralaine said, "Well put, dear. It seems even the deans should remember not to judge a book by its cover." She shot a brief glance at Lady Lee'shan before turning towards a beaming Éolan in the corner, who quickly regained his composure.

"Éolan, Lisle and Davian are discussing lodging in one of the cottages. I assume you will want to accompany them..." As she trailed off, Mim locked eyes with Lee'shan again. "Very well spoken, Miss Hart," she said. "You surprise me with your thoughtfulness. But then again, I think you are full of surprises, aren't you?"

Mim had no idea how to respond, so she remained polite but short. "I'm sorry, Lady Lee'shan, but I don't know what you mean." Lady Lee'shan smiled back and said no more.

Lady Caralaine turned back around. "We wish you the best of luck, my dears, and are excited to welcome you into the throng. I hope you find your stay here all that you have dreamed it would be. Lady Lisle will be out shortly to show you to your cottage and I will be in touch." With a nod she strode back into her office with Lee'shan in tow and closed the door, leaving Mim, Éolan, and Bette in the anteroom.

Éolan was all smiles and gave the girls a huge hug. "This is the best news we could have possibly asked for!"

Lady Lisle came gracefully flowing into the room and approached the three. "Your lodging assignment has been chosen and I've decided to lead you down myself," she said.

"Where have you decided to put them? I was hoping for room in the castle, but you seem to be full due to the repairs," he said.

She smiled as she spoke again. "I'm putting them in Gracemere, which I thought you'd be happy about."

Éolan then took on an appreciative tone that seemed to mingle with relief. "Please do not feel as if you have to do that. It is not your burden to have them," said Éolan.

She gracefully put her hand on Éolan's arm, and Mim swore that a halo formed around the two. It was very fine, almost unnoticeable, but clear enough to spot with the naked eye if you were paying attention. It was the same phenomenon that happened when he had touched the amulet back on the road, and when she looked to Bette for confirmation, her friend just stood there and didn't seem to notice.

"I am rarely there and I need help with its upkeep. We have been very busy of late and I'm only able to stay down there once a week, if that, and I think the girls will do great there. Not to mention Camilla will need some attention as well."

Éolan let out a short, boyish laugh. "I can't believe Camilla is still alive."

Lisle smiled before she turned towards Mim and continued on. "It is very comfortable and I'm sure the two of you will find it suitable. It also has a lovely stable in back for your horse. However, there is current resident who also lives there, but I assure you she won't be much of a bother."

Jessel crept out of Mim's bag on the floor. She arched her back into a large stretch and jumped onto the red leather armchair. Lisle arched her eyebrow as Mim grabbed the cat. "I see that you have a feline friend. This should be *quite* interesting," she said.

As Mim wrestled Jessel back into her large bag, she received a few scratches and a desperate howl. Jessel had been cooped up for too long and was losing her patience. "Lady Lisle, I assure you that she is very well trained and remains outside most of the time. You won't even notice she's there, I promise," Mim said.

Lisle smiled. "Oh my dear, I'm sure I won't. However, I'm not the one to be worried about." With a quick glance at Éolan, she led the way out of the doors and back down the spiral stairwell.

Once they reached the hall they made their way back out into the sun and the sweet valley air once again filled their noses. They headed right and followed a few paved walkways through the courtyard before exiting through a small and ornate stone gate. Mim let Jessel climb up on her shoulder and enjoy the walk as she and Bette took in the dazzling surroundings. They made their way down the small lane, which was aptly named Springfield due to all the tiny natural springs bubbling up here and there.

Along each side were many of the different looking cottages with their neatly tended beds and screened in front porches, and Bette pointed out that each had a small sign on the front designating its unique name. As they passed by a cute yellow one with a large porch and hundreds of yellow flowers along the front and sides, she noticed its name read *Daisy Dell*.

Most students on the road waved at them as they walked by, and Mim felt much more welcome by them than she had the girls on the tower stairs. As they continued along the lane, it began to switchback and made its way down towards the stream at the base of the valley. At the bottom, they cut off onto a small cobblestone lane named Jersey.

At the very end on the left was a small blue wooden cottage

with two huge maple trees out in front. A small wooden sign with fancy metal letters read the name: *Gracemere*. Lady Lisle opened the front door and led them onto the screened in porch, which held a swing and three ancient looking brown wicker rocking chairs. Before entering she bade them to take off their shoes.

Inside was wonderful, and Mim couldn't believe that this is where she and Bette would be staying. It was decorated with antique wooden furniture, and a large stone fireplace anchored the exterior wall to the left. To the right was a small hallway that had the washroom at its head, with two bedrooms that split off to the sides. Looking straight ahead and to the right was a spiral stair leading up to what looked like a loft, and atop them was something that Mim thought was a giant grey-blue pillow. That was until it blinked, stood up, and hobbled away on its three remaining legs.

"Oh, Camilla, come now, we have new guests and you better just get used to them. They're here to stay," said Lisle softly from the base of the stairs. Camilla made no return appearance and Mim didn't see her again for quite some time.

Lisle led them towards the back of the cottage and showed them the small dining area that led to the kitchen, and then out onto the back porch, which looked over the stream and stable. Mim could hear the water from here and loved it. A sudden melodic tone of chimes came drifting through the window.

With a sigh, Lisle paused and looked towards the girls. "If you'll excuse me, ladies, I had not realized the hour grew so late and am going to have to cut this short. The Caroline signals the hour is five o'clock and all the students will be returning to their residences for supper. However, today it is my cue to get to the main hall to help with preparations for the ceremony this evening. But Éolan will fill you in on most of the details you will need," she said.

She turned and left, letting the porch door close gently behind her. "And don't forget to feed Camilla!"

Éolan smiled and murmured, "Mothers..."

He passed the girls a drink and Bette snatched hers and chugged it down, immediately wanting a refill.

Mim was suspicious, however, and the drink smelled strange.

"It's called *oasic* Mim, and if it's too tart you can add some sugar."

As Mim took a sip the bitter and sweet liquid made her lips pucker a bit, but she found the drink refreshing enough. "I'm fine, thanks," she said, taking another sip.

Éolan explained a few things to them as they sat and sipped their drinks. Apparently, Camilla dwelt upstairs and hardly ever came down. This alleviated Mim's anxiety about Jessel, whom she told to remain downstairs at all times. Whether or not she would listen, Mim didn't know. But as Éolan continued on, a cart with two trunks pulled up, and on the seat sat Chessa, Alrik, and another very strong and tan skinned young man. Carmen was with them also, and looked vibrant. She had been fed, watered, and brushed, and as Alrik began leading her around back to the stables, Bette ran out and grabbed her reins. "I'll take her from here," she said.

As the boy began to heave the darker colored trunk towards Mim's room, she stopped him.

"Umm, sorry. You have the wrong place. I don't own a fancy trunk like that."

The boy looked down at his piece of parchment and back up at Mim. His dark skin and brown eyes were like Chessa's, and although he was a bit heavyset, he was handsome. "You are Mikky Hart are ya no'?"

"Yeah, that's me, but..."

"You're alright, Iwai, it's hers, take it on in," said Chessa as she came in from the porch.

Éolan walked up to Mim and smiled. "Consider it a welcoming gift to start you on your new journey."

Iwai came back out and heaved Bette's trunk into her room. Mim walked in and found a large silver skeleton key on her bed. Éolan lingered in the doorway for a moment, smiling.

Mim unlocked the trunk and pulled its lid open. It was full of pants, boots, leggings, nightgowns, undergarments, clothes for every season, toiletries, books, quills, ink, and on top of it all rested two pieces of shiny silver jewelry. One was a petite silver bracelet, the other a locket.

"I can't accept this, it's, it's..." She trailed off, speechless.

She felt Éolan's hand on her shoulder.

"Mim, you can accept it, and it makes me very happy to give it to you. You have lived with nothing your entire life, and somehow have made light out of it. You and Bette have both risen from the ashes of your past and are starting a new journey, and most of the people in this school haven't struggled as hard as you have to get here. So a roof over your head and a trunk of necessities to make your days and nights comfortable is nothing extravagant," he said.

The porch door slammed and Bette entered the cottage, whistling a merry tune. Éolan stood and walked out.

"Bette dear, I have a surprise for you in your room," she heard Éolan say as he led Bette inside. After some low murmuring and a few "Oh no's", Mim heard Bette start saying "Thank you" over and over again from across the hall.

Mim wrapped her hands around the softest and warmest cloak she had ever felt and looked out the window. Inside she became calm and closed her eyes, and for the first time in her life felt a little bit of peace.

Jessel jumped into the trunk and began to purr while making a nest on Mim's new belongings. Mim grabbed her cat and pulled her in close, letting the warmth of her body and rumbling of her purrs soothe her. The melody of the Caroline echoed in through the window, mingling with the sounds of laughter from passing students on the lane, the rushing of the stream, and the chirping of crickets from the wood. Mim whispered into Jessel's ear. "We made it, Jess. We finally made it."

XVIII

Remains

J UST OUTSIDE OF THE VALE, high atop a nameless peak that most birds wouldn't frequent, stood three black-hooded shapes. They looked foreign against the white crisp snow and vibrant rays of the sun as they watched the coach carrying Éolan, Mim, and Bette roll past the guardian's gate and into the Charis Vale. Morra Losis let out a low and guttural growl, and crushed the large rock she was holding in her right hand to dust. The figure next to her, a small and pitiful man, cowered backwards until collapsing by a low rock, shielding himself. After a long moment, he dared to speak.

"Mistress, what should we do now? We cannot enter the Vale to retrieve the girl." She remained motionless for a moment before turning her head towards the man, and only her head. It swiveled slowly, a full hundred eighty degrees until her black eyes landed on her servant.

"I cannot enter the Vale past this point, you are correct. But there is nothing saying that you cannot. And had you captured her in Iccobar as instructed, we wouldn't be standing here," she said.

The man cowered before speaking again. "But if I'm not mistaken, servants of Izman cannot pass the guardians. It is said the Graces put an enchantment around the vale before leaving. Is that not true?"

The woman's eyes narrowed. As the rest of her body turned to catch up to the position of her head, she moved slowly forward in her odd, disjointed manner. When she got to the man she reached down and plucked him from the ground. With his throat in her hand, she walked him over to the edge of the peak and stretched out her long arm, dangling him over the side.

"I am a servant to no one. And you will *never* speak of the Graces in my presence again," she snarled.

The man was flailing now, unable to breathe, but nothing could break her grip. And even if he had, the next ground he touched would be 10,000 feet below.

He wailed as she launched him back behind her and onto the flat promontory of rock on which they stood, not even bothering to look where he had landed.

"The *Graces*," she spat, barely being able to speak the name aloud, "did leave some of their filthy residue behind, yes, but that was nearly a thousand years ago. What remains are a group of old pig-teaching sows, and they will not stop me from my purple-eyed prize."

But it did puzzle her how the enchantment around the Vale

had lasted for so long. The Graces had been weak, wasting their efforts and power on teaching the five races how to better themselves. The thought of it almost made her smile. She walked forward, putting her pale hands up against the unseen barrier. It did not harm her, yet would not allow her to cross and stood stronger than iron. She walked to and fro, but the barrier held in every direction. Yet a stone cast from her hand passed through unhindered.

The human had crawled forward on all fours, petting at the hem of her cloak. She looked down at him. He was sobbing now, with his forehead pressed on the cold stone that had been cleared of snow by the flailing of his wretched body. But beneath the snow she saw something, and her eyes widened as she reached down and threw him backwards once more.

There, on the rock beneath the snow, was her answer. It was so small that no mortal could have seen it, but to her it was unmistakable. The ancient writing of the Esmë was etched upon the surface, no thicker than the threads of her robes, and running the full length of the precipice on which they stood. She followed it to the edge, where it continued to run down towards the surface.

She stood up, and for the first time in over a thousand years a small smile came to the corner of her mouth. *How juvenile of them*, she thought. The human behind her was still sobbing, but her need for him was now quite finished. She cared nothing for groveling humans. In fact, she cared for nothing at all.

She looked to her right, where the third figure stood. It was one of her children, and when her gaze fell upon it, a red eye began to glow beneath its cavernous hood, beating like a pulse.

"Make it quick," she said as she looked back down upon the vale. The creature floated silently towards the whimpering man and before the screams of terror left his throat, the sound of tearing flesh and breaking bones echoed amongst the ancient rock.

Within a few moments it was done, and as it slowly rose its black robes now glistened in the sun. It spun and moved silently forward with crimson drops falling from its cloak, splattering starkly upon the white snow and grey rock. When it reached its master, it stretched out its pale red-stained hand, and clutched within its seven fingers was the beating heart of the poor fool. It was now the only part left of him, save the pile of polished bones scattered upon the precipice.

Morra Losis took the heart and put it to her nose while taking in a deep breath, filling her gurgling lungs with its scent. "You preserved it well, my darling, catching it right before it left the body."

As the beat began to slow, she turned her head towards the sky and quickly devoured the heart whole. She licked the blood from her fingers.

"Ah. Nothing tastes as good as fear."

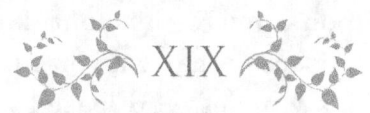

XIX

Éolan's Next Move

T HE NEXT MORNING BROUGHT HEAVY rain to the Vale, and it fit Éolan's mood. He was high atop the eastern tower in the same room where the girls had awaited their fates the day before, and was lost in the fire crackling low in front of him. He was brooding and he knew it, but so much had happened in the last week that he could hardly make heads or tails out of it.

He had written to Callan, but just like his husband he feared putting any details in writing. He missed him terribly, but Éolan had finally accepted that it was going to be much longer before he made it back to Alamarayn than he had first thought.

This had also prompted a letter to Naveen, who was his viceroy in Nausica and in charge during his absence. She was very capable, and Éolan trusted her to keep things in order during his absence.

He had called upon a few of his confidants from Charis to meet with him and discuss what was on his mind. He had no answers and all of his worries were based on speculation, but the bag weighed heavily on his mind.

Absentmindedly, he moved his hand down the soft fabric of his dark blue robes, finally stopping on the pouch where the coins were tucked away. *Perhaps I am just being overly paranoid*, he thought to himself. But as the rain picked up outside a harsh and cold wind blew in the cracked window. He drew his robes more tightly around him. He knew this was not the case.

The door opened and Caralaine gracefully walked in, followed closely by Lee'shan.

"Good morning," he said clearing his throat and making his best attempt to sound happy. He should have known better. There were very few individuals he couldn't fool, and these two women were among them.

"Good morning, dear," said Caralaine.

"Hardly," said Lee'shan. She crossed the room and tossed her soaked cloak onto a hanger before reaching over and forcefully shutting the window before moving towards the fire. She grabbed a number of logs and tossed them into the fire, and picked up the bellows from the stand on the side and began puffing air into the flames. "It seems you brought all of this lovely weather with you from the south, my dear."

Caralaine spoke up from the corner.

"Oh come now, Lee'shan. A rainy day is nice once a while," she said as she took the kettle off the burner and started preparing for tea. "I assume ginger peach is still your favorite?" she asked Éolan.

"Yes, thank you," he said absently, once again lost in the now roaring fire.

"You need to get whatever it is that bothers you off of your chest, dear," she said as she handed him his cup and saucer.

"That is why I have called you here. Strange things are moving in the unseen and I have no idea where to start making sense of them," he said.

Caralaine sat down across from him in the low red leather chair and lit her long white porcelain smoker. "Yes, I have felt it as well."

"As have I," said Lee'shan as she poured her tea and sat down. After a moment of silence only filled with the crackling of the now hearty fire, there came a knock on the door. The rest of those he had called upon had begun to arrive. Davian and Lisle arrived first, with the others coming quickly after. They were ten in total, and made up the master deans of the Charis Vale, and all now sat silently with their eyes on Éolan.

He did not speak right away, because he didn't know where to start, and sat wondering how to explain everything. After a moment he decided the best course was to get down to the more pressing issue first. He took the bag of coins from his pocket and set them on the low coffee table in the middle of the room.

"One of the young girls I brought with me had these in her possession when we met on the clipper from Iccobar. There is over five thousand of Laurasian currency inside."

Davian leaned towards the coins that were now in a red felt bag, not the black silk one that Mim had before. Éolan still kept that in his pocket.

As Davian opened the bag and dumped them out, he whispered, "I'll be..." before leaning back and stroking his chin.

The group said nothing and simply stared at the coins, all looking hesitant.

"Miss Hart had these, did she?" Lee'shan asked, not taking her gaze away from the coins. "It seems she is full of surprises. I knew it the second she stepped out of the coach and I looked into those eyes."

She took a sip of tea and slowly looked around the room. "And I'm sure no one here needs reminding of the last time we saw a woman with platinum blond hair and striking violet eyes." The other deans remained silent and motionless, because they all knew the exact time they had. And that memory was difficult for anyone to linger on too long.

Lisle then spoke gently from her seat. "You have many things on your mind, Éolan. But something else weighs on you that is much heavier than these coins. It is ok to show us, that is why we have come."

He produced the bag from his pocket and tossed it on the table. Although it was empty and weighed no more than an ounce, it thudded on the wooden surface as it landed. "This is the original purse the coins were carried in. I barely noticed it at first, but there is writing on the bag that I no longer have the skill to read. It is Esmë script in nature, but does not share its form," he said.

"What do you mean?" asked Lee'shan skeptically as she picked up the bag and began examining it. "It is very old. And yes you are correct; the writing is definitely from the Esmë language family. I'd recognize that anywhere. Strangely, it uses the same symbols but yet the patters are diff—" Lee'shan eyes widened as she stopped and slowly put the bag back on the table.

"Oh Éolan. You cannot be suggesting what I think you are? It is not possible," she said.

"It is possible," said Éolan. "But I need proof."

"Proof of what? What would be the significance of the writing?" Davian asked.

Caralaine stood and picked up the bag. She had it by its strings and held it at arm's length, treating it as if she handled a dangerous animal.

"No volumes of the ancient languages still exist that can positively identify the runes sewn on this bag, and only one person on the sphere still has the skill to read them." She turned and walked towards the fire. "And Éolan is hoping that he will not reveal what is suspected."

"Which is?" asked Lee'shan.

"That these symbols are Rura Voran," Caralaine said, tossing the bag onto the burning logs. Éolan couldn't believe what she had done and stood to run towards the fire, but stopped.

As it landed on the burning logs it should have caught like any other fabric would have, but instead the black bag sat on the embers and hissed as if laughing at the flames that danced around it.

Caralaine calmly grabbed the tongs and removed it, placing it back on the table. She said, "Something dark shields that bag. I felt it the day you and the girls arrived, but until now I could not pinpoint it."

The others were now staring at the tiny black coin purse as it sat unharmed on the table.

"Rura Voran?" Lisle asked. "That speech has not been seen or heard since Atlan met its doom. And now we see that the bag itself is shielded somehow. How can this be?"

Éolan shifted uneasily. "That is not all. Before fleeing Slaidburn, Mim was given these coins and bag by someone she describes as a demon woman. She said that it was surprised at her appearance because the creature couldn't *smell* her. And when I asked for its description, she said her eyes were black pools."

"Black?" asked another of the deans fearfully.

They all began murmuring, and Lee'shan then cut in, aggression and fear now in her voice. "Well it sounds to me that we need to get Miss Hart and Miss Brooke up here straight away and figure it out!"

Caralaine stood and put up her hand. "That is enough," she said calmly, yet still commanding the mood of the room back to a state of order, allowing Éolan to continue.

"I have already talked with both of them on board the clipper, and what they know, we know. Mim is just beginning to realize the seriousness of the situation she is in, just as we are. But she is young and has been considerably sheltered living down in the swamps, and while she definitely plays a larger part in this, until I know what questions to ask or what to look for, she has given me all I need for now."

"However," Éolan said, leaning forward and putting his elbows on his knees, "there are other forces at work that make the discovery of Mims eyes and this heirloom all the more strange. As we sit here and speak, King Jehrym is pulling all of his people in from the outlying districts and into Iccobar. He said the summit in Volaris was more volatile than he had ever seen, with the Chancellor being unable to keep order for the first time in centuries. The eastern nations are now like set like explosives, and someone or something is working masterfully from the shadows and holding the match."

"Bronwyn is fleeing the plains of Kaiair with her people, and seeking refuge in Alamarayn. A deep fog has settled over southern Endmoor and the black swamps are now moving steadily northward at an alarming rate, swallowing whole towns in a matter of months. The people speak of a terror that dwells in the mists, and whether it was from them or not, I felt real fear for the first time in many long years. And to ice the cake, we have the biggest mystery of all here in the Vale, which is Mim."

"I have been having dreams of her for longer than she has been walking on the sphere. She claims to have been abandoned in southern Endmoor as a babe and raised as an orphan, making it nearly impossible to trace her roots. She also carries an amulet with her that is very much Esmë in origin. It is older than any relic I have seen in recent years save those that are locked away beneath this very castle. In my company she wouldn't touch it with her bare skin, which makes me think that she possesses at least some knowledge of the craft and the power of the relic. And unless I am mistaken, the last time anyone on Aldaya saw a maiden with blond hair and purple eyes was during the Trial of the Heart. And that was over 1,000 years ago," he said.

No one in the room moved as they processed the news he had just delivered. But after a moment, Caralaine spoke. "You were right to come to us, and I believe you are correct in what your first move should be. The writing on the bag has to be deciphered. Once we know the answer to that riddle, I feel that the other pieces of the puzzle will become clearer. We will then be able to move forward with more confidence."

Lee'shan spoke, "And as for young Miss Hart, if she possesses skills with the craft and has an amulet that can intensify those abilities, we must address it sooner than later. If there is Tari blood in her as suspected, she could be very strong and a danger to herself and those around her if she loses control."

Caralaine said, "And we will have to approach that matter carefully. We have remained hidden for far too long and sacrificed too much to compromise our positions now. If agents of Izman feel it is safe to walk amongst us, our efforts and plans are working. I will think of a way to approach Mim about this, but we will not look before we leap."

She turned towards Éolan. "But leave that matter to us. Go and find the answers you need and return as quickly as possible. The vale is still well protected and we are far from the mists of Endmoor," she said.

Éolan took a deep breath and looked up. "I hope far enough. But even the Charis Vale cannot be fully removed from full-scale war, nor can the power of the Graces keep Izman's foul craft at bay forever," he said.

Davian spoke. "I know where this conversation is headed, and I do not believe we can afford to jump to any quick conclusions. We must look at the facts at hand and try not to interject our own fears and anxieties into them. From what we know, this 'demon woman' is more likely a rogue mage of some sort, or perhaps even an Elven sorceress that has turned to darker craft; and nothing more."

Éolan sighed. "I am not trying to jump to any conclusions, but the signs are becoming too obvious not to say it aloud. There is something foul working on Aldaya, and we are its guardians. It has been our task to keep a watchful eye, and now that things have begun to take a darker turn we must investigate to the fullest extent of our abilities."

He turned towards Caralaine.

"We need to send word to Proveglia and make sure the master seals on the subterranean prisons are still intact and strong. If there are agents of Izman daring to show themselves on the surface, their first goal will be to unleash their master and free the others. That cannot be allowed to happen," he said.

With a flash of lightning and rumble of thunder, the attention of everyone in the room once again turned towards the bag lying on the table.

"You could be right," said Lisle quietly. "I do not remember the last time I heard thunder in the Vale." Éolan stood up and walked to the window, staring through the sheets of rain towards Mim's cottage.

"The first of the riddles is to decipher the speech on that bag. As soon as the weather gives, I will make for Ashmantle. Liator is the only one that can tell me for certain what it reads, and hopefully he still holds me in high enough esteem to be of help."

The deans stood. "I am going to have Chessa remain here and keep watch on the girls, but I would appreciate extra eyes from you as well. I fear for their safety, and until we figure out the mystery of the bag they cannot be allowed outside of the Vale alone," he said.

"You leave the girls to us. They are strong and already making progress, and you have nothing to fear while we have our eye on them," said Caralaine.

The others nodded and left immediately. Lisle strode up and put her hand into Éolan's. "The path is dangerous, and there is no guarantee he will reveal the answers you need. Is there no other way?" she asked, turning towards Caralaine.

"I wish there were. With some digging in the vaults below the castle we would surely come across traces of the runes, but that could take months or longer. All volumes of that twisted speech sunk with Atlan. Our quickest chance is to go ahead with Éolan's plan," she said.

Éolan squeezed his mother's hand gently. "All will be well.

Luckily for me it is still summer and the trails should be clear. But could we meet at the cottage this evening for a bit to go over a few things?" he asked.

"Certainly. I will be down around seven," she said before exiting, followed closely by Davian and Lee'shan. The room now only held Éolan and Caralaine.

"Something lurks closer to us than the mists in the south or what festers in the central lands. It eludes me, but it is dangerous. It is strong, and growing stronger. The Vale is safe for now, but we must move quickly." She looked down at the bag and then into the flames. "I do not need to remind you of the cost of not moving fast enough."

Éolan shook his head. "Indeed you do not," he said before walking towards the door and exiting the room.

As he wound the corridors and stairs towards his rooms, he noticed no one and remained completely inside his head until he heard someone shouting his name from a distance. He turned to see Mim and Bette walking towards them, with the young Hornsby girl in tow.

"I was shouting your name so loud I thought the ceiling was going to cave in!" Mim said with a smile.

"Hazel is taking us around and giving us the grand tour. She's also filling us in on how it all works. Orientation helped, but there is still a lot to learn. You care you join?" Bette asked.

"I would, but I have some meetings to attend. But if you could both meet me at the cottage at five, I would appreciate it. There are some things I need to go over with you," he said.

"Of course, my Lord. We will see you then!" said Bette. She and Hazel began walking forward and chatting.

Mim, however, stared up at him quizzically. "Is everything alright?"

He could tell she was trying to sound lighthearted, but Éolan could hear the concern. "Everything is fine, Mim. I think I am just exhausted from the traveling. Meet me at five though, correct?"

Mim's purple eyes seemed to be probing him, but she didn't push the issue. "Yes, my Lord," she said, "five it is."

As she walked off to catch up with Bette and Hazel, Éolan kept his eyes on her for a moment. He knew deep down she was the key to the riddles and must be protected at any cost, but it was becoming more than that. He was beginning to care for Bette and Mim deeply, and felt responsible for them. As if sensing him, she turned for a moment at the end of the hall and the two locked eyes. He smiled and waved, as did she, but Éolan knew she was on to him. Mim knew him well, too well for an average girl who he had met just days before. But amidst all the uncertainty and questions, he was sure about one thing. Mim was not average in the slightest.

XX

Dream On

THREE WEEKS HAD PASSED SINCE the girls had settled into Gracemere and Éolan had departed. Before he left, he had informed the girls that he was traveling home to take care of some issues, but that he would be back as quickly as possible. Mim knew he was lying the second he spoke the words, and even as she and Bette had stood at the main gates with Chessa and watched him ride away with Alrik, she knew he was up to something. Bette didn't seem to have any suspicions about it, but she was too wrapped up in her studies and research to give it much thought.

Chessa had moved into the cottage, and at first it hadn't gone very smoothly. For the first week her reaction to the cats made her miserable. But after a few treatments and some herbal remedies from Lady Lisle things had gotten better. Chessa was a wealth of information and knew a lot about the world, and Mim had already learned quite a bit from her. Hazel had also joined their ranks and become her and Bette's closest friend. They were largely ignored by Sesame, Deidre, and Moya, and Mim liked it that way.

The process of integrating into their new environment had proved to be more daunting than either of them had expected. Bette was doing much better than Mim was, partly because she had started her classes when the other students had. Lady Lee'shan had made the two of them do pretesting so she could place them in the appropriate levels, and Bette's scores were pretty close to the norm. Mim's, however, had been terrible.

She scored so low that her first four weeks had been in remedial tutoring to get her up to standard levels. But she was a quick learner, and with the help of the deans she was making good progress. She had been focusing on the general studies like reading, writing, and rhetoric, and she was nearing proficiency.

But getting used to the coursework was only half of the battle. Every student was part of the vast workforce that kept the Charis running smoothly. Lee'shan had explained to them that each student got two credits per semester in service work, which was mandatory. This could be gardening, cooking, cleaning, or anything that they picked from the service list. Most students had signed up long before fall term started and had their pick of the best, but Mim got lucky and found a position in the bakeries.

She got along well with the kitchen staff and found them to be a bit more her speed than some of the other students and professors. It was her prior years in service work that made the shoe fit so well, and they got her humor, and she theirs. It also hadn't hurt that on her second day Mim demonstrated her cooking abilities with two of Miss Barley's recipes from the Last Stand. The sweet bread had gone over particularly well and was now being served with most of the meals, which made Mim feel happy and useful.

Bette had also got herself a nice job in the libraries. Mostly she cleaned and re-shelved old books, but had also begun spending most of her free time there as well. She spent hours poring over old dusty books, which Mim loved to help with. She didn't have the patience Bette had for the long hours, or the ability to read as quickly, but the information they had learned was worth it. However, it brought up almost as many questions as it answered.

After Éolan had told them of the Tari and their purple eyes, she and Bette had begun researching them first. The only one listed in the historical volumes was named Merope, who was the focal point during the terrible Trial of the Heart. Apparently she had been the most powerful of the spirits that dwelt in the outersphere, and during the period of the northern dawn on Atlan she would frequent the twin isles.

During this period was when Izman had dwelt in the north as well, and after a time he had become enamored with her and she with him. But Merope's desires also lingered on another, and upon hearing of her treachery, Izman captured her and cut out her heart. But the heart of a star is not like that of humans. It is radiant and filled with light and power, containing the core essence of that Tari's spirit.

By taking this, Merope had become a dark and wicked queen to Izman, and a puppet completely under his control. Maia and the other Esmë had petitioned the Varot to uphold the ancient canon of laws and imprison Izman then, but there was no proof of his crime. He denied ever having anything to do with the treachery, and so he had gone on unhindered. All of the Esmë knew the truth, even the Varot, but they had no choice. After the trial, Izman and Merope disappeared, and within a few short years the Great War had begun.

Other than this tale, they had found no more information on the Tari, nor anything giving more than a brief description of her appearance. And any hope Mim had of finding a link between her and they remained out of her reach for now. She and Bette had spent every waking free moment down in the cavernous libraries beneath the castle, but the amount of material would take a person their entire lifetime to cycle through. And although Bette had quickly mastered the cataloging systems, many of the books they needed and wanted were not placed back properly, causing even more problems.

Mim took a deep breath and looked out of the window. Today was Sunday, and she had convinced Bette that they needed some fresh air. Students had the run of the grounds today, and Mim intended on taking a break and enjoying herself a bit. She was at her favorite table in the commons area that was located far in the corner. It sat by a nice window that always let in the cool mountain breeze, and when she looked back towards the front of the hall she spotted Bette coming towards her. She was smiling and waving.

Just over a month ago, Mim hadn't known Bette, and now she couldn't imagine life without her. And secretly, seeing Bette happy made Mim feel fulfilled. She felt responsible for her in a way, and was the reason Bette was there. Although she hadn't brought all the poor kids from the south like she had planned, helping one was enough for now.

Bette flopped down into the chair across from her with an exasperated breath. "I'm starving. You want to get some lunch and go down to the cottage for a bit? Hazel said she'd stop by at some point and I feel like cooling off in the creek." Mim agreed and the two made their way to the large buffet that lined the far wall.

On Sunday's, the kitchen staff prepared and left the buffet out all day for students to munch on as they passed through. There were no formal meals inside the hall on weekends. As they filled their plates and headed outside, Sesame, Deirdre, and Moya came floating into the hall and as usual were dressed to attend a ball.

The three rarely said much to Mim and Bette, especially now that Hazel spent most of her time with the two of them. Today was no different, and they barely spared them a glance.

"Nice to see you too," Mim said.

As they passed they turned and glared but Mim just waved and walked out of the big doors and into the sunny courtyard.

Both her and Bette's appearance had changed a bit over the last month. They both had a full and healthy look to them now, with their hair, skin, and nails looking much better due to Mim's sack of goods that she had taken from the clipper.

They also looked pretty in the clothes that Éolan had got them, which accented their bodies well and actually did a good job at fooling people into believing they were semi-affluent. As they neared the cottage, Hazel was already on the porch swing with her monstrous dog tied to the maple outside. "Where have you two been? I've been sitting on my duff for almost a half hour waiting for ya!"

Mim threw Riken a treat from her plate. "It's good to see you, Hazel!" said Mim. The three walked inside and Bette veered off towards the wash room. As Mim neared the kitchen the hulking form of Camilla came thumping down the spiral stairs. She had been rousted from her loft by smells of the food that Mim had brought. The ancient three-legged cat had grown very fond of her, and treated Chessa warmly, but still remained a bit cold towards Bette.

Mim gave the old girl some pieces of cold chicken from her sandwich that were quickly devoured, just like the half piece of cheese and small chunk of bread that came after. Mim had never seen a cat eat table food like Camilla did. The week before she had seen her eat a child's portion of casserole that Chessa had made. "One of these days you're going to explode," Mim said as she scratched the cat behind the ears. Behind her, Jessel jumped onto the sill of the bay window from outside. She was covered in cockleburs from nose to tail, and had a mouse hanging from her mouth.

"And just where have you been? You're a mess! And give me that mouse. I told you that you don't need to hunt anymore."

Once life had settled down and things hadn't gotten so desperate, she had tried to train her cat to quit killing the small things needlessly. It half worked, and Mim now had to settle for live "presents." This had been fine until Jessel brought a small garden snake into Mim's bed, which landed her on the front porch for a night. Since that incident she had turned her focus onto field mice only. Mim pulled her cat onto the table and removed the rodent, which was unharmed, and tossed it out the window before she began removing the burs from her fur. Bette entered the room and noticed Camilla.

"Cammy!" she squealed, clapping her hands. "Come here, my little pumpkin!" Camilla knew she was too old and slow to make it up the stairs in time, so she just hunkered down and waited. As Bette bent down and heaved her over her shoulder, the cat growled and put her ears back. "I know, that mean old Jessel is scaring you again, but don't worry, I've got you." Bette walked to the stairs and put Camilla down, who immediately waddled up and out of sight as fast as she could. Bette turned towards Mim. "You know, Jessel really does make her nervy."

Mim rolled her eyes. "Oh yeah, I'm sure that must be it."

Bette huffed a bit before continuing. "Anyway, there's a lecture tonight on astronomy and they take you up to one of the really high mountain towers and let you look through the scopes! Hazel is going, we should too."

It actually sounded like a fun idea to Mim, and Astronomy was the class she was most excited about taking. "Sounds great. What time?" she asked.

"The flyer said to meet in the entry hall at 7:45, so we've got plenty of time to relax for the afternoon." Hazel said. She had long ago made herself welcome, and walked to the cold box and took out the pitcher of oasic and helped herself. "And we can't forget to bring cloaks; it gets cold up there."

The girls spent the rest of the afternoon lounging down by the creek in their bathing suits and taking in the sun. Autumn was creeping steadily closer and the girls knew their days outside by the creek were numbered. Hazel told them that during the winter months there would be snow, and by her demeanor it seemed she detested the stuff. Mim and Bette were excited. They had only heard of snow and never actually seen it.

As the afternoon wore on, Riken had chased Jessel up a tree twice, and after the second time she decided to remain on her branch until Hazel finally tied the dog up out front. Bette had tried to bring Camilla out for some fresh air, but received two gashes on her back as the frightened behemoth spotted the large bloodhound and launched off her shoulder and back inside.

As the sun disappeared behind the mountains, the girls realized they had about an hour and a half until they had to meet in the hall, which gave them enough time to bathe and eat a bit of supper. As Mim munched on leftovers from the fridge, Hazel brought something called The Far Darron Festival to their attention.

Every year the town threw a large festival to celebrate the beginning of autumn and to welcome the students back. Hazel said it was packed with gaming booths, song and dance, foreign foods and drinks, and loads of other entertainment. There were also people called pyromancers that attended, which Bette seemed floored by but Mim remained ignorant of.

At 7:45 on the dot the three girls strode into the hall and sat down at a table, and after a minute or two a wrinkly old man who looked to be nearing the century mark came around the corner followed by a group of younger students. He introduced himself as Professor Cary and passed out a brochure entitled Paint the Sky with Stars.

It gave a brief explanation of the night sky and what they would be seeing. She liked the pictures best and was particularly interested in the constellations and star groups, especially one called the Nontet Cluster.

"Ahem, if I could have your attention." The old man stood on a rickety old stool so he could see everyone in the group, but two of the younger students braced him in case he lost balance. "Thank you for attending tonight's lecture, and I'm excited to say that you are in for quite a treat. We couldn't have asked for better viewing weather tonight. We will be ascending the Vellorian stairs up to the summit where I have already set up the scopes. It is quite a trek, and the air is particularly thin up top, so we are going to take our time. If everyone is ready, let's head out!"

Mim thought the old man's enthusiasm was cute and hoped he was her professor when she reported for her first class on Tuesday evening. As the group marched forward the younger students were in front behind Professor Cary, followed by Mim, Bette, and Hazel bringing up the rear.

As they walked through the main dining hall they cut to the back left corner and went through a door that Mim had never taken before. It led out into a small section of courtyard that sat between the castle walls and those of the mountains. The small path led towards a smaller stone archway and into the mountain itself. The hallway had electric lights on the ceiling, which led the group directly to a flat stone wall that had six small doors on it. Here, the old professor stopped and explained how they were going to proceed.

"These are the dobos that take us most of the way up. They are a bit tight, so we will be going five at a time." He stopped and looked back behind where Mim was standing. "Lady Lee'shan, Lord Davian, what a pleasure! Will you be joining us on our trip up to the summit?"

Everyone turned around and bowed or curtsied as the two walked up.

"Yes, we thought we would join you if it's not a bother. As you know, astronomy is one of my favorite pastimes." Lord Davian said with a smile.

Lee'shan didn't offer an excuse as to her presence and simply smiled at everyone and remained quiet. She could have just been paranoid, but Mim swore the woman had been following her.

"Oh there is plenty of room, plenty of room!" Professor Cary said. "Let's get these lifts going so we can see some stars, shall we?" the small man said.

He went over and pulled a large metal lever on the wall. A whirring could be heard from behind the tiny doors, and suddenly they slid open, revealing a small room inside. As they stepped in the small square room and the doors closed, Mim immediately began to feel claustrophobic and wanted out. But they had started to climb and so all she could do was wait. As the lift rumbled upward it gave a shake here and there, and Mim swore a few times they were going to plummet to their deaths.

When they stepped out, Mim thanked Hazel for her previous advice. It wasn't just chilly up here; it was downright cold. As they pulled their cloaks over their shoulders, they made their way towards the stairs. Being so high in the mountains was very new to Mim and Bette, and by the time they got to the top they had to sit down and catch their breath along with some of the younger students.

The large observatory tower was empty save for the observing lenses, and Mim was in awe at how close the stars seemed. She felt as if she reached up on her tippy toes she could have plucked one from the sky. The moon had not yet risen, so its light didn't mask the stars, and they twinkled brightly and created a wonderful light around all of the students.

She listened intently as the professor explained the different lenses and how to use them, and then he set them loose to try them all out. Mim, Bette, and Hazel made their rounds, checking their books and trying to figure out what was what, and Mim realized she had never been this interested in a subject in her entire life. As the night wore on, Professor Cary took the younger students down to get them settled, leaving them with Lee'shan and Davian.

Mim had finally gotten a telescope to herself and was focusing in on the cluster. Her book described them as the nine sisters, and this immediately brought Mim back to her dreams of the woman. The song she sang was about a group of sisters as well, watching the world from above. They had to be the same ones, and she became flooded with excitement! Her dream must have been a memory, because she was certain she had never heard of these stars before tonight, *except* in the dream. She was almost giddy as Lady Lee'shan walked up beside her.

"You seem to be enjoying yourself tonight, Miss Hart," she said.

Mim said, "Hello, Lady Lee'shan. And yes, the stars have always fascinated me. Especially this grouping here."

Mim pointed to her book and began blabbering off facts and names before Lee'shan cut her off. "I'm very glad you find it so interesting. However, I am afraid it is time for us to head down," she said.

So, with great reluctance, Mim rode down the claustrophobic lift. Once they reached the ground, the three girls bid the deans good night and headed towards the gate that led out onto Springfield and towards their cottages. Lee'shan stopped at the threshold and bid the girls a safe walk home with a smile, but when Mim turned back around she noticed the woman was still there, waiting until they were completely out of sight.

Hazel cut off from them as they passed a little street named Bluff, and just as Mim and Bette were about to hit Jersey, her friend gasped. "Oh no! I forgot my notepad in Hazel's bag and I need it for tomorrow. I'll meet you at the cottage." She turned around and took off, running up the street and out of sight.

Mim slowed as she hit Jersey and walked with her eyes and her mind up in the night sky, having a rare moment to herself. The more she thought on the stars, for the first time ever Mim felt beautiful inside. Had she been looking into a mirror she would have seen her eyes glowing in the starlight with no help from the amulet.

As she took in a deep breath of the warm nighttime air and started walking, she heard a twig snap somewhere off to her right. It had come from a dark cluster of trees that sat between two outcroppings of the mountain. It was darker down here than in the upper glades, and with fewer street lamps the only light she had was from the stars and rising moons.

As she looked into the shadow of the trees, the warm breeze slowly grew colder and stopped. The drone of the bugs ceased, the fireflies quit glowing, and suddenly Mim felt afraid. Something was moving amongst the trees, but whatever it was eluded her. She tried to focus her eyes on it, but it seemed darker than the nighttime shadows that surrounded it. A single red orb began to glow from within the shadows, and it pulsed with the beating of her heart. A humming entered her mind and began to dull her senses, and everything began to slow down.

She reached into her pocket and retrieved the amulet, putting it around her neck. The second it touched her skin, her eyes shone fiercely out into the night. The humming stopped, and her senses were heightened. She was even more aware of her danger now, and as she looked towards the trees her eyes could now see a dark figure within. She took a few steps forward and the violet light from her eyes pierced into the orb. A terrible noise rang out, and the shadows beneath the tree lunged outwards, knocking her onto her back before disappearing.

Suddenly Bette was above her.

"Mim it's me! Calm down!"

Once their eyes locked, Bette became silent and a look of calm came over her face. She said nothing and just stared straight into the purple light. Mim took off the amulet and shoved it into her bag, and Bette came around.

"Are you alright?" Mim asked.

Bette seemed confused, but nodded as her memory returned. "Yes, I'm fine. But, what just happened? Why were your eyes glowing like that?" she asked.

But Mim was still scared and ignored her friend for the moment. She looked back into the cluster of trees, but all seemed normal. The fireflies were back to their rhythm and all of the nighttime sounds had returned as well. "Come on Bette, we need to get to the cottage. I'll explain there."

They continued on down the lane and Mim looked back a few times towards the trees but saw nothing. Bette was silent, but when Mim sat her down on the rocking chair near the hearth, she could see the color had drained from her face. Mim didn't know how to start, so she decided to go with the beginning. She calmly told Bette about her outburst on the bridge, and how

Jennah had given her the strange amulet and what happened when she put it on.

Bette said nothing, but stood up and went around pulling the drapes closed and locking the door before sitting back down. "Put it on again," she said.

Mim was reluctant, but after another prodding she took the amulet out of her bag and placed it over her neck. She could feel her eyes glowing and her senses become heightened again. But now that she was calm and her mind was quiet, the experience was different and much stronger than the other times. Strangely, serenity and clarity seemed to amplify its affects even more.

As she looked down at her hands, they seemed to have the same light halo around them that she had seen on Éolan. She closed her eyes and could hear every insect outside and every creak from the trees in the woods. She could feel the age of the mountains around the Vale, and a great force that surrounded the perimeter. When she opened her eyes and focused on Bette, she could hear every beat of her friend's heart and sense her presence beyond that of her physical being.

But as more power flooded into her from the amulet, the noises from outside grew louder, and the beating of Bette's heart was thumping in her head. She sensed something dark somewhere in the mountains, and the fear started multiplying inside of her chest. She screamed as it began to overwhelm her, but suddenly it stopped.

Across from her, Bette sat with the amulet in her hand and the broken chain still dangling from it. Mim was drenched in sweat. "Bette," she said breathlessly. "You cannot tell anyone about this. Promise me," she pleaded.

Bette shook her head up and down quickly and put her shaky hand into Mim's. "I won't. I promise. But have you told anyone else about this? Does Éolan know?" she asked.

"He knows I have it. He took it from me for a moment when we first met near his coach. I could tell he recognized it somehow, but he didn't say anything. But when he held it in his hand, a halo went around him too. It wasn't nearly as bright as when I have it on, but I could definitely see it. I also saw one when he and Lisle hugged the first time we arrived." Mim said.

Bette's eyes narrowed for a moment, and she shook her head slowly up and down. "That is *very* interesting. I've suspected that there was more to Lord Éolan than meets the eye for quite some time now, as well as the Master Deans of the Hall. There is something about them that is just not quite...normal. I can't put my finger on it yet. But it's in their eyes, the way they walk, and the way they talk. I can't explain it, but surely you have noticed it too. And now that you told me about the halo around him when he held the amulet, it all makes much more sense. There is not halo around me when I hold the amulet, is there?"

Mim noticed excitement in her voice when she asked the question, but there was definitely nothing.

"No Bette, at least I can't see one if there is."

"Well, then at least we answered one major question. You have the ability to use the craft, as does Éolan. But Mim, you have to tell him when he gets back. No questions asked. If I wouldn't have been here to rip it off of you, I don't know what would have happened. I've heard terrible stories of people losing their minds or literally burning away when they lose control over it. And why did you have it on when I found you on the road? If anyone had been watching your secret would be out." Bette asked.

"There was something dark moving in the woods near the glen. It felt like the demon from the Last Stand, so I panicked and put it on. But it has never done that before. I had it on for hours when I was traveling through the marshes," Mim said.

"Well I think you should hide it away and not use it until we figure out more about it. Or at least until Éolan returns," Bette said.

But Mim didn't agree. Whatever was chasing her was dangerous, and the only thing that had saved her life just moments before had been the amulet. She knew she couldn't wear it everywhere, but that didn't mean she couldn't keep it on her in case she needed it.

"I'm going to keep it near me, but I promise I won't wear it again until Éolan comes back," she said.

Bette nodded in agreement, but even though she had said the words, all Mim wanted to do was put it back on. She was frightened of how it felt when the power had begun to overwhelm her, but the clarity and rush it had given her beforehand made her feel completed inside unlike anything in life ever had.

A knock at the door made her jump, but she could hear Chessa outside hollering about being locked out. Bette ran to the door and let her in, while Mim rushed into her room.

"Oh-ho! I have been lookin' for you and Mim around da grounds for over two hours. And just where have you two been off sneakin' about?" she asked. Mim was still in her room and composing herself while Bette ran interference.

"We were up on one of the Star Towers looking through some of the scopes with the deans and some of the other students. It was a lecture night," Bette said. She was trying to sound nonchalant, but Mim could tell that Chessa wasn't buying it.

"And where is young Mim?" asked Chessa.

"She's in her room resting. She got a bit of altitude sickness up on the tower and I was just going to make her some tea," Bette said.

Mim quickly changed into her nightgown and curled up under her covers just as Chessa came in through the door. She glanced suspiciously down at her, and Mim managed a weak smile.

"Hi, Chessa," she said.

"Mm-hmm," she said.

She walked over and placed her hand on Mim's forehead.

"Well, you two are in for da night that is for certain! And da next time you go climbing around da peaks of mountains, you tell me first. Is that fresh-water clear?" she asked.

Mim actually managed a true grin as Chessa finished. She loved the way she talked.

"Of course!" said Bette. She cheerily brushed by and came in with everything for tea and pulled the desk chair up to the edge of the bed. "Would you like some, Chessa? I put enough in the kettle for you as well. It won't be long."

Chessa shook her head. "Oh no. After doing laps around this valley I am in the mood for something stronger. But make sure to put some *tansy* leaves in with her water. It'll help the nausea." she said.

As Mim put her head back on the pillow, she could hear Chessa rooting through the glass bottles of vexor in the kitchen. It was the last thing she remembered before falling asleep, and nothing disturbed her dreams until dawn approached.

She was enjoying a lovely picnic with Alrik on an island somewhere. She had never been there, but it seemed familiar in her dream, and lovely birds the likes of which she had never seen were flying above her in the afternoon sun. As the two sat and ate fresh fruit, bread, and cheese from their basket, they laughed and joked about school and their friends. Then Alrik leaned over and kissed her stomach, but when he looked up it was no longer the same person. It was a tall, handsome young man with light brown hair and piercing blue eyes. Around him was a halo of white light, and although she didn't know him, Mim felt safe.

"Let's name him Ojen, after the Lord of the Seas," the boy said, grinning from ear to ear.

As Mim put her hands down on her enlarged stomach, she felt a kick. "That sounds wonderful," she said, smiling back at him. She was truly at peace for a moment, but then everything changed.

The sun became veiled with dark thunderclouds. As she looked over at her handsome companion for comfort, his blue eyes were now pools of black, and his face was expressionless. Then she was running through the center of the island as fast as she could. Her stomach was so large that she couldn't move quickly, and the shooting pains emanating from it were so bad that she nearly collapsed as each one came on. The black-eyed man was chasing her, and she struggled through the trees and vines. Just as his hand clasped onto her shoulder, she screamed and stumbled out onto a beach.

Ahead of her and to the right stood Éolan and with him was a shorter man of blond hair. They were standing on a wooden dock that jutted out into a lake. She yelled for Éolan and groggily stumbled towards him. The pain in her abdomen was nearing unbearable as she finally reached him and fell to the boards. But suddenly the pain was gone, and Mim looked down to see her stomach was as flat as it had always been.

She looked up at Éolan, but he said nothing and stared down at the canoe that was tied to the side of the dock. Inside was something wrapped in a dark, tattered, and bloody cloth. It was shaped like the body of a small child, but its head was far too large and its limbs too long. As Mim bent down and cautiously began to unwrap it, the back of the head became visible and revealed raven black hair. Whatever it was, it was facing downwards into the puddle of cold dark water that stretched across the bottom of the leaky boat.

As Mim slowly removed the final layer, the oversized head turned with bone crunching snaps until it faced upright, and Mim realized it was the face of the demon woman. Her icy hand reached out and clasped around Mim's throat.

"Caught ya!" she squelched.

Mim jerked up in bed with a gasp, barely being able to breathe, and a few hundred miles to the west, Éolan did as well.

XXI

The Watcher

HIS EYES JERKED OPEN AND he sat up onto his elbow. The wind was howling around him and, although the sun was barely gracing the horizon, the air around him was already muggy and holding the heat of the approaching day. The small patch of grass he and Alrik had found between two stone outcroppings had given them some shelter for the night, but it did nothing for the knots in his back. Whether they were from stress or sleeping on the ground for the last three weeks he didn't know, but he guessed a mixture of both.

As he fully sat up and rubbed his eyes, the trivial complaints of his sleeping arrangements were not in the forefront of his mind. He had already drifted back to the nightmare that had just awoken him, and although he had no desire to dwell on it, he felt that any dreams involving Mim were important enough to try and remember.

He had been on an island, and briefly the sun had been shining. His feet were dangling off the edge of a wooden dock, with his toes barely touching the surface of the water. Callan was with him, and they were both lying on their backs as they gazed up at a flock of strange sea birds that flew overhead. They were beautiful, with large blue and white wings that spread ten feet out in each direction. They made no noise as they gracefully rode the thermals through the air, and for a brief moment, he was truly at peace.

"Do you think we will end up like them someday, my love?" Callan asked as he slipped his hand into Éolan's.

For a moment Éolan did not understand his husband's question and sat in silence. But as he watched them more intently, he realized that the beautiful birds had left the world long ago.

But before he had a chance to answer, Callan spoke again. "My heart tells me so, as does yours, but as long as you are with me I can think of nothing that could bring me to despair."

He kissed Éolan's hand and smiled at him gently before looking back up at the sky, but suddenly fear flooded into his eyes. The light of the sun quickly vanished behind the large black storm clouds that now came barreling down over the mountains. As they surrounded the lake, he pulled his love in close to him and closed his eyes, and they braced for the worst.

Then a scream echoed out from the island forest that sat behind them. As the two stood, Éolan turned and started towards the forest before Callan grabbed him.

"Don't!" he cried. "She is already dangerous. You know she will never stop hunting her. Let us go, far away. Please come with me!" he pleaded.

Éolan wanted so badly to go with his husband, but another

scream drew his attention back to the dark trees, and shortly after he saw Mim stumble onto the beach clutching her enlarged stomach. Suddenly, he felt his husband's hand leave his and turned to see him dive into the lake and disappear. He wanted to jump in after him and find protection under the water, but the shrieking female voice began echoing inside his head again to help her.

Once Mim got to him, she bent down and had begun unwrapping the cloth from around a strange bundle in the canoe, revealing the body of a pale and grotesque creature. The digits on the hands and feet were twice their normal length and looked more like a spider's legs than fingers and toes. It looked pale and lifeless, but as she removed the last strip of cloth, the face of an ancient terror had stared back at them. It reached out its spidery fingers and wrapped them around Mim's throat, and as it started to pull her down towards its mouth, she screamed and he woke.

Even though the breeze held no chill, a shiver ran down his spine as he dwelt on the image of the face. As he took a drink of warm water from his canteen, he looked north towards the rising sun. Within a few short hours he would arrive at his destination, and with all luck would have the answers that he so desperately needed.

He stood up and moved towards Alrik. He had been on watch duty near the beginning of the outcropping, but was asleep sitting up. He prodded the young man and with a grunt he came to.

"I am sorry, my Lord. I should never have fallen asleep on guard."

Éolan could tell he was furious at himself, but gave the young man some leeway. "No. You shouldn't have. But we are exhausted Alrik. I most likely would have done the same." Éolan said.

He slowly stretched his body, twisting his back to and fro until he had achieved a few good cracks. Alrik was over at the packhorse and getting some food from the packs. He brought back the last bits of dried fruit, nuts, and bread and handed them to Éolan. "This is all that is left, my Lord," he said.

Éolan took some of the fruit and a hunk of bread and left the rest. "You need strength as much as I. Eat up," he said.

As he took a bite of a shriveled peach slice, he wondered how much longer they would have been able to last. But he knew the distances of travel well and had brought them just enough for the journey. On Aldaya he was barely unmatched in the knowledge of the many networks of roads and trails, and his memories held the secret ways to destinations that had long been forgotten in the modern age. And it was to one of these old and lost places that Éolan and Alrik were finally nearing. They had been off of the main path now for days and he was riding completely off of his memory. It had been many years since he had crossed this rough terrain, and moving as stealthily as possible was key. They were north of the Vellorian Shield now, which put them into the lands of Taris Muur.

It was a dark and mysterious place that very few from the south dared to enter. They were commonly called the Wild Lands because many strange and magical creatures fleeing from the ruin of Atlan had settled here after the sinking. In the aftermath of the Great War they had carved out a labyrinth of fractured territories, and the remnants of them that still survived adhered to no rules but their own. The southerners called them "the Forgotten," and thought of them as long bereft of loyalty and great deeds, hiding in the lost places and tending to their dwindling numbers in fear.

Éolan smiled at their ignorance, for he knew better. There was an ancient strength in the north that was much greater than anyone guessed, and if they ever united under one banner the south would have been hard pressed to repel them. However, there were no alliances here, nor trade agreements, and no uniform standard of law or government. They each looked out solely for themselves, which was the main reason Éolan moved as quietly as possible. It was simple; those that dwelt north of the shield didn't want to be found, nor did they appreciate intruders.

But for sixteen days they had skirted along the humid foothills of the Somerset Range, keeping the rainforests at a distance to the right, and all had gone well so far. At first it had been the great jungle cats that had stalked them, but as he approached Vöth they had respected their neighbors and finally backed off. But once they had entered their realm, the treetop warriors had watched them every moment of the day and night, and had yet to give any trouble. But as he and Alrik moved deeper and deeper into their territory and closer to their homeland, he wasn't sure of how long this uneasy truce would last. Luckily for both parties, his incursion wouldn't be for much longer.

As the rays of the rising sun finally cleared the horizon and hit his back, sweat began beading up on his forehead. But this didn't stop him and Alrik from keeping their dark green cloaks up over their heads and moving forward at the usual pace. Éolan dared not move too fast, for the path was too narrow and difficult for their horses to maneuver, but moving too slowly would also raise suspicion, so he did his best to remain as steady as possible.

A few hours passed and the sun was nearing its zenith when they finally stopped at their destination. He knew he had arrived after rounding a bend and coming face to face with a boulder that was very unlike its neighbors. It was monstrous, and within its grey stone wound ribbons of black obsidian. Large veins of it ran throughout the entire range, and long ago Dwarves had mined it and sold it far and wide across the Great Isles.

It was strong and beautiful, but also revered by many as an effective and powerful means of protection against negative forces and the dark craft. The old stories even told of a powerful sorceress that had built her castle from the stone, and that where it graced the western shores of Atlan was the last place to fall to the shadow. Éolan knew the story true, and had always thought this was the main reason his old acquaintance had taken up residence here in his subterranean realm. Other than its very private location so far abroad, the added protection had probably helped guide his decision.

As he led his horse around the back of the boulder and to his left, he searched for a few minutes until he found a large crack in the sheer wall of the mountain. It was just wide enough for him and his steed to enter, and just as he was about to remove his cloak, a female voice rang out from somewhere up above him.

"What business do two southlanders have with he who dwells inside the mountain?"

Éolan and Alrik froze, just like they had discussed if something like this were to happen, and he briefly looked up from deep within his hood. He took in the small but dangerous looking woman that looked down at him from her ledge. She was feigning a relaxed state, but Éolan could tell she was poised to pounce on him at a moment's notice. She had dark skin and piercing eyes, one emerald green and one like silver silk. In her hand she held a long wooden spear with a smooth and deadly looking obsidian blade strapped to the tip. Her long brown braid drooped over her right shoulder and down to her waist, and on the dark green cloth that surrounded her chest she wore a carved wooden pin that depicted a strange jungle bird. By her look she was a Vöthan, but her silver eye alerted Éolan to the possibility of something else.

"What is your name, young warrior of Clan Esso?" Éolan asked politely. He remained calm, but also kept his face concealed under his hood.

The woman nimbly jumped down from her ledge and now had her blade pointed directly at Éolan. "I am Signa of Clan Esso," she said proudly, "and how you know of its name is treason. Drop to your knees Lord of the South. You are now my prisoner."

Éolan smiled to himself beneath his cloak, because now he understood. "Warrior Signa, I know your clan name by the pin you wear on your breast. It is the Esso, deadliest of the avian hunters that dwell within rain forests. You, like it, are a canopy warrior, and I know this because I am no stranger to the north. Although it has been quite a long while since my travels led me to this part of the world," he said. But the woman was not in the mood for banter.

"On your knees! Or I will run this spear through your gut and send your head back to the Sea Palace on a spike."

Beneath Éolan's hood, his face had grown serious. He had listened to enough and was through with games. He spun and quickly threw back his hood, brandishing his sword, and Alrik did the same. As the afternoon sunlight struck Éolan's eyes, they shone brilliantly like lit sapphires. He stood tall and his voice echoed off the rocks that surrounded him.

"The business I have within the mountain is my own and no other's. I will pass unhindered, unless you wish to tell more lies before you are disarmed?" he asked.

The woman lunged forward, wielding her spear with deadly precision. But her style was much different than the warrior women of the jungles, and older. Against what Éolan had taught him, Alrik lunged forward clumsily and the woman made quick work of him. In one swift move and some quick work of the hands, Alrik went down in a heap and she advanced quickly. But Éolan was too fast for her.

He backed away while calmly and decisively thwarting her advances with ease. She spun tirelessly, jumping from rock wall to rock wall, lashing down with her black blade. But Éolan had found his center and moved with grace and precision. It had been years since he had fought an opponent this skilled, but he was still superior. After exchanging for a few moments, he found his gap, and with three fluid movements he took her spear and rested its deadly black blade directly on the pulsating vein in her neck.

She smiled and nodded her head. Although most people would have been perplexed, Éolan wasn't surprised in the least. She backed away slowly and began to spin in place and the black veins in the rock began to glow all around them. As her speed increased, orbs of purple and silver light began shooting from her like sparks. But after a brief moment the spectacular show ended, and where the Vöthan warrior once stood was someone quite different.

She was the same height as the previous woman, but different in all other aspects. Her raven black hair framed her pale face and was stark against her silver eyes and white skin. It fell in many long layers down to her waist, and was barely discernable from the midnight purple dress that barely reached her knees. Her only jewelry was a thin silver chain around her neck, and on it hung a large obsidian crescent moon pendant that was still glowing slightly. She looked odd against the bright sunlight and lush greenery of the foothills.

"Hello Ardra," he said.

"Hello, Éolan," she said. "It has been quite a time since you last visited us. So long, in fact, that I had nearly forgotten what you looked like. I am glad you are here, because the world is growing darker. But unlike the others I almost welcome it, and am growing tired of this charade," she said.

Éolan gave her a serious look of warning, but she didn't make any effort to change her demeanor. "Do not worry. Your guard is out cold, and will be until I wake him," she said.

"Yes, I am aware of your defensive styles, but you should also be aware of the risks of exposing yourself. However, I am not here to lecture and I have no more time for games. Will you be seeing me in, or will I be going alone?" Éolan asked.

The woman looked up at the sky for a moment as a few gray clouds veiled the sun. "You don't have much time. A storm is brewing, but I gather that is why you have come."

Éolan nodded his head, and she walked over to Alrik. She moved her fingers along the base of his neck, finding a few pressure points, and he opened his eyes in confusion.

"On your feet, Alrik," said Éolan, helping him up.

Alrik looked around and laid eyes on the new woman that stood before him. "But, my lord, where—?"

Éolan cut him off. "We don't have time for that now. This is Ardra and she is a sentinel for Liator who dwells within. Hurry, gather your things," he said.

As Éolan and Ardra walked on, she spoke so only they could hear. "I promise, no more games. But do tell me one thing. What gave me away?" she asked.

"Three things. Firstly, I never told you I was a lord from the south, or that I resided in the Sea Palace. Second, your unique fighting style is certainly not that of a Vöthan. And thirdly, you forgot one of your eyes when you shifted. Only one turned green," he said.

"You were always too smart for your own good, which is probably why I never particularly liked you," she said.

They walked in silence, and slowly the green vegetation became less as the crack narrowed and deepened. As they rounded a sharp bend, the path ended abruptly at a jagged and haphazard doorway. It was more circular than square, and by its shape looked as if one of the giants had punched one of their fists through glass. The razor sharp edges had not dulled over the passage of time, and were far too low and deadly for him to bring his horse inside. Alrik stood a few paces away.

"Your guard and I will wait for you here," said Ardra.

"Why will you not enter?" he asked.

The woman walked him back away from the entrance before she continued in a hushed voice. "It has been a very long time since any have come to see him, and he believes that he has been forsaken for using his powers. If this is true, then your reasoning is flawed. He watches because it is his duty, and all the while he knows it is harming him. In our Taar forms, practicing without the gifts for too long is almost suicide."

Éolan could sense her sadness, but anger burned underneath as well. When she turned back her poised demeanor had been traded in for frustration, and her voice grew harsh. "You know the price that we all pay if we open ourselves without a proper conduit. But since the gifts were taken, what choice does he have?"

Éolan suddenly put up his hand and she immediately stopped. As a crow cawed eerily from somewhere out of sight, they both looked up cautiously at the greying sky.

When she continued on she was calm once more, and spoke so low that even the rocks around them seemed to be straining to hear her whisper. "I do not know what questions you have for him, but do not be disappointed in the answers you receive. If you tell me your purpose, maybe I can help."

Éolan produced the small black silken bag from his pocket. "I need to know what the runes sewn on this bag mean, and he is the only one that still holds that knowledge."

Ardra stared at the bag intently and although she brought her hand down towards it, she could not bring herself to touch it. When Éolan spoke again, his voice was tired. "I have never asked him, or any one of us, to needlessly put themselves in harm's way. He chooses his own actions, just as we all do."

"Do we?" she asked as she tilted her head inquisitively and narrowed her eyes.

"Of course we do. And I care deeply for him as well. Never have I abandoned a friend, and I promise you I will do what I can to help," he said.

"Don't you think you've done enough already?" she asked. Without answering, he passed into the utter darkness of the mountain, and somewhere deep below him came a distant echo of eerie chanting. He pressed on towards it. He wasn't leaving without an answer.

XXII

Ashmantle

AS ÉOLAN GOT TO THE bottom of the winding stairs, he walked out into one of the largest caverns that sat beneath Aldaya. It was called the Dün Kehyrn, or Hollow Mountain, by the Dwarves. After the sinking of Atlan, the surviving Dwarves had founded the nearby subterranean kingdom of Khalamet. It sat beneath the area where the Somerset, Fair-Weather, Valhalla, and Seelie ranges converged, and was an area known as the *Vandine*. It meant "razor ice" in the old tongues, and nowhere else on Aldaya could you find a more dangerous labyrinth.

But the Dwarves had persevered, and with the help of the giants and Esmë they wrought a new homeland beneath the peaks that was nearly impenetrable. The mountains were rich in metals, precious gems, and minerals, and the Dwarves mined feverishly for them. And as they sent scouts along the Somerset range towards the sea, they came upon the largest deposit of obsidian that had ever been discovered. It filled nearly the entire inside area of a single peak, and quickly they had begun to mine.

The Dwarves said that as they emptied the mountain, a sorcerer had appeared with precious star jewels from the goddess Maia and asked for their assistance. The deal had been for them to mine and empty the mountain but leave him its heart, and help bring his design for it into reality. In return, he would give them the coveted jewels and let them keep all of the extra obsidian they could take back to their kingdom. They accepted, and created what now lay before Éolan's feet; the kingdom of Ashmantle.

As he looked out from the doorway, a stone outcropping jutted out towards a single bridge that led across the black lake. The water took up nearly the entire floor of the empty mountain, except for some small pockets of shoreline around the edges and the large island that sat in the middle. As instructed, the Dwarves had left the heart of the mountain intact, and it spiraled gracefully upwards from the island and into the unseen peak several thousand feet above.

But where it met the island, a strange structure had been carved out of the black obsidian. Although it looked smaller at this distance, Éolan could see the eerie blue light radiating out from its many openings and lighting the gems and veins of moonstone that twisted upwards within the heart. They reflected off of the polished black walls of the cavern, giving the illusion of a night sky above. This, in turn, also reflected onto the surface of the lake, and as Éolan started across the bridge it was like walking within a never-ending sea of stars.

The bridge was narrow, just wide enough for a wagon to

cross, and had no railings to keep anything from slipping into the water. As he walked, Éolan could see some of the strange lake dwellers coming to the surface. They were iridescent and glowed internally, and were beautiful as they drifted gracefully within the dark lake. Some made strange songs as they floated along the surface, and Éolan stopped for a moment to admire them. He had nearly forgotten how beautiful Ashmantle was, but as the strange chanting came echoing out from the island again, he walked on.

As he approached the structure, two women walked out of a jagged doorway at its base. They looked very much like Ardra, and stopped him as he neared the door, speaking in unison. "State your purpose, Éolan of Alamarayn," they said.

"I have come to see Liator, my brother, friend, and confidant of old. I am in need of his council," he said. But unlike the women, his voiced echoed around the interior of the mountain. The chanting came again, but this time was followed by a man's voice. It started soft, but by the end was echoing so loudly that Éolan had to cover his ears.

"Well. It seems that old *friends* only seem to have the time to visit when it suits their needs. I alone have kept watch, opening myself up to the terrors of practicing unaided, with no help from my *confidants*. But now that the days begin to grow darker, my expertise is needed again. Is that not so, *BROTHER!*" screamed the voice.

"Liator!" Éolan shouted. "You know you are not the only guardian keeping watch over the sphere. We all work on different fronts, and if our communication has fallen by the wayside, it is both of our doing," he said.

A laugh echoed throughout the mountain, and the two women moved from the doorway to let him pass through. Once inside, Éolan walked towards the center. On a tall black dais sat an orb of blue misty light, and behind it was Liator. He was floating in mid-air and his eyes were swirls of white, and when he talked his voice seemed to echo out from the air around the room and not his mouth. "You say you have come for my council. What is it that you want?" he asked.

"I will not discuss the matters at hand until I have your undivided attention," said Éolan. Liator laughed again, and after a moment the light from the orb lessened a bit and he floated to the ground. His eyes turned to deep brown, and as he steadied himself on the dais, the two women came rushing towards him. He waved them off and shook his head violently before looking up to Éolan. His demeanor changed, and a smile came to his face.

"Éolan!" he exclaimed. "I am sorry about my actions. It is difficult to communicate while embracing. Please, come and sit," he said.

He led Éolan out of the room and into a sitting area with a few chairs. He withdrew a pipe from his dark purple robes, but before he could pack it Éolan produced a small bag. "This is a gift," Éolan said.

Liator smiled and clapped him on the leg as he took the bag and smelled the contents. "Aaah," he said. "Peacebloom is always a wonderful way to get back on my good side," he said, giving a wink. He packed his pipe and lit it, and after exhaling spoke again. "Now, what is so urgent that you traveled all the way to Ashmantle? And by horse, no less!"

Éolan explained his reasons, filling Liator in on the details of his travels and the fears that lingered in his heart. His old friend was particularly interested in Mim, and when Éolan asked if he had seen anything about her in his practicing, he shook his head disappointingly. "Of late, opening myself up to the essence has proved very difficult and has begun to take a toll on my mind. For many years I could manage unaided, but something blocks me now. It is as if a moth-eaten blanket has been draped over my eyes. I get images, but most are so fragmented that I cannot make any sense of them," he said.

Éolan then produced the bag. "I must know what these runes mean. I suspect they are Rura Voran, but I can no longer read it. You are the only one with the memory to translate them," he said.

As Liator looked down upon the bag, he gently traced his fingers over the runes. For a long while he said nothing, but after another long pull from his pipe, he leaned back with a sigh. "It is Rura Voran, you are correct. And it is a riddle. Strangely enough, one that has been coming to me as I try and penetrate the darkness of my mind. I had disregarded it in the jumble, until now. It reads:

> 'ONE EATS,
> ONE DRINKS,
> TWO BY TWO.
> ONE STOMPS,
> ONE SLINKS,
> TWO BY TWO.
> BLACK AS NIGHT,
> RED AS DEATH,
> TWO. BY. TWO.

Éolan leaned back and stared out of a jagged doorway towards the lake. *Black as night. Red as death. Two by two. Black as night. Red as death. Two by two.* The riddle kept repeating in his head until he thought back to the dream. He closed his eyes.

The woman that had given Mim this bag and revealed her hideous face in his dream was the fallen Esmë goddess Tar Channon. After being seduced and mutilated by Izman, she had become the creature called Morra Losis. She had been one of the most terrible foes to the light during the northern wars, and her appearance amongst the living meant only one thing. One of the days he had dreaded most had finally arrived, and terror once again walked amongst the world of the living. The Twins had arisen.

"Have you seen them in your practicing? Have they given you any glimpse of where they are or what they might be doing?" Éolan asked.

The bag was floating in front of Liator's face, spinning slowly as he studied it. "Oh no, and I wouldn't expect them too. The twins are far too cunning for me to just stumble across them, especially when working unaided. However, there is a strange enchantment on the bag that I think you'll find of interest. She has made it so she can track anyone that carries it or the contents within."

Éolan's stomach dropped. How could he have been so daft? Just like him, Morra Losis had seen the mystery of Mim the second she had laid eyes upon her. But she could not smell her, and was not yet strong enough to track her on her own. So she given her the bag and had been following her. He stood up and looked towards Liator.

"I have to return to Charis. Now," he said.

He rushed towards the doorway, but just as he neared it Liator spoke again. "You and your guard will never make it in time by horse. A storm is bearing down upon the Charis Vale, but it is not just of air and water. She may not be strong enough to assail it on her own, but if she is loose then so are her children; and her sister could be with her also. She is powerful, Éolan, which is why she is still exists above the surface at all."

Éolan turned around, his anxiety growing. "But there is no other way for me to reach them in time," he said.

A small smile came to the corner of Liator's mouth. "I do believe there is a way. We have an old friend nearby that I think would lend a hand," he said.

One of the women that had blocked the doorway now joined them, and Liator gave quick instructions for her to bring Ardra and Alrik up to the peak that rested above them.

"Follow me," he said.

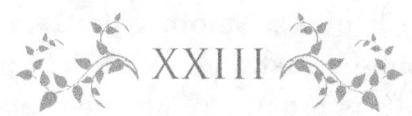

A Gathering Storm

S THE GIRLS' OIL LAMPS burned lower and lower, Mim leaned back and rubbed her eyes. Since Bette had witnessed what had happened to Mim after putting on the amulet, and knowing about the attack near the glen, their researching had doubled. But any books that focused on the actual powers of the Esmë were very hard to come by. There were some brief historical descriptions here and there of some of the more powerful, with the focus mostly being on the great works they had achieved. But they had found nothing that had to do with the practice of magic, or as the texts called it, the "Harnessing of the Essence."

It was mentioned constantly here and there, but they couldn't find anything relating to what it actually was. Bette had also noticed that there were no volumes, ledgers, or even a scrap of parchment that predated the disappearance of the Esmë. Nor was there anything about why they had left or where they had gone. They seemed to be at another dead end, and Bette was becoming increasingly frustrated by the lack of information.

Mim was also frustrated, having tried for days to produce anything without putting the amulet on, but getting nowhere. She tried becoming angry, sad, peaceful, happy; nothing. She had tried putting the amulet in front of her so she could see it but not touch it; nothing. But at the urging of Bette, she was resisting the temptation to put it on again until Éolan returned; which she hoped was sooner than later.

But she had experienced a number of moments where the urge to wear it was almost irresistible. Before the dark presence had come to her mind, her last experience had been wonderful. She had felt connected to everything in a way that she couldn't describe, almost as if she had become part of a great rhythm that ran through everything and everyone around her. But the fear of losing control, and maybe even hurting Bette, Chessa, or Jessel, kept her from wearing it again.

Bette had also prodded her to tell Lady Caralaine about the attack in the glen, but she had avoided it so far. She didn't want anyone to know until Éolan returned, and was nervous that the deans would try and take away the amulet. Although they hadn't learned too much more, they knew for certain that the Master Deans practiced the craft in some way. How much they knew, or how powerful, they hadn't figured out.

The girls also noticed that they had been watching Mim like hawks, being ever present and just around the corner or just across the hall. Down here in the vaults seemed to be the only place that she felt a bit of privacy. Even at the cottage Chessa was constantly checking in on her and keeping constantly informed of where Mim was going, when, and with whom. All of this had to be Éolan's doing, and although she appreciated the concern, her privacy was beginning to dwindle less and less by the day.

Bette now had both of their lamps next to an old book as she squinted in the dim light. It was nearing midnight, and although the library above was technically open all night, Mim wasn't quite sure about the protocol for being down within the vaults. However, Bette had decided that it would be better to ask forgiveness than permission.

But Mim was tired, and with the Far Darron Festival starting the next day, she wanted to get some rest. She was looking forward to getting out of the Vale with Bette and Hazel and experiencing her first trip into the town, but the threat of being attacked again weighed on her mind. She knew she was being watched, but staying inside the Vale alone didn't seem any safer than being at the festival and surrounded by her friends and all of the deans.

"Bette, come on. We have a long day tomorrow and I'm falling asleep. We can pick it back up later," she said, stifling a yawn. Bette said nothing and slammed the book she was reading shut. As a cloud of dust billowed outward, she stood up and began gathering her things, grumbling crossly.

"We attend the most prestigious learning institution on Aldaya, and somehow cannot find one scrap of text telling us *anything* about the Esmë or their powers. I know that some of the eastern territories don't worship them any longer, and I know that the Holy Deeds of Pretoria consider talk of them or magic as heresy, but for the love of Maia, they were the creative force behind this world for five ages before they disappeared! Did they just take all of their history with them on their way out?" she said.

"Maybe they buried it," Mim said.

Bette didn't appreciate the sarcasm, and she shot Mim a glare. "Well you can make jokes all you like, but I find it odd," she said. "It took me two days just to unearth this old book of runes. And how did that help? Not one bit, because I can't find use of them anywhere! The ones etched in the vines throughout the Vale are all just of the five elements, and I learned what they were when *I* was five." she said.

They talked a little about it as they walked towards the cottage in the brisk night air. Bette had been going at it for so long that she started talking of conspiracy and began to sound as if she was losing her sanity. But Mim was so tired that the moment they got to the cottage and checked in with Chessa, she flopped onto her bed and fell asleep.

———◦◦◦———

Early the next morning, the time to leave for the festival was closing in, but Mim almost couldn't bear to pull herself off of the porch swing. As a brisk wind blew in through the screens, she pulled her grey cloak even more tightly around her shoulders and closed her eyes. Autumn seemed to have arrived overnight, and throughout the vale the cottage doors no longer stood open to the summer breezes, but were now tightly closed against the chill that had come down from the mountains.

Smoke rose from the chimneys now, and work had already begun in the castle and on the upper cottages to prepare them for the approaching winter. But luckily for Mim, Gracemere sat at the lowest point of the valley and would be last in line to receive its glass panes and heavy shutters. So with the brief time she had left, she was trying to enjoy every moment possible before they sealed up the little blue cottage until spring.

As she closed her eyes and took in the earthen smell of the first falling leaves, her moment of peace was suddenly shattered by a loud shriek that came from inside. As she ran in, Chessa was sitting at the table and in the middle of enjoying her first meal, but laughing merrily at Bette who was crouched atop a small wooden chair. She had one of her shoes in her hand, and was just about to smash it down upon a particularly large terrace spider before Mim intervened.

"Hey! You know I hate it when you kill bugs. It's not doing

anything wrong by trying to stay warm. Now go get a cup so I can throw it outside," she said.

"I don't mind if it is trying to stay warm, but it isn't going to use my leg to do it!" she said. She very carefully stepped down from the chair, and sped off towards the kitchen to grab a cup. Mim easily caught it and opened the bay window and threw it out, letting a gust of cool air in which hit Chessa head on.

"Close that before I catch a snow sneeze! And go stoke da fire while you're at it. Lettin' all of da heat out for a spider..." she said, trailing off and taking a large sip of her herbal tea. Mim looked at her crossways, and couldn't understand how Chessa always drank it. There were more flower petals inside of the glass than liquid, but she swore by it. And as she took another sip, she also devoured one of the large white petals from within the cup. Mim wondered where she was going to get flowers in the dead of winter, but wasn't going to bring it up.

"Now. You two are heading out with da other students right at nine from da main gate. Most of da deans will be there and accompanying you. I am heading down by coach as well, if you care to join. You stick by me as much as possible, but if not, stay close to your friends. Do not leave da town without finding me first. Da festival goes all night, but da deans want all of the students back by sundown. Clear?" Chessa asked.

She had been over this with them at least four times now, and the girls agreed. They also told her once again that they wanted to ride Carmen down instead of taking a coach, and that Hazel would have her horse as well. So as the bells tolled once, signaling the students that is was at the half hour mark before departure, Mim and Bette headed out to the stables and got Carmen ready to go. As the happy old horse trotted onto the lane, Mim thought she could smell saltwater on the breeze, and for a moment it reminded her of being back in the south.

As they got to the main gate, Bette stopped Carmen and waited for Hazel, who arrived on top of her large stallion. Some of the students were already leaving, and the girls wanted to ride alone and catch up. Mim kept watch, and when she thought all was clear she quickly jumped onto Carmen and they trotted out towards the gate.

As they passed under the archway of the guardians, she smiled proudly to herself and spouted off to Bette and Hazel. "I guess Lady Lee'shan can't be everywhere all of the time, now can she?"

As they emerged on the other side a moment later, the sun hit her eyes and Mim jumped as she heard, "I would not bet on it, Miss Hart." Off to the left stood the Ladies Lee'shan and Lisle, and another she knew as Lady Cody, each standing next to their beautiful Cavalla Whites and looking ready to ride.

"I'm sure you wouldn't mind some riding company, seeing that we were just about to depart?" Lee'shan smiled at her, and although she asked it as a question, Mim knew she had just gained three riding companions whether she liked it or not.

"Not at all," she said.

Lee'shan was much nimbler than Mim had expected, and easily pulled herself up onto her horse. Unlike the sisters, she rode traditional like Mim, and wore a cream colored riding suit that split at the waist. Once up, she wrapped a light blue scarf around her head, and the way it framed her face and lit her eyes, she thought Lee'shan looked even more formidable today than normal.

The sisters were even more graceful as they mounted their large twin cavallas, and how they managed in their beautiful riding dresses without a stepladder was impressive. Their horses were just as large as the ones that pulled Éolan's coach, and she could tell they were meticulously cared for in every detail. They also wrapped scarves around their heads, which complemented their long amethyst and emerald colored gowns. As Mim looked upon them, they reminded her more of beautiful and powerful queens than schoolteachers.

Once ready, Lee'shan motioned for the girls to start first, and the group took off towards Far Darron. Once out of the valleys, the road finally became wide enough for them to spread out a little. But Mim noticed that the deans stayed very close, so she tried to break the silence.

"Lady Lisle, I beg your pardon, but may I ask if you have heard from Lord Éolan? Does he plan on returning soon?" she asked.

"I have heard nothing since he departed, but I am sure he will be back a soon as possible." But as composed as she tried to be, Mim became anxious by the look in the woman's eyes. She was worried for her son. This confirmed Mim's suspicions that Éolan was somewhere much more dangerous than his home in the south.

As a coach appeared in the distance along the horizon, the women moved like clockwork, with Lee'shan moving slowly forward and in front of Carmen, while Cody took her place on Mim's left. Once it had passed, Lady Cody dropped back into her normal position, as did Lee'shan.

Mim sighed with frustration as she finally made the decision to let the cat out of the bag. "May I ask how long this will continue?"

"Continue what, my dear?" asked Lee'shan.

Mim smiled to herself. She had tried her best, but could no longer keep up her façade. "You have been watching me since Éolan departed," she said.

But before Lee'shan could answer, a distant rumble of thunder made them all turn around and look back towards the Vale.

Two days prior to the festival, the deans had informed the students of an approaching ocean tempest that was raging across the Sea of Storms and heading towards the mountains. The notice that went out said there was no cause for alarm. But it warned of heavy rains that would be swelling the streams, and that everyone should be prepared to go to lamplight. This was especially true for those that chose to stay down in their cottages.

Since the storm was hitting over the extended festival weekend, the girls fully planned on staying at their cottage, having no intention of moving into the cramped rooms of the castle until they were forced. They had already invited Hazel down to ride out the storm with them as well, and the three were looking forward to it.

But as they neared Far Darron, Mim couldn't help looking back at the deepening clouds over the mountains. She was no stranger to ocean storms, but this one felt different to her. Lady Lisle also caught her eye. She too looked ominously towards the storm, and Mim knew she sensed the same thing.

As the two locked eyes for a moment, Mim absently reached towards her pocket and felt the amulet. She hadn't told Bette she had brought it, but she wasn't going to risk leaving the Vale without it. With another large rumble, she grasped it tighter.

Lee'shan spoke. "We will make for the stables and rendezvous there. In case we are separated, follow this main road and turn to your right at the central clock tower. Head straight and you will see them. I would not recommend getting down from your horse!"

But as they had neared the town, Mim and Bette were immediately swallowed into the crowd. Bette carefully started weaving Carmen into the throngs of people that filled Far Darron and making her way towards the stables.

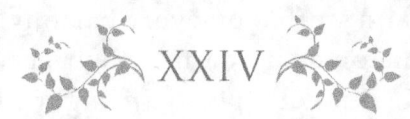

XXIV

The Far Darron Festival

MIM HAD NEVER SEEN SO many people in one place in her entire life, and it was thrilling. Every street seemed swollen beyond capacity, and luckily for her she was high up on Carmen and had a bird's eye view of where she was heading. At her height she would have easily become lost down on the ground and could have been swept off to who knows where.

Hazel had gone off to meet with members of her family and would be meeting back up with her later on, and the deans had been swallowed by the crowd as well. Although still on horseback, they were some distance behind her now. But Bette wove Carmen through the crowds with great skill, slowly making towards the center of town.

As they looked at the homes and businesses lining the boulevard, the friendly people of Far Darron were hanging out of every window and stuffed on every balcony. With the help of the free flowing ale on every corner, their cheeks looked much redder than usual, and not a person in sight wore anything but a smile. A man had given her a large mug full, and as she took a sip she spat the bitter liquid out. But she had nowhere to put the large mug for now, and had to keep it for the moment. This proved to be a smart move. As the ambled through town, she was offered at least three more. But upon seeing her full mug, the people would laugh merrily and move on.

As she looked down to her right, an elderly man who seemed to have had more than his fair share stumbled backwards over an empty cask and fell with a thud to the ground. But instead of getting angry, he began laughing so hard that tears came to his eyes. She laughed at the sight, and tried to choke down another sip, but it nearly made her sick.

The large banners above them stretched across the wide boulevards, each advertising some wonderful food, drink, or attraction. Balloons of all colors, sizes, and shapes floated through the air, and bursts of rainbow confetti rained down from the sky. Through the alleyways she could see the tips of the large tents on the eastern end of town.

Although they weren't the only people on horseback, it did seem to draw some attention towards them. As Bette passed them closer to the buildings along the side of the street, young men and women started throwing flowers down towards them. When Mim caught them the people cheered. She hadn't remembered a time where she had so much fun, and all she wanted to do was hop down and get lost in the town for days on end.

As they rounded the corner towards the giant tent city and stables, something hard struck the side of her face and nearly knocked her from Carmen's back. Whatever it was had fallen into a crease of her grey cloak that was now bunched up on her lap. As she slipped her hand in, her fingers wrapped around something cold and metallic. When she pulled it out she realized it was a large coin, and as she held it up to her eyes the joy instantly disappeared. It was the same ancient style as the ones she had been given by the creature from the Last Stand.

Anxiety flooded into her and her chest tightened. This was no coincidence, and whoever had thrown this was close. She looked around to try and spot anyone in black, but there were so many people her search was in vain. "What was that?" Bette asked. "Are you alright?"

Mim immediately jumped down from Carmen and drug Bette off as well. She showed Bette the coin, and without a word they began shoving their way towards the stables. They would be safer once they met up with the deans.

Now that they were in a hurry and on the ground, the drunks around them became more of a nuisance than a fun spectacle. After a few nasty words, some crunched toes, and her cloak dripping with spilt ale, they two finally arrived. Bette tethered Carmen and the two rushed inside, hiding behind the flap of one of the large tents. But as she stood there, the seconds turned to minutes, and before long Mim was getting worried that they had gone to the wrong place.

The same humming sound she had the night near the glen drifted up to her ears, and she turned to run. She grabbed Bette's hand and they disappeared into the tent city. But as they wove in and out of the canvas flaps and into the different canopies and rooms, Mim realized she was now alone.

Bette was no longer behind her, and she searched tried frantically to retrace her steps. "Bette!" she shouted. But there was no answer. As she wound her way through the paths between the white tents, Mim realized she was lost. Every time she tried to retrace her steps it only seemed to worsen the situation, and when she tried to guide herself by the noise of the thunderous crowds, it only wound her further into the labyrinth.

As she ran through another set of the canvas flaps, the temperature of the air around her dropped, and the noises of the crowd became distant until they vanished completely. She was fighting for control of herself, just like she had the night after coming down from the star tower, but this was even more intense. The blood in her veins felt as though it was turning to ice, and as she took a deep breath and blew it out, her breath froze on the air and fell to the grass below her, shattering like porcelain on stone.

That was when she heard it. Although distant, there was no mistaking that gurgled high-pitched laugh. Out of the corner of her eye she thought she saw a black flash move past her, but when she turned there was nothing. Then the laugh came again, this time louder, and she turned and made a run for it.

As she took off down the path, her legs were barely working. The cold had grown so intense that Mim began to fear if her exposed skin would survive. But she had no choice and knew if she stopped now that her death would come swiftly. As she weaved down the endless corridors, with each door she passed stood the woman. There was no mistaking her razor sharp teeth, or the eyes that looked like deep wells of the blackest ink. Her laugh had now grown to a shrieking scream, and as Mim tried to cover her ears with her hands, her legs finally gave out and she fell to the ground.

For a moment all was still, and everything ceased. But as she looked up towards the white ceiling, two cloaked figures appeared above her, and their red pulsing eyes seemed to match that of her slowing heart. She knew they were the same creatures that had accompanied the woman back in the Quilt. But as she stared into their dark and cavernous hoods, she knew that they were not from the world of the living.

She could feel herself fading, and whatever strength she had was waning quickly. But something warm was vibrating against her leg; it was the amulet. Mim reached her frozen fingers and grasped the warm metal, sending violet rays of light into the dark hoods. The creatures shrieked loudly and disappeared from her view. Mim put the amulet around her neck and tied the broken chain. She was warm again and standing, and her senses were heightened. She could feel the evil straining against her, tainting the rhythm of the world around her.

The winds of the fast approaching storm were blowing the canvas doors to the tents back and forth, and from their depths her foe floated forward. She snarled at Mim as she approached, and although the wind lashed around them, her black robes and hair remained still.

The two locked eyes, and although she was afraid, the power flowing through the amulet gave Mim the strength to stand her ground. The creature snarled, gnashing her teeth and throwing her hands forward. Rays of what looked like liquid black ink erupted from them, and without thinking Mim threw her hands up as well. The darkness radiated violently off of the halo, like oil and water. But Mim could feel the amulet beginning to become too powerful. It was growing hot on her skin, and she was losing control of her mind.

The more power the creature threw at her, the hotter the amulet became. It began searing her skin, and Mim screamed in pain. She couldn't hold on any longer and dropped to her knees. But as she closed her eyes and prepared for whatever was about to come, she heard a distant call of her name. She turned towards the sound, and when she opened her eyes she saw Lady Lee'shan and Lady Lisle standing in the billowing wind.

As they looked upon the demon towering over her, Mim expected them to run for help or out of fear, but instead they slowly walked forward. Their eyes were fierce, and their cloaks lashed out behind them as if caught in a gale force wind that Mim could neither see nor feel. Brilliant flashes of light hurled from their hands, quickly overwhelming Mim's attacker. All she heard were two terrible screeches before she lost consciousness.

"Mim! Mim, wake up darling. I know you can hear me, now listen to my voice. Come back to me. Follow my voice. That's it, come on."

As Mim opened her eyes she saw Lady Lisle bent down over her, staring intently. "What happened?" she moaned groggily.

Lee'shan was there also and stooped over her. "We don't have time to explain, Mim. It will have to wait until the castle. Come on now, up on your feet."

As she and Lisle drew her up, Mim noticed the tents around them were shaking much more fiercely in the strong wind. Outside there were people shouting, and as a large flash of lightning cracked overhead, Lady Cody and Bette entered. The often quiet and gentle woman now stood tall and her demeanor was serious. "We must not waste time here. The storm is nearly upon us, and they could return. We must get back to the Vale, now."

A large rumble of thunder boomed so loudly that it shook the ground below them. Bette rushed forward and grabbed Mim and hoisted her arm over one of her shoulders and began guiding her outside.

Lisle and Cody were flanking them on both sides like sentinels while Lee'shan strode out in front. When they left the shelter of the tents, Mim's breath caught in her throat as she looked towards the sky. The storm clouds that issued over the mountain were blacker and more terrifying than any storm she had ever seen. As they swirled above, bolts of lightning struck whatever stood highest, sending sparks flying onto the street. The townspeople were running frantically here and there, trying to find shelter in the already overcrowded buildings or screaming for loved ones lost in the fray.

A huge gust of wind swept through the town, turning garbage and glass bottles into airborne killers, and behind them one of the tents gave way and was lifted high into the air before landing on a large mob of people.

Lee'shan led them through the crowds and to their horses, and when they arrived, she untied Carmen while the sisters hoisted Mim onto the back of one of the large Cavalla's. Once secure, Lisle floated up gracefully behind her and made to take off. A large coach appeared, with Chessa sitting atop the driver's box, and right behind them galloped up Hazel.

"Bette, take Carmen!" Lee'shan yelled. Her friend didn't hesitate and quickly mounted her horse. "And Chessa, get as many students as you can into that coach and get back to the Vale." Chessa nodded and swung the coach around masterfully and sped off. "Everyone else, follow me and stay together!"

The wind was so strong that even a few feet away Mim could barely hear her. Her mind was still fuzzy, and her body felt so weak that she could barely keep her head up. The group galloped off and Mim held on as tightly as she could.

Within a minute they were already clear of Far Darron. As they rode, Mim was surprised that horses could run so fast. Looking back, even Carmen's legs were moving so quickly that they had begun to blur, and Bette looked as queenly as the deans as her auburn hair whipped fiercely behind her in the wind.

The closer they neared to the entrance of the Vale, the more violent the winds and lightning became. They twice passed coaches that had been tossed onto their sides like toys, and Mim could see the drivers struggling to loosen the horses from their traces. The students that had been inside were running up the road to safety, and Lee'shan, Cody, and Bette had stopped to get as many of them onto their horses as possible. As they rounded a bend and disappeared out of the view of the students, Lisle raised her hand upward and a brilliant emerald shaft of light radiated up into the sky.

A few moments later they neared the entrance to the Vale, and host of the deans issued out on horseback and stopped. Lord Davian, and the Ladies Trulane, Christiane, Robyn, and Amanda were there, each looking fiercely towards the approaching storm. "Morra Losis is loose in Far Darron and nearly killed Mim. And I fear that the approaching storm is being driven by the dark craft. She will devour everything in her path, including the students. We have to get them back inside the Vale," Lisle said.

Without a word, the group galloped out and across the bridge.

Exhaustion was flooding over Mim and all she had the urge to do was close her eyes. The wind was getting so strong now that she feared she might be blown off of the horse. She heard the clopping of the Cavalla's hooves on stone as they galloped beneath the guardians and all went dark.

Lights Out

MIM HAD NO IDEA HOW long she was out, but the high-pitched whistle of gusting winds and the rattling of the windowpane off to her right had drawn her out of sleep. She didn't recognize the room she was in. It was dark, but she could tell it was grand, and in the low light she could see large the outlines of wooden furniture. As she tried to sit up, her movement had awoken something next to her, and as she looked down she saw two green eyes staring up at her. It was Jessel.

Her cat purred for a moment and gave Mim some comfort,

and as she became more aware she realized the walls around her were made of smooth stone and not wood, which meant she must be somewhere in the castle. She felt something else move next to her before it suddenly jolted upright, which she quickly realized was Bette.

"Mim? Mim are you awake?" she whispered.

"Yeah, Bette, I'm awake," she said.

Her friend then flung off the covers and jumped off of the bed before disappearing into the darkness. After a second Mim heard the thud of a pillow and a groan from across the room.

"Hazel! Come on, Mim's up." As the two sets of footsteps came padding back across the carpet she heard a low moan.

"Quiet, Riken! You stay right where you are," Hazel said.

With another moan, Mim heard the big dog's head hit the carpet. As the two girls climbed up in bed, Bette risked the wick of the oil lantern on the side table. As the girl's faces came into the light they both looked exhausted, but their gazes were intent on Mim.

"Where are we?" she asked quietly.

"We're in the castle," whispered Bette. "Everyone has been evacuated from the cottages and are now inside. It took us almost all day, but everyone finally fit. And the two lower main halls under the castle are being used to treat and house refugees from town."

"Are we in one of the towers?" she asked.

Bette nodded and explained that they were high in the eastern tower in Lord Éolan's rooms, right below the apartments for the deans. Mim could also hear Chessa snoring heavily from across the room.

"Hazel, could you fetch me some water?" Mim asked.

"Sure thing," she said. And as she disappeared through a doorway Mim turned towards Bette.

"Where is my amulet?" she asked.

"It is right here." Bette said, opening the drawer of the side table. Mim grabbed it quickly and got out of bed. She put on her clothes and shoved it into her pocket.

A bright flash shone through the window and a large rumble of thunder shook the tower. Immediately, the gong of the castle bells erupted in warning the wind grew silent.

Chessa jumped up. A tremor began to shake the castle, and as Chessa ran to the window and looked out, a flash of lightning lit the sky. She turned around and yelled to the girls to get down just as a terrible rushing sound met their ears. Mim grabbed the large down comforter from the bed and dove over the group just as the row of round glass windows along the wall shattered inward.

As the wind and rain whipped through the openings, Mim heard foul laughter on the air. It was the demon woman, and Mim knew her name now. Lisle had called her Morra Losis, and there was no mistaking it; she was somewhere out in the tempest searching for Mim. Adrenaline rushed into her. She felt trapped inside the castle, and wondered how long the protection spells would last. She ripped the blankets off of her and the others and grabbed the oil lamp off of the dresser. It was rain soaked but the wick was still dry inside the glass shade, and as she fumbled around found a pack of matches.

Hazel yelled from the doorway. "Come on! Back here!"

As Mim looked up, her friend was standing off and to the left in an alcove that looked to be sheltered from the wind and rain. Jessel, Camilla, and Riken were already there as well, and Bette helped Mim up and they ran together.

As they all got in, Mim turned to see the crumpled shape of Chessa lying on the floor in the middle of the room. The three girls ran and began heaving her back towards the doorway. They finally got her inside and slammed the door shut, and Mim realized they were in the lavatory. She bent down and surveyed Chessa, who had a large bleeding gash on her head, but no other injuries. "I think she was just knocked unconscious," she said. After a few moments the winds had passed, and Mim wasted no time.

She lit two other lanterns on the counter by the sinks and turned back towards her friends. "I've got to hide somewhere until the storm is over. I need to find Lady Caralaine or someone to help me find a way to get into the tunnels that lead back into the mountain. Does either one of you know how to get there?"

"I do," Bette said.

"Then you and I will go. Hazel, you stay here with Chessa and wait for help."

Her friend nodded, dabbing blood from Chessa's head. Mim grabbed one of the lamps and wrenched the bathroom door open and marched out into the darkness. The wind had died down a bit, but rain still blew in the tiny dark portals that now only held shards of broken glass. The rest of the windows lay scattered all about the room, with some of the larger shards driven deep into the sides of the wooden furniture like spears. Mim grabbed her pack with the compass, map, and elinine from Jennah, and shoved her amulet inside. She threw Jessel onto her shoulder and followed Bette out of the door.

As they entered the hallway, Lady Caralaine and Lee'shan were rushing towards them, with three of the Dwarven smiths on their heels. They were shorter and stouter than the women, and in leather and fine metal armor. Each had deadly looking pieces of smithy tools in their hands. Their black beards came down in braids to the middle of their chests, and their eyes shone like dark jewels beneath their helmets. Had it been any other time, Mim would have been excited, but other than their appearances she barely noticed them.

"Lady Caralaine, Chessa is hurt and locked inside the lavatory with Hazel. She needs help. But I have to get back inside the mountain somewhere and hide. Morra Losis won't stop until she finds me," Mim said.

Caralaine didn't miss a beat. "Lee'shan, take Mim, Bette, and the smiths as an escort back into the mountain and seal yourselves within the relics vault. I will be there shortly."

"Follow me," Lee'shan said. Mim and Bette walked behind her as the Dwarf smiths fell in behind them, and they began making their way stealthily through the castles dark corridors and down towards the vaults.

The wind rushed through Éolan's hair as he glided above the storm. Alrik still had his hands wrapped tightly around his waist, but he had finally begun to relax. They vast wings of the ancient creature they rode rose up and down as they soared through the air. Her name was Annon, and she was among the oldest creatures to still grace the sphere. She was counted amongst a group called the Kem, who had been awakened by the Esmë upon Atlan before the Five Races. Her teal, gray, and yellow feathers were soft but strong, and Éolan's grip tightened on them as she dove down towards the Vale.

The storm that stretched below them was monstrous, and its great eye wall was just about to pass over the Charis. They had been circling above, waiting for it to arrive and giving them the chance to land. Just as their window came open, Annon swooped down within the castle grounds. Éolan and Alrik dismounted and ran towards the castle doors as the fair creature took off and ascended back towards the clouds.

The eye wall of the storm was almost upon them, and they had barely made it to the castle in time. He could hear the foul laughter on the wind as he had glided above the storm, but he could now feel it all around the Vale. The ancient protective spells around the castle were strong, but against the tempest raging down upon them, he was not sure if they would hold.

As they ran towards the main gate, he knew it would be barricaded, so he ducked to his left and wound around towards the side entrance that led out towards the cottages. He and Alrik sped across the courtyard as fast as they could in the ankle-deep water, and when he reached the gates to the main hall his fists thundered loudly against the wood and iron. After a tense moment of shouting his name, he heard the clinking of the large locks from the other side, and suddenly a crack appeared and they slipped in.

When he threw back his hood, Caralaine and Davian stood before him, each with a lantern in hand. Caralaine ordered the ten Dwarven smiths that stood with them to seal the doors once again, but before she had a chance to ask him anything, Éolan interrupted. "There's a funnel headed directly at us. You need to get everyone inside the mountain as quickly as possible."

She looked to Davian, who immediately motioned for the Dwarves to follow him and they disappeared into a dark tunnel off to the right.

"Where's Mim?" he asked. "Is she safe?"

"Lee'shan has taken her and Miss Brooke down into the vaults under the castle in the hopes of hiding. But she barely made it out of the festival alive."

Éolan stopped and turned to her. "What do you mean?"

"If it hadn't been for your mother and Lee'shan, she most certainly would have died. Morra Losis and her henchmen attacked her in the venue tents."

The warning bells in the towers above them began to pierce the onslaught of the raging storm outside, and everyone still left in the hall began running back and into the passageways leading into the mountains. Then all went quiet. "Everyone take cover!" Éolan yelled.

He ran over and grabbed Caralaine before dashing towards one of the small storage rooms on the backside of the stairs. As they ducked inside, the wind screamed and the castle shook. The sound of shattering glass met their ears. Laughter echoed through the mountains and down into the Vale, and sounded as if the storm itself was taking joy in its destruction.

As it passed, he and Caralaine stepped out and took in the destruction that lay before them. Glass was everywhere, and large cracks now worked their way up the eastern tower like large veins in the ancient stone. Alrik was pulling himself off of the ground, with shards of glass falling from his armor.

"She knows she can't enter here while the barrier spells are in place. She's trying to use the storm to bring down parts of the mountain. If she succeeds, and the scripts are broken, there will be nothing stopping her," he said.

"I'll get the others and meet you back here as quickly as possible," Caralaine said.

"She wants Mim as badly as we do and means to take her. She's ready for a fight," Éolan said.

But Caralaine calmly kept walking forward with her cane in one hand and her lantern in the other, and answered without turning around. "I'm counting on it."

It took her less than ten minutes, and she soon returned with Davian, Lisle, and the other eight of the master deans. With one last shudder from somewhere within the mountains, the wind died down to a mere breeze, and a light knock came at the door. No one answered, and the knock grew louder and louder until the ancient doors began groaning under the pressure.

Caralaine turned to Éolan. "We can handle her. You get to the girls and keep them safe," she said.

Éolan took off towards the back of the hall with Alrik in tow, and just as he was about to go through, he looked back.

The trembling doors wouldn't hold much longer, and as Caralaine threw her cane off to one side she now spoke as a battle general defending her keep. Her voice echoed throughout the hall. "Form a line behind me," she said. A halo of light formed around the nine of them, but as the locks gave way and the doors burst open, the three horrors that stood before them were not the three Éolan expected.

They were tall figures hooded in black, and Éolan knew the terrible creatures as the Reemen; stealer of souls and foulest of the dark designs of Morra Losis. But as the deans moved forward and the dueling began, he realized that their master was not with them; which meant she was already somewhere else inside the castle.

<hr />

The group made their way down from the tower and all had gone smoothly. As they snuck out from the service stairs, Mim thought she caught a glimpse of Lady Caralaine on the far side of the hall heading away from them. But whoever's lantern it was had been so low and so far away, that she couldn't be sure.

They made like ghosts across the hall, and when they reached the back wall, Lee'shan led them down the large tunnel that led back towards the inner halls. Mim had been this way before once or twice, but in the darkness it seemed unfamiliar. Moving straight into the library and towards a large hallway at the back, they reached a small door and she produced a key from her pocket.

Inside was a dark and steep stone stairwell, and Lee'shan moved quickly downward after locking the door behind them. She led them through hallway after hallway, zigzagging in-between old doors and tapestries. Occasionally they would hear the noises of townspeople and the other teachers echoing through the hallways, but not once did they see them.

As they continued on the sound of voices stopped, and the farther down they went the air became so cold and stuffy that breathing was becoming more difficult. They came upon an old but strong iron door and then out into a large cavernous hallway. The lamplight flickered off of the large purple crystals, moonstones, and diamonds that jutted down from the ceilings, and Mim noticed the Dwarves look up hungrily at them. But Lee'shan continued on.

As they neared the end of the hall, the darkness around them deepened and a vicious cackle came to their ears. The second it had started, a halo formed around Lee'shan, and the three Dwarven smiths rushed in front of her. Mim withdrew her amulet and put it on, grasping Bette's hand, and the light from her eyes pierced into the shadow in front of them.

Power flooded into her body, and her senses heightened. The taint of the shadow around her made her want to vomit, and the anxiety and fear she was sensing from Bette made her heart begin to beat furiously in her chest. But the energy from Lee'shan was different than all of the rest. It was centered, calm, and powerful.

The laugh continued and grew nearer, and the light around

Lee'shan grew brighter as well, radiating out into the darkness. Shafts of black shadow flooded outward, smearing across the shield around Lee'shan like black oil in crystal water. The unprotected smiths in front were raised from the ground, with the terrible blackness issuing out from their mouths, eyes, ears, and pores. As they fell to the stone floor their bodies shattered like glass.

Mim could see Lee'shan trembling, and the closer the shadow advanced against her the dimmer and smaller her halo became. Mim could see Morra Losis in the gloom, delighting in her assault and slowly pushing her way forward against the light. They began backing up as the shadow ebbed and flowed against the halo. Mim was desperate to do something, but had no idea how to control the forces that were flooding through her.

The halo around Lee'shan began to flicker, and she turned and yelled for them to run. Mim had no intention of leaving, but Bette tugged at her hand and drug her backwards away from the battle. As they got to the end of the hallway, Mim saw the shadow envelop Lee'shan entirely, and her heart dropped into her stomach. But Bette continued to pull and Mim turned to run.

XXVI

What Bette Knew

HE HALLS THEY FLED DOWN were all identical and made of the same smooth rock. Mim could feel the age in the stone, and the memory it held as she ran by. She could feel every heartbeat from her and Bette, and every thought and anxiety also. As they neared a junction of the corridors, Bette dragged them to the right and into a room that was filled floor to ceiling with thousands of dusty books, furniture, stone statues, and ancient looking trunks. Mim heaved the door open and ran around to the other side and slammed it closed. They shoved the rusty iron lock into position and ran back into the labyrinth.

They were frantically looking for somewhere to hide, and took off towards the back of the room and dove behind a massive pile of old cloth-covered furniture. Jessel crept from Mim's bag and stared cautiously around, and Bette told her to remove the amulet so the light wouldn't give them away. It was hard for her, but when she took it off the light of the amulet died away, as did the wonderful sensations, but something just in front of them glowed dimly. It was underneath a thick canvas cloth and very tall, and Mim stood and pulled the corner of the fabric away.

Beneath it was a very old and ornate mirror, and for a moment Mim thought she recognized it. As she got closer, she finally realized where she had seen it. Although it wasn't identical, this was definitely related to the one that she had seen on the third floor of the Inn. It had the same strange shapes around it, all interconnected with the vine writing. The white stone inlaid within the carvings had kept some of the light that had been coming off of her, like she had powered it somehow. Bette stood up and was next to her now.

"Do you have any idea what this is?" she asked.

"No. I've seen one like it in Slaidburn, but we don't have time—"

Bette put her hand up to shush her and dug into her pack, pulling out the book of runes they had been studying from the library. She made Mim hold the lantern over the book as she furiously flipped to a page in the middle and gasped. Mim looked down and saw a very lifelike drawing of a similar mirror on the page, but couldn't read any of the words around it. However, it seemed Bette knew enough to give an answer.

"Mim, this is one of the lost traveling mirrors. Lord Davian said there used to be thirty of them during the golden age of Atlan, and that the Esmë and mortal leaders would use them to travel to all parts of the lands in just a single step. But after Atlan fell he said they were all destroyed," she said.

Behind them and up the hall they heard the locked wooden door explode, and a cloud of dust rolled into the room. "Well, can you make it work? I don't care where we end up as long as it's not here. This could be our only chance to survive!"

The temperature in the room plummeted, and at their feet Jessel howled. Mim turned towards the stairs and saw a faint glow of lantern light that was growing, and the bearer of it was singing a tune merrily to herself.

"ONE EATS,
ONE DRINKS,
TWO BY TWO.
ONE STOMPS,
ONE SLINKS,
TWO BY TWO.
BLACK AS NIGHT,
RED AS DEATH,
TWO. BY. TWO"

"Bette, you work on this while I try and stall her. Just do your best."

Mim ran back out into the center of the room and walked a bit towards the stairs. She put the amulet around her neck, and its power flooded into her. She could hear every speck of dust hitting the floor around her, and the evil that approached threatened to wash over her with every breath. But she tried to focus and find her center. The song echoed closer and she stood as bravely as she could, waiting.

Morra Losis rounded the last corner and paused as she laid eyes on Mim. She smiled terribly.

"Hello, my little piglet." She took a deep, gurgling breath in and the air became even colder. "I knew you were special the moment I laid eyes on you back in that sty you call a town. But I must admit, you surprised me today. I just hope that my queen will find you as interesting as I do."

The sound of her heavy footsteps echoed throughout the room, and her black eyes widened hungrily as she walked towards her prey.

Mim thrust her fist out at the woman's grotesque face, but she easily dodged it. Her cold hand wrapped around Mim's wrist, and she squeezed, her long razor-like nails digging deep into the skin. Shadow entered Mim like poison, and the veins within her arm began to blacken.

Mim swung with her free hand but Morra dodged it and hit Mim squarely in the chest. She flew backwards and landed with a thud, skidding along the floor. She was bleeding from the back of her head, and as much as she tried, her eyes wouldn't open.

Morra Losis was quickly on top of her, and her rank breath filled Mim's nostrils. All Mim hoped was that when the demon was finished with her, Bette and Jessel somehow would make it out alive. All that was left was the sound of her feeble heartbeat in her ears and the pain coming from her jaw beginning to crack in the woman's icy hand. But suddenly the image of the beautiful blond woman appeared in her mind. It was the same one she had dreamt of all her life, but this time it was not in the context of her normal dream, nor did she disappear.

Images began flooding into Mim's mind: Jessel and Bette, Éolan and Hazel, all of her old friends from the Quilt and all of her new ones at Charis. As each one passed, her heart beat a little faster and her body grew a little warmer, and Mim felt life coming into her once again.

Suddenly they stopped, and the blond woman was there once again, but this time her smile was gone. She was serious now, and her purple eyes glowed fiercely. Mim knew she couldn't give up and forced her eyes open again.

As the violet light erupted from them, it pierced deep into the black pits of her enemy's, searing them like ice in a hot skillet. Morra Losis howled in agony as she let go of Mim's jaw, and seizing the moment, Mim punched her as hard as she could and rolled to her right. The force of the blow, backed by the strength of the amulet, sent Morra Losis flailing violently backwards and into a large pile of canvas covered furniture.

When Mim staggered upright, the dark terror was already

advancing once again. The skin around Morra Losis' eyes was blistered and bubbled, and where Mim had struck her, the skin was cracked like glass.

The madness and hunger in her eyes was now even more harrowing and ghastly. Mim thought back to the battle upstairs, and how calm and centered Lee'shan had been. The energy from her had almost been serene, and Mim tried her best to channel that feeling into the amulet. It was her only hope.

As Morra Losis advanced, the halo around Mim strengthened and became brighter. The demon unleashed the shadow from within her and it flooded around her. She moved to plunge her icy hand deep into Mim's heart, but instead she grasped the amulet. She screeched in agony, as did Mim. The amulet grew white hot and burned them both. It seared into Mim's skin and Morra Losis drew her hand away in pain. Blood oozed down Mim's chest now, and the woman's pale hand looked deader than the rest of her.

Taking the opportunity, Bette came out of nowhere at a full run and heaved her shoulder into the demon, who was thrown out of the way and into an ancient-looking machine and out of sight. She grabbed Mim and started to drag her towards the mirror.

"I've almost got it figured out! But the runes are starting to fade and we need the amulet to light it again. I just need one minute more," she said.

Mim used her friend to help get her off the ground and keep herself steady, but had no idea how bad her wound was. She felt as though the amulet had melted all the way into her frozen lungs, and blood oozed from beneath her shirt. Bette set her down at the base of the mirror, and although pale and half dead from the freezing temperature, looked as determined as ever.

"Just look at it, Mim. Concentrate!" Bette said.

When she looked at the mirror, the light from her radiated against the strange inlaid carvings and all of the runes but two were glowing back at them. Bette clumsily bent down and picked up the book in her frozen hands and began tracing her fingers over the edge of the mirror.

Morra Losis appeared at the end of the row and screeched and came at them. Bette threw the book down and started pressing and turning the last two runes on the edge of the mirror haphazardly until they heard a click. The glass pane of the mirror rippled as if someone had dropped a stone into the surface of a smooth lake. She had done it.

Bette picked up their bags and Jessel and heaved them through the mirror, and as they disappeared, she shrieked in a mix of excitement and fear. She grabbed Mim and put her arm over her shoulder. As they backed towards the mirror, blinding waves of shadow erupted from Morra Losis's hands. With what strength she had left in her, Mim threw her free hand up and concentrated on the halo that surrounded them. But as the darkness enveloped them, the amulet once again grew hot, burning into her already fresh wound.

Bette spun them around. They were only two steps from the mirror, but just as they reached the threshold, the demon grabbed Bette's hair and yanked them to the ground. From their right, a blinding flash of light blasted Morra sideways. At the end of the hall, Mim saw Caralaine and Lee'shan standing there. The two women glowed in the gloom of the cavern, and their eyes sparkled brilliantly.

The monster reared her head but continued to take a beating from the deans. Every time she would hurl shadow from her hands, Lee'shan would meet it head on, allowing Caralaine to strike. She was amazed at the display of strength and power, but Mim could see they were growing weary quickly, and with each volley their halo seemed to grow dimmer.

Then Lisle was there, and the three women combined proved too much. Morra Losis sprung back into the darkness to flee, bringing down a large stone statue near the mirror. As it started to fall, Bette tried to move herself and Mim out of the way, but her foot caught on a piece of the rubble and the two stumbled backwards. Éolan rounded the corner behind the deans and yelled, "NO!" before they fell into the mirror and all went dark.

———◇◦G◉◦◦———

As the women moved off to track Morra Losis, Éolan heard more of the deans enter the vault. He reached down to the ground and picked up the torch that lay amongst the debris. As he surveyed the outside of the mirror, he tried to remember the rune patterns and decipher where the girls had traveled. His heart dropped as he thought of the odds. Of the thirty traveling mirrors, Éolan only knew the whereabouts of five. The others were presumed lost or had been shattered during the war upon Atlan. And if the girls had chosen one of them, their fate was already decided. His stomach felt like an empty pit as he thought about them trying to emerge from a shattered mirror.

Caralaine, Lee'shan, and Lisle rounded the corner behind him, followed by the others. "Where are the Reemen?" he asked.

"They have escaped. They disappeared shortly after you left the front gate. As for their master, she seems to have slithered out through a crack somewhere in one of the caverns," Davian said.

Éolan spoke without turning around, keeping his gaze on the mirror. "Lee'shan, I need you to help me figure out where they've gone. Get every book that we have on the mirror combinations," he said.

Lady Cody came up quickly. "I have left Robyn, Christiane, Trulane, and Amanda to guard the entrance. But the students and other deans are out of bed and beginning to ask questions. What should we tell them?" she asked.

Caralaine turned around. "If there are any wounded, tell them we will be setting up additional healing stations in the lower east hall. If not, they are all to remain where they are. As for the other deans, tell them that the storm was much worse than anticipated, and that we are inspecting the foundation of the building and will be up soon," she said.

She nodded but stayed rooted to the spot, staring at Éolan. Lisle strode up and put her hand gently onto his shoulder. "What do you intend to do?"

It took him a moment, and he could feel all of their eyes on his back. The entire world had changed in a matter of days, and they were among the few who were aware of it. But he knew what had happened tonight was only the beginning; like a small stone that triggers an avalanche. The others in hiding had to know as quickly as possible, but that would be easily accomplished by the Graces that stood behind him. His first priority, however, was different.

Just before the girls had fallen through the mirror, he and the others had seen the Essence radiating from Mim. She had a power within her that was far greater than any of them could have imagined. But it also meant she was dangerous, and far more so than she realized. He could tell she had been severely wounded, and he needed to find them as quickly as possible. When he turned around, the light of the Esmë radiated out from his eyes, which burned like molten sapphires in the gloom of the vault.

"I'm going after them."